A MATTER OF HONOR

Nina Pykare

No one knew the secret sorrows of Agatha Trimble. To all, she was the paid companion to Lord Winthrop's spoiled daughter, sworn to see the newly orphaned Cecilie through her first London season before making any future plans. Then suddenly fate delivered them both into the hands of the Earl of Denby, Cecilie's new guardian – and the everlasting flame Agatha had tried to extinguish from her heart.

Five years ago he had deserted her. Now, she was in his grasp again, knowing he would never let her go. He vowed to make her his once more. But could she ever trust him again.

NINA PYKARE

A Matter of Honor

John Curley & Associates, Inc.
South Yarmouth, Ma.

Library of Congress Cataloging-in-Publication Data

Pykare, Nina.
    A matter of honor.

    1. Large type books.   I. Title.
[PS3566.Y48M38   1988]   813′.54   87–30377
ISBN 1–55504–483–2 (lg. print)
ISBN 1–55504–484–0 (pbk. : lg. print)   *88B9438*

20.95

Published in Large Print by arrangement with Donald MacCampbell, Inc, in the United States and Canada, the U.K. and British Commonwealth and the rest of the world market.

Distributed in Great Britain, Ireland and the Commonwealth by **CHIVERS BOOK SALES LIMITED,** Bath BA1 3HB, England.

Printed in Great Britain

A MATTER OF HONOUR

Chapter One

The mid-April day was lovely. The English countryside basked under a warm sun. The hedgerows along the London road were all abloom, the meadows were waving with wild daffodils, and the smell of spring suffused the warm air. But the two occupants of the closed carriage had no eyes for the beauty around them. The younger, with blond hair wildly tossed in the current style à la Titus, a small pert face, and a stubborn jut to her strong chin, was crooning to a creature in her arms. At first glance it appeared to be a wizened little baby clad in a red suit, but closer inspection revealed that the baby was, in sober fact, a monkey.

"Now, Dillydums," crooned the girl, who was obviously his mistress, "you must not be afraid in London. It's a big, big city, as Papa used to say, but I'm sure we shall deal famously there. Shan't we, Aggie? Aggie!"

The sharpness of the second calling of her name caused the other woman to raise her head. There was nothing fashionable about her, but a discerning observer would have found the rich dark brown of her hair and the deep intense blue of her eyes quite a fascinating combination. "Yes, Cecilie, we shall manage," she said patiently, and then, seeing that her charge had returned her attention to the monkey, she resumed her own musing.

If Cecilie had been a more perceptive and less selfish young woman, she might have noted that her companion was not her usual calm and placid self. But young Cecilie had never given much consideration to others, intent as she was on satisfying her own whims. It was partly this circumstance that disturbed her companion. Cecilie's papa had always given in to her and the five years that Aggie had served as her companion had been uncomfortable ones.

Agatha Trimble turned to look out the window, but she saw nothing that passed before her eyes. She was remembering. Her own papa had died when she was just eighteen, the year after her coming out, and his death had exposed to the world what had previously been a well-kept secret: his substance was completely gone. There was no dowry for her, nor any money upon which she might subsist. She had counted herself fortunate to find the position with Lord Winthrop. Cecilie, though willful and selfish, was not really bad. With the right attitude and patience, one could usually bring her around. But now – Aggie suppressed a sigh. Cecilie's papa had died last fall and a new guardian had been appointed, the Earl of Denby. She did not recognize his name; she had not been to the city since her own coming out. At that time, too, many of the young men had been away, fighting Napoleon. Thankfully, that was now over. Had *he* survived? she wondered, and then scolded herself sharply. There was little point in thinking of the Viscount Acton or of the days when he had loved her.

She stifled another sigh and found that she was twisting her hands together in her lap. He had not *really* loved her. She knew that now. But it had seemed so then, in those golden days of youth and happiness. If she closed her eyes, she could see him still. Tall and dark, with a shock of unruly black hair, a high aristocratic nose, bushy black brows, and those smoky gray eyes that seemed to burn with hidden fires. She swallowed over the lump in her throat. She had been young and foolish, believing his whispered words of love, surrendering herself to kisses stolen in dark corners at balls, and waiting with longing for the day he would ask for her hand in marriage. But that day never came.

3

One night he was waltzing her around Almack's, every fiber of her being alive with his touch, and the next he had vanished, without so much as a word. It had taken her a week to realize that he was really gone; and even then she did not give up the hope that he would return with some explanation for his abrupt departure. She had refused the young men who had clustered around her, refused them all because her partiality for him had been so great. Now, of course, she knew that he had been amusing himself with a naive young girl. But then, then, she had thought the fire smoldering in those smoky gray eyes was love. She sighed. Such men knew nothing of love. They only took what they pleased and went their merry way.

Finally she had forced herself to realize her mistake in giving her heart to such a man, but by then it had been too late. The next year Papa had died and then no one had wanted her.

She pushed absently at a wisp of hair that had escaped its bonds. Probably all had worked out for the best. Had she married one of those other men with the image of Acton still in her heart, life would have been intolerable. Better to have no kisses than those of a man she could not love. Slowly her eyelids sank against her cheeks and in her

4

memory she felt again the pressure of Acton's strong arms around her, the feel of his lips on hers. Her whole body had responded to his kisses, kisses that ran like liquid fire through her veins and dissolved her bones into so much melted butter.

The tears welled up behind Aggie's closed lids. She was three and twenty now and would never know a man's kisses again. But she had a secure position and, thanks to Lord Winthrop, once Cecilie was safely married, she was to have a small inheritance. Not enough to live royally, of course; but she thought she might open a small day school for young ladies. She had learned a lot about guiding recalcitrant misses in the last years and she could profit from it.

There was much to be done before she could even think of that. Cecilie must be outfitted for her coming out. The come out itself must be planned and given. A suitable husband must be settled upon, the marriage planned and held. Only then, with Cecilie safely taken care of, could she pursue her own plans. If Cecilie's papa were still alive, or if she had it to do on her own, Aggie was confident of the outcome. But there was this new guardian to be considered. She knew nothing of him except his name, the Earl of Denby. The solicitor had said no more and she had not thought it proper to ask questions. Certainly his first orders had been sensible enough: to stay in the country during the cold months while Cecilie finished her mourning and then he would advise them when to come to London.

And so he had, and here they were on their way. Aggie could only hope for a man with the sense to trust her judgment. However, as she well knew, many men thought *they* knew best. Indeed, it was only because Lord Winthrop had given up in despair that she had had such a free rein with Cecilie. But if this new guardian decided to interfere and began high-handedly ordering Cecilie around...

Aggie stifled another sigh and determined to concentrate on the scenery. It was quite foolish of her to be acting like this. It was pointless to borrow trouble, as Papa had always said – although his actions in those last years had sometimes been so strange as to cause her to wonder. And surely a little more forethought might have kept him from going so often to White's. But that, of course, was all water under the bridge. At least, Acton's desertion had not been based upon Papa's poor financial prospects. Unconsciously, she sighed again. Perhaps that would have been easier on her pride. At least she would have known his reason for leaving so abruptly. But she must put all that behind her. No doubt by now he had a wife and little ones. The thought was not a comforting one and Aggie blinked rapidly to stop the gathering tears. It was addlepated to weep over such a man. Far better to forget him and concentrate on her plans for Cecilie's future.

Dusk was falling when the carriage reached the city. Cecilie, who had been dozing, now sat erect, the monkey chattering excitedly on her shoulder, and looked around with great interest. She had never led a particularly sheltered existence, her papa being a man well-known to the *ton* and so accustomed to having houseguests, though always those near his own age; but he had never allowed her to come to the city. So now her eyes fairly sparkled, and the monkey, sensing her excitement, hopped about on her shoulder.

"Oh, Aggie, look! Isn't the city wonderful?"

Aggie nodded. "Yes, dear."

"Oh, look!" Cecilie leaned perilously out the small window. "They're lighting all kinds of lamps."

Aggie looked and smiled. "Those are the illuminations, Cecilie. To celebrate the peace."

"Look! That one says 'Thanks Be to God' in variegated colors."

"I see," answered Aggie. "We should indeed be grateful that Napoleon is no longer free. That monstrous man has been responsible for the deaths of many brave Englishmen." *Pray God, not Acton,* she added silently.

"Now all the young men will be coming back," said Cecilie happily. "And I shall have my pick of them."

To this Aggie raised a silent eyebrow. Cecilie was a bewitching creature, to be sure, with blond ringlets, hazel eyes, and a delicate feminine form. But that delicate form housed a will of iron and a temper known throughout the Dover countryside. It was Aggie's devout wish to keep that same temper from ruining Cecilie's matrimonial chances. And it was not going to be an easy task.

"Oh my! Just look at that! Hampton, stop the carriage. Oh do!"

The coachman, used to the young mistress's strange demands, pulled the horses to a halt and sighed deeply.

Cecilie grabbed at Aggie's arm. "Oh, Aggie, do look at that one!"

Aggie, leaning out the window, recognized Ackermann's in the Strand. She drew in her breath. It was not surprising that Cecilie should be amazed. This transparency was beyond doubt a work of great ingenuity. Bonaparte was represented as lying with the foot of grisly Death upon his breast. In one hand Death held an hourglass, its sand almost run out, and in the other a massive iron spear. Under and around the fallen tyrant could be seen the broken eagles and torn flags of his command, while in his hand he grasped the shattered and bloody remains of a sword. On the walls of Paris the allies of England – Russians, Prussians, Austrians, and others, were rising the Bourbon standard. The whole was surmounted by a brilliant circle of gaslights, showing the union of the world in this Holy Cause. Over this flew the fleur-de-lis in triumphant display above the tattered tricolor of the Revolution.

"Oh, Aggie," cried Cecilie. "Look at the smaller transparencies to the sides. See, there is the tyrant blowing bubbles which keep bursting, and there he is building houses of cards which keep tumbling down."

"Yes," said Aggie. "The whole is very well done. But we really should be getting on."

Cecilie nodded. "Yes, I know. Hampton, drive on." With a last look she pulled in her head and turned to her companion. "He was such a little man, that Napoleon. He didn't look at all like an emperor."

Aggie smiled, wondering what Cecilie would think when she saw the prince regent, whose corpulency had been the talk even during her own come out. "Don't trouble yourself over Bonaparte, dear. The world is safe from his depredations now."

Cecilie nodded. "Yes." She smiled in satisfaction. "I'm so glad it was all managed in such timely fashion. I shall never forget my first sight of the city, all lit up like this."

"I'm sure you shan't. But listen, my dear. We'll soon be approaching Grosvenor Square." She cast a look at the monkey, busily searching among the artificial flowers in Cecilie's bonnet. "And there are a few things we should talk about."

Cecilie turned quickly, dislodging the monkey, who came tumbling down into her lap and cast her an accusing look. "Really, Dillydums," she told him. "Don't be silly. I told you before that there's nothing to eat on my bonnet. But never mind." She pulled the monkey into her arms. "We'll be there soon and then you shan't have to be cooped up in the carriage. You'll have a nice large house."

Aggie sighed. "Please, Cecilie, the Earl is not likely to be overjoyed by the addition of a monkey to his establishment. If you want to keep him, the monkey must behave."

"Keep him!" cried Cecilie, clasping him to her violently. "Of course I shall keep him. The nasty old Earl wouldn't dare to order me about." Cecilie's pink lips formed a stubborn pout and she pulled herself dramatically erect.

"The Earl may not be old," said Aggie patiently. "And even if he is, it is unwise to form an opinion before you have met a person."

"If he can't appreciate Dillydums, he must be nasty," exclaimed Cecilie with the illogic of youth.

"Never mind," said Aggie. "Just quiet the monkey. We must go in."

The door was opened and the coachman appeared to help them descend. Cecilie was the first out and Aggie heard her exclamation of surprise. "My goodness! What a great tall house."

Aggie hurried to descend before her charge should say anything unfortunate, but Cecilie stood silent, lost in wonder.

Aggie herself bit back an exclamation of surprise. She had expected a fine house, but nothing quite this magnificent. The house seemed to take up the space of several normal houses and it rose at least four stories into the air.

"Well," said Cecilie, finding her tongue at last. "It appears that the Earl is well-larded. I shall have quite a royal come out."

"Cecilie!" Aggie could not help the annoyance that crept into her voice. If the Earl were to hear such candid remarks, he could hardly be expected to be impressed with them.

"Quiet now," warned Aggie, and together they went up the walk, leaving the coachman and grooms to follow with their bags and bundles.

The door opened as they approached it and they were greeted by a tall lean butler whose round face looked out of place on his thin angular body. "His lordship left orders to show you to your rooms. He had some business out and, not knowing the time of your arrival, thought it best to handle it now."

Aggie nodded and, gently pushing Cecilie before her, followed the butler up the great staircase.

"There'll be a maid along to help you unpack," said that worthy as he opened the door to a suite of rooms. "When his lordship returns, he'll be wanting to see you. Until then, perhaps you'd like to freshen up and rest a little."

Aggie nodded. "Thank you,..."

"Bates," he said. Then he was gone.

Aggie gently closed the door and turned to her ward. It was as if the closing of the door had opened Cecilie's lips and a torrent of words came pouring out. "Oh, Aggie, this is capital, just capital! Look at this place! Why, the Earl must be rolling in the ready. I shall have dozens of new gowns, and slippers and gloves, and shawls and fans. Oh! I can hardly wait to get to Bond Street."

"Cecilie," Aggie reminded her charge. "Please, be sensible. The Earl's money is his own. What your papa left for your come out is quite sufficient, I am sure. You must not expect the Earl to spend his funds on you."

Cecilie gave a stubborn shake of her blond curls. "I don't know why not. Surely he can afford it."

"That is not the question," said Aggie patiently. "It was very kind of a man in his lordship's position to take on your guardianship. It is an imposition on his time."

Cecilie's face began to take on an aggrieved expression and Aggie knew she had said too much. "I'm not any trouble, Aggie. You know that!"

Aggie swallowed a sigh. "I did not mean that, my dear. I simply meant that the Earl must have other responsibilities and arranging a come out is time consuming."

Cecilie smiled. "He needn't even bother himself about it. You and I can handle it quite nicely."

Aggie managed to remain calm. "We know nothing at all about the Earl," she said patiently. "He may leave all to us or he may insist on running things himself."

Cecilie's small chin seemed to jut out even further. "Well," she said with a finality that ended the conversation, "if he tries to run my life, I shall certainly find him nasty."

It was over an hour later and their boxes and bundles had all been unpacked, when a tap on the door caused Aggie to call out, "Yes, what is it?"

The door opened to show Bates. "His lordship has returned and he wishes to see Miss Trimble in the library."

"Just me?" said Aggie.

Bates nodded. "Those were his lordship's orders. He said to tell you that he has some matters that must be discussed with you first. He will meet his ward later."

"Very well, Bates." A glance at Cecilie's face warned Aggie of a gathering storm and she hurried from the room before the girl's anger should become a full-fledged tantrum. Though she knew the day was inevitable when her charge's temper would become apparent to all, Aggie hoped to forestall it, for a little while at least.

She descended the front staircase as calmly as she could and, following Bates's gesture, made her way to the library. Outside the door she paused momentarily, hoping to steady the trembling of her knees. But they seemed determined to tremble despite all her efforts and, taking a deep breath, she stepped through the door.

Across the room stood a man, his back to her. He was tall and lean, with broad shoulders that strained the material of his coat of blue superfine. His dark hair curled down over his cravat and touched his coat collar.

"Milord?" she said softly, and then, because he had not heard her, she repeated a trifle louder. "Milord? You wish to speak to me?"

"Yes, Miss Trimble," the Earl said, his deep voice raising vibrations along her spine. Then he turned, and, staring into those smoky gray eyes, Aggie's mind told her what her body already knew. This was the man who had deceived and left her!

She reached out blindly for some support, but there was nothing close by and she felt herself slipping into unconsciousness.

"Aggie!" She thought she heard him cry her name, but by that time the comforting darkness had closed over her.

When she opened her eyes some moments later, she was lying on a divan and the Earl was looking down at her. She struggled immediately to rise. He had carried her there – the man whose protestations of affection she had once believed. Her only thought was to escape his presence and the scrutiny of those terrible gray eyes. She struggled to sit up, but he pushed her back with a strong hand. "Lie still, Miss Trimble. You've had a bad shock."

"You –" Aggie formed the word with stiff lips. "What are *you* doing here?"

"In good time," he said brusquely, drawing a chair closer. "Lie still and I will enlighten you."

Much as she wanted to run away from him, Aggie knew it was impossible. Her legs simply would not hold her.

After a quick glance at her, his lordship continued. "You came here expecting to see the Earl of Denby?"

Aggie nodded.

16

He smiled dryly. "You see him before you."

"But then, then –"

"Then I was the Viscount Acton. I succeeded to my uncle's title, you see. And you have before you the Earl of Denby."

"Oh," said Aggie, her tone barely audible. A little of her strength was returning now. She swung her feet to the floor and sat up slowly. The Earl eyed her carefully, but he said nothing. "You knew – that I was Cecilie's companion," she said, forcing herself to meet his eyes.

"Yes," he agreed. "I knew."

"Why – why did you let me make this journey – knowing that I could not stay?"

His eyes grew darker and the line of his mouth hardened. "I did not know any such thing," he said gruffly. "As Cecilie's guardian I am conversant with the terms of her father's will." When she did not reply, he gave her a long searching look. "I know the terms," he repeated. "I know that if you leave her before she is safely married, you will lose what was left you. That is why I did not tell you before you arrived here." He rose suddenly and strode across the room.

"I – you must know that I cannot stay here." She stared at the hard muscles of his

17

back, her heart pounding heavily in her throat.

He swung toward her then. "I know no such thing," he said curtly. He drew himself up to his fullest height and she felt herself seem to grow smaller. "You not only *may* stay here, you *must*. I will not be responsible for your losing your inheritance. Do you understand me?"

Aggie pushed hopelessly at her tumbled hair. "But – but – you must see. It's impossible. I cannot."

A strange look, almost of pain, crossed his handsome features, but before she could look closer, he turned his back again and resumed his pacing. "I am well aware of your antipathy toward me," he said sharply. "But in this case you must consider yourself. Also, you might give some thought to your charge. It would be rather hard on her, would it not, to lose her companion so soon after losing her father?"

Aggie found herself twisting her hands nervously and was glad that he had his back to her. He was right, of course, she could not very well desert Cecilie at this important time. But to stay here, in the same house with *him* – to see him every day. To know how once she had loved him. To remember how he had simply vanished from her life. She didn't know if she could manage that.

And yet, what was the alternative? As the Earl stood, his back still toward her, she considered the possibilities open to her. If she left now, she had no place to go and no money to go with. The inheritance would not ever be hers if she left Cecilie now. And she did have a duty to the girl. Also, to be entirely practical, how could she even go about finding a new position if she left this one so precipitously? She swallowed hastily. There really seemed nothing to do but stay, painful as that would be.

Almost as though he had divined her decision, he turned again. "You must be sensible, Agg – Miss Trimble."

Her heart skipped a beat and leaped high into her throat as he almost spoke her given name. In what tender tones he had once whispered it, tones of love. She felt the color flooding her cheeks at the thought.

The Earl continued to stare at her, his eyes clouded with some indefinable emotion. "Well, you will stay?"

His words echoed curtly in her ears. She forced herself to her feet. She wavered there unsteadily for a moment, his eyes heavy upon her. "I will stay, milord," she agreed. And then she drew herself proudly erect. "As you are well aware, I have no other recourse. If I had, matters would be quite different, I assure you."

Again that strange look crossed his face and his eyes raked her over. "Good. I suggest we forget our differences from the past and concentrate on getting our charge safely matched. Agreed?"

"Agreed," replied Aggie, forcing her voice into a steadiness she was far from feeling.

"Good. Since I have a dinner engagement, I shall leave you to your settling in. Tomorrow will be soon enough to discuss our plans." He bowed gracefully and, with another searching look at her, left the room.

Aggie stood trembling for several minutes before she sank back on the divan. She could not go upstairs in her present state of distress. Even Cecilie would notice this unsteadiness that had overtaken her. Oh, why had fate taken such a cruel turning – to force her back into contact with the man who had once broken her heart. Well, she would simply have to go on. She had conquered her partiality for him. It was only the shock of seeing him so unexpectedly that had undone her. They would let the past go and think only of the task of getting Cecilie settled. Dear God, she wished that to be done quickly. Then she would be free of him.

Chapter Two

The next morning began with disaster. Cecilie had insisted on waiting up quite late because she wanted to see her new guardian. However, they did not hear him come in and finally she had been persuaded into her bed. It was because of this that they both slept very late the next morning. And that's when it happened.

Aggie had just opened her eyes and was making her plans for the day, considering what was best to do first, when a startling roar of male rage went reverberating through the upper hall. "Bates!" shouted his lordship in obviously irate tones. "Come here! Get this – this thing!"

Aggie, dragging on her robe, hurried into the hall. As she reached it, she heard a wild chattering, punctuated by the Earl's pungent curses. The sound made her want to cover her ears. The sight that met her eyes was equally appalling. The Earl stood thundering in the hallway. He was only half-clothed. He wore his breeches of ribbed buff cord and his Wellingtons, but the upper half of his body was unclad. Aggie stopped in her tracks, the sight of his bare chest making her clutch at her robe and avert her eyes.

His lordship, however, did not seem aware of his state of undress. His dark brows were drawn together fiercely and the shadowy mat of hair on his chest rose and fell with his shouts. "Bates! Exactly how did this – this thing get into my establishment?" And he waved the wretched monkey which he held off by the scruff of its neck.

Without more thought, Aggie moved to rescue the poor thing. "Give me the monkey, milord," she said softly, gathering the terrified creature into her arms. "You are frightening him."

He scowled at her, but he released his grip and the monkey came gibbering into her arms. He clung to her in terror, hiding his head in the folds of her robe. She turned her attention to soothing him, making the kind of little crooning noises that Cecilie used.

"Miss Trimble!" The Earl's words boomed like thunderclaps in the hall. "Is that *thing* known to you?"

Aggie nodded. She forced herself to look up into his eyes, blazing now with indignation. In those long-ago days she had never seen him angry, but a man's anger was no novelty to her. Cecilie had often driven her father into paroxysms of rage. The best approach in such a case, Aggie knew, was to remain calm and dignified.

"Yes, milord. This is Dillydums, Cecilie's monkey. He must have slipped out while we slept. I thought we had shut the door tightly."

Bates coughed discreetly. "If you please, miss, I believe the maid Millie might have opened the door to see if you were awake yet. She might have left it ajar."

Aggie turned to the servant with a smile. "Yes, Bates. Quite probably that is what happened. We shall have to be more careful from now on." She began to move toward the bedroom.

"Miss Trimble!" The sound was enough to make even a brave man quiver and Aggie had to swallow twice before she could reply. It was difficult to remain calm under such rage.

"Yes, milord." She hated meeting his eyes, but it was improper to look at his bare chest and to look at the floor seemed too abject.

"Why did you not inform me of this creature?"

Aggie frowned. This was getting to be too much. She did not intend to spend the next weeks being bullied. "I thought, milord, that you already knew. I sent Cecilie's guardian several reports during the winter. Among them was a report on the purchase of Dillydums."

The Earl looked slightly discomfited by this and Aggie could not forbear driving the knife a little deeper. "Had I know that your lordship was uninformed on this point, I would have been most certain to tell you."

His lordship did not take kindly to this. His face clouded over again and his frown was terrible to see. "Do not pick words with me, Miss Trimble. I read all your reports. I simply did not expect that such an animal would be brought to the city. Therefore I was not prepared, or amused, to find it swinging from my bed curtains and waving my razor around as though it had gone mad."

"If Dillydums was bad, it was your fault," said a shrill young voice.

Aggie turned in dismay to see Cecilie standing there. Evidently the commotion in the hall had wakened her, and, without robe or slippers, she had come to find out what it was about. She stood in her long white nightdress, rubbing the sleep from her eyes and glaring at his lordship. "I think you are a mean, nasty man," said Cecilie with the blunt honesty of the young. "And you're not too smart either."

A gasp from Bates was not stifled quite in time and Aggie shuddered. It did little good to reflect that his lordship had brought this on himself. And, she supposed, he would discover soon enough that this was the wrong way to approach Cecilie.

"Anyone with any sense at all," continued the girl, "would know better than to yell at Aggie. It's not her fault if Dillydums got out. Nor that *you* don't like monkeys." She gazed reproachfully at the Earl. "Besides, if you'd come home at a decent hour, I wouldn't have sat up half the night waiting and slept so late this morning. And then he wouldn't have gotten out at all."

The Earl's look of dire wrath did not seem to bother Cecilie one bit. "It's no use your glaring at me like that. I only said what's true. Dillydums is a little dear. He wouldn't hurt a fly."

She took a step closer and gazed at his lordship with wide curious eyes, as though she had just then become aware of his state of undress. "How very curious. Do all men look like that?" she asked, her gaze held by the mat of dark curly hair that covered his chest.

"No!" said his lordship sharply. "Bates, we will finish dressing now." His eyes met Aggie's and for a moment she thought she

25

saw a hint of merriment there. But surely that was impossible. And anyway, the Earl's eyes were deceptive. A woman should never trust what she saw there. Never.

"I suggest," said the Earl in an even tone, "that you ladies also dress and meet me in the breakfast room. We shall continue our discussion of monkeys there."

"Very well, milord." Aggie shepherded an unwilling Cecilie back to the room where she carefully shut the door before releasing the monkey. They were certainly not off to the best of starts.

"I don't like him," said Cecilie. "He's all puffed up with his own importance. And he doesn't like animals."

Aggie forced herself to smile. "His lordship was startled," she explained. "He did not expect to find a monkey in his rooms – and armed with a razor. It was really rather natural for him to be upset."

"He does it very well," observed Cecilie. "Being upset, I mean. Papa was never very good at it." Her eyes widened. "Imagine him having a chest like that. Still, he's a mean man and I shan't like him."

Aggie judged it better not to discuss his lordship's chest, which for some odd reason seemed to have impressed itself firmly in her mind. "It doesn't matter what you think of him. You must be careful not to aggravate him. You were lucky today. Remember, Cecilie, he is able to deal with you quite severely. And what he says in a temper he may well stick by, even though he later regrets it."

"He doesn't scare *me*," said Cecilie, combing at her tangled blond curls while the monkey perched cheerfully on top of the mirror, his ordeal quite forgotten.

Aggie shook her head. How could she persuade her young charge that Denby was a very different man from her father? Smiles and pouts, Cecilie's chief weapons, would be lost on the Earl, Aggie feared. There was no doubt that Denby was a hard man, quite accustomed to having things his own way. How irritated he must have been to have the guardianship of a young girl thrust so summarily upon him. And a willful, stubborn girl, at that, she thought, as she slipped into a morning dress of rose-sprigged muslin, one of the few pretty gowns she still owned. Releasing her luxuriant hair from its night braid, she brushed it and swiftly confined it to its usual knot.

"Are you almost ready, Cecilie?" she asked, careful to keep any hint of anxiety from her voice. At times Cecilie could be fiercely partisan, and, although Aggie

27

appreciated being defended, such blunt honesty was hardly politic when dealing with a man like the Earl. He seemed more accustomed to having women speak softly and look submissive.

"I suppose so," pouted Cecilie. "But I really don't see why we need to bother with him. You and I are perfectly capable of running my affairs."

"*We* may believe that," said Aggie with a small smile. "But the law says differently and it has put your affairs into the hands of a guardian until you have a husband to take over."

Cecilie tossed her blond curls and her eyes danced with mischief. "Men are such bores," she said. "So stuffy and solemn." Her chin jutted forward. "Well, one thing I know. I'm going to find a husband that will be fun. We'll ride and dance and enjoy ourselves. We're going to have *fun.*"

Aggie swallowed a sigh. It was useless to try to tell Cecilie that there was more to marriage than dancing and fun. She could only hope and pray that they would find the child a decent man who would not curb her high spirits so sharply as to break her completely.

Cecilie put the monkey on his leash and fastened it to the bedpost. "Now, Dillydums," she told the little creature whose small black eyes watched her so closely, "you must be a good boy. We have to go see his nasty old lordship, but we'll be back soon."

Together they left the room, carefully shutting the door behind them. "I do hope Dillydums doesn't get too lonesome. I don't see why we couldn't bring him along."

"Perhaps on other mornings," Aggie replied patiently. "But today the Earl is not in the best of moods. We don't want him to remain angry."

"I don't care how mad he gets," said Cecilie with an impish grin. "I've never seen anyone get so incensed. He's very interesting in that condition."

Aggie strove for patience, but her nerves were so on edge from her confrontation with the Earl that she found it difficult to be her usual calm self. "You *must* understand the situation. The Earl is a man of great power. He will not hesitate to use it. If you cross him, you may well find yourself sitting at home, without a carriage, without new gowns, perhaps even without a come out!"

Cecilie stopped in her tracks, her mouth open in astonishment. "He wouldn't! He wouldn't dare!"

Aggie shook her head. "Do not be too

sure, Cecilie. There is no telling what he may do."

As her charge walked on, seemingly sobered, Aggie smiled bitterly. That was certainly the truth. Once she would have staked everything she had on Denby's character, but now she knew better. How could one trust a man who spoke words of love in a woman's ear, whose eyes promised heaven on earth, whose kisses transported her into ecstasy, and who then vanished, as it were overnight, not to reappear for five long years?

Aggie brushed away the tears that had suddenly filled her eyes. Dear God, how she had loved him, loved him through a whole long year of waiting until common sense had finally convinced her that he was gone for good. She swallowed another sigh. She must get Cecilie married as soon as possible and get out of his house where every meal and every turn in the corridor might result in a meeting with *him*.

She hated him, of course, she told herself as they descended the great staircase. And she certainly had just cause. He had ruined her life with his whispered words of longing, words that had led her to believe in his love. And then he had abandoned her. Surely that was cause enough to hate any man. And yet

30

she knew, much to her dismay, that had he come back and offered an excuse for his behavior, had he whispered those words of promise again, she would have fallen into his arms. It was a rather disconcerting thought and one she did not care to pursue any further.

Cecilie preceded her into the breakfast room and Aggie could tell from the set of her back that this was not going to be a pleasant meal. The Earl was seated at the head of the table. A shirt, cravat, striped waistcoat, and coat of blue superfine had been added to his costume. He was still a fine figure of a man, thought Aggie, and then reminded herself of his nature. Good looks were one thing, character another. And a man who trifled with the heart of an innocent young woman...

"Good morning, Miss Winthrop, Miss Trimble." He rose and bowed gracefully, his expression gravely formal.

"Good morning, milord," Cecilie's reply was a trifle sullen, but Aggie's was quite even.

"If you will be seated, Bates will serve you."

"Yes, milord." Aggie led Cecilie to a chair and then seated herself. She did not trust herself to look at Denby and so gazed down at her plate.

"I trust that Dillydums is a prisoner in your room," said his lordship to Cecilie in what was obviously an attempt to regard the morning's outbreak with humor.

Cecilie did not, however, respond in kind. "Yes, the poor thing is tied up like some terrible felon. It's absolutely heartless." And her eyes widened in innocent reproach.

The Earl seemed somewhat discomfited by this rather dramatic reply and his eyes sought Aggie. She, however, was steadily regarding her charge and did not meet his gaze.

"I hardly think it is *that* terrible," said his lordship. "Surely he did not run free at the house in Dover."

Aggie suppressed a smile. The Earl obviously knew very little about monkeys – or girls like Cecilie. But he would learn. Normally Aggie was of a very kindhearted nature, but it would have taken a veritable saint not to enjoy Denby's present discomfort as Cecilie fastened him with another wide-eyed gaze and declared, "Of course he did. We never tied the poor thing up."

The Earl did not have to reply to this immediately, having taken a bite of muffin. When his mouth was again empty, he said in a tone that did not quite achieve evenness, "This is London. Here we do not have animals running about loose."

"That's quite silly," said Cecilie, tossing her golden curls. "Animals are nice to have around. Better than people a lot of the time." And she gave the Earl a look which clearly indicated that in his case the truth was obvious.

"In London we have many callers," said his lordship, striving for a calmness he did not quite achieve. "We cannot have animals all over the house."

"Can't see why not," replied Cecilie through a mouthful of muffin. "The Duchess of York has animals everywhere at Oatlands. No one complains. Except of course the Duke, when he can't find a place to sit."

If Denby was surprised by his ward's familiarity with the royal family, he did not indicate so. "I'm afraid you are not yet a Duchess," he said in a firm tone. "Therefore the monkey must not be let to run about loose." He fastened a stern eye on Cecilie. "If he gets out again, I shall have to find him another home. Do you understand?"

For a long moment Cecilie stared at him in surprise. Then two big tears appeared in her eyes and rolled slowly and pathetically down her cheeks, to be followed by a steady stream of the same. The picture she presented was truly pitiful; and Aggie, if she had not experienced the same scene times innumerable, might well have been affected by it.

Denby was not. "I believe you should know that female tears will fail with me," he said. "They may have gained you your point in the past," he continued with a swift look at Aggie that seemed to hold her to blame, "but they will no longer serve for anything."

"You – you –" sputtered Cecilie. "You are a terrible, terrible man. I cannot understand why my papa left me in *your* care."

The Earl smiled dryly. "I assure you, Miss Winthrop, that the matter is no more to my liking than yours. However, that's the way it is. And the sooner we learn to deal together the better. We have one task: to get you properly married. Then we'll be rid of each other. I suggest that you cooperate with me. For your own good."

Cecilie refused to reply to this, disdainfully stuffing her mouth with eggs and sausage.

Denby turned to Aggie and this time there was no escaping his gaze. His smoky eyes were dark and clouded as he regarded her. "I understand that you have had a free hand with Miss Winthrop."

Aggie nodded. "Mostly her papa wished it that way." There was no time to offer excuses.

The Earl frowned. "That was well enough in Dover. Here things are different. I expect frequent conferences so I may be acquainted with your plans for Cecilie. When you leave the house, you will inform Bates of your destination and your time of return. All purchases, of clothing, and so on, will depend upon my approval. Is that clear?"

Aggie felt her hackles rising. He needn't imply that *she* was responsible for Cecilie's character. She had done her very best for the girl. Her eyes grew a deeper blue as she returned his gaze. "I understand your orders, milord," she said stiffly. "And I shall obey them." For another long moment their eyes held. Then Aggie could stand it no longer and let hers fall.

Denby turned to Cecilie. "Do you understand these rules?" he asked.

"I heard them," replied Cecilie, cramming another muffin into her mouth.

The Earl had a surprise in store for him if he construed this as a statement of assent, Aggie thought; but she doubted that he would appreciate being told so. However, he surprised her.

"You'd better *remember* them," said his

lordship. "And *obey* them. If you do, we shall deal well together. If you do not –" He frowned deeply and his dark brows met in a straight line across his forehead, giving him a grim, threatening look. "If you do not, I assure you that you will regret it." His expression softened. "However, I trust that you are a good sensible girl with an eye to the main chance. And, since you've got a proper dowry, we should have no trouble finding you a good husband."

Cecilie made no reply to this, continuing to stuff food into her mouth in a way that caused even Aggie, aware of the girl's intent to annoy, to feel a little nauseated.

Denby turned to her and his gray eyes held clear reproach. "I trust that before Miss Winthrop's come out, you will take the time to instruct her in the proper table manners. Otherwise, we shall never get her to the altar."

Aggie felt the color flooding her cheeks, but it was the color of anger, not of embarrassment, that stained them. Her blue eyes blazed at him, but she managed to keep her temper under control. There was no point in antagonizing his lordship further, not when she had to stay in this house until Cecilie was safely married. "Cecilie knows good manners, milord," she replied evenly.

"And I use them – when the occasion requires," added her charge in cutting tones.

"Cecilie!" Aggie could not stop the exclamation that burst from her lips or the look of dismay that she instinctively gave the girl. This was *not* the way to get along with Denby or with any man used to running everyone around him.

The Earl's lips set in a grim line and he rose from the table, pushing back his chair. He fastened his smoky gray eyes on Cecilie as he did so. "Miss Winthrop." The chill tone of his voice made Aggie's knees tremble and she knew from the set of Cecilie's shoulders that in spite of her bravado, the girl was frightened, too.

"I suggest that you reconsider your manner of behaving. The next time I am forced to undergo such a disreputable display of ill-conceived boorishness, I shall send you to your room to contemplate your sins." His eyes swung around to Aggie and rested on her coldly. "As for you, Miss Trimble, I suggest that you take this occasion to speak severely to your charge." His eyes seemed to scorch her and she fought to keep from dropping her gaze. "After all," he added with a sardonic humor that did not sit well with her at all, "your interest is at stake, too."

Then, before she could summon her wits

to tell him just how despicable she found his behavior, he turned swiftly on his heel and strode off, leaving her to stare after him in consternation.

Chapter Three

The rest of the day passed with a minimum of fuss. Together Cecilie and Aggie made long lists for the come out. They debated over the various kinds of refreshments they might serve and the kinds of flowers to be used in decorating the ballroom. In both cases Aggie acceded to the girl's wishes. She was not at all sure, however, that the Earl would. He had not been much amused by Cecilie's childish display of bad manners. If only she could persuade the girl to act in a reasonable and mature manner. But this was the forlornest of hopes. Aggie had never been able to prevail upon her charge to act reasonably. The girl was far too spoiled. And that was due, not, as the Earl seemed to think, to Aggie's laxness in regard to her charge, but to the very bad beginnings made by Cecilie's papa. He had absolutely doted on the girl and every time Aggie had attempted a firm hand about some matter, a few smiles or tears had soon turned things to Cecilie's way of thinking.

Aggie looked across the room to where Cecilie was playing with the monkey. With her tousled golden curls and her wide eyes, she presented quite an entrancing scene. Aggie stifled a sigh. If only they could get Cecilie married without anyone coming near her! The rude and vulgar young woman at the breakfast table had been quite different from this enchanting creature. But the Earl had not yet seen Cecilie at her worst. And when he did . . . Although she was concerned, Aggie could not help smiling just a little at the thought. Cecilie provoked was apt to do one of two things. Either she would throw herself upon the floor and scream and kick like an infant, or she would turn red in the face, begin screaming, and throw whatever was closest at hand. Neither of these ways of behaving, Aggie judged, was apt to make the desired impression on the Earl. He was too experienced a man to be moved by such childish behavior.

Aggie sighed again. "I am going to take a turn or two in the courtyard," she told the girl, who was busy dressing the monkey in an old scraf and a strong of pearls. "Do you want to come along?"

Cecilie shook her head. "No. I think I'll just stay here and play with Dillydums."

"Very well," said Aggie. She closed the door carefully behind her, fighting down the impulse to remind Cecilie of the Earl's dictum. She knew that to remind her about keeping the door closed was more likely to lead to it being left open out of sheer perversity.

She made her way to the courtyard where the spring flowers were blooming in profusion. Aggie sniffed appreciatively. For some moments she wandered contentedly among the blossoms, filling her eyes with their bright color and her nostrils with their scent. Then, discovering a little stone bench, she sank down upon it. As the weight of her thoughts began to press in upon her again, the beauty of the little garden receded. If only Cecilie were already married...Or if her guardian were not the Earl...A shiver swept over Aggie, though the sun was quite warm. Cecilie and the Earl were both strong-minded and spoiled. They were going to come to cuffs often – that seemed apparent. It was also clear that Aggie was apt to be caught in the middle – a most uncomfortable position, as she well knew.

But try as she might, she could think of no way to avoid trouble. Cecilie listened to no one and Aggie could hardly see the Earl condescending to take advice from a mere governess/companion, especially one he thought so little of. A sob caught in Aggie's throat and took her unaware. It would not be easy to be near the Earl even if Cecilie were the best-behaved young woman. And with her carrying on in this fashion, it was going to be very difficult.

A sparrow landed on a bush nearby and began to chirp merrily. Aggie swallowed again and blinked back the sudden tears. Spring, with its reminders of her own Season, always made her a little sad. For a moment she slipped back into the past, into those golden days when she had lived in the exciting knowledge that a man cared for her. Aggie stared unseeing at a rosebush while her mind presented her with a series of pictures: herself, flushed and nervous at her come out, surrounded by flattering, admiring young men. Then he had appeared, so dark and so heart-stoppingly handsome. From that moment on all other men had seemed like cheap imitations. And later, at Almack's and at other balls, he had swept her round and round the floor to the pulsing rhythm of the waltz, all the while staring down at her from those smoky gray eyes filled with tenderness. Or so she had thought at the time. Her eyes closed as Aggie relived in her memory the feel of his arms around her, the strange sense of excitement his nearness gave her, and the shuddering ecstasy of his kisses.

The sound of footsteps on the stones startled her and her eyes flew open. For one brief moment her heart leaped in happiness at the sight of that beloved form, and then sense returned, and with it the fear of what her face might have revealed to him.

The Earl had evidently just returned to the house. He was wearing trousers of buff kerseymere, Wellingtons, and a coat of brown superfine. He looked quite well, just as handsome as he had the first time she had seen him, those five years ago.

But when she looked closely at his face, she saw that something was wrong. His dark brows met over his nose and his eyes were now hard and cold as the stones beneath her feet.

"Milord, what is it?"

He was obviously under great stress, the strong line of his mouth grimly firm. "Have you taught that idiot child nothing at all?" he demanded fiercely, towering over her like some angry god of old.

Aggie, wrestling with the strange fear she felt, got to her feet. "I did the best I could with Cecilie," she replied evenly. "What has she done to upset you now?"

"Upset me!" thundered his lordship. "That girl would drive a saint into hell itself!" He glared at her.

"I am well aware that Cecilie is difficult," said Aggie, her hackles beginning to rise. "What has she done?"

"Difficult! The girl is impossible. I shall never find anyone stupid enough to marry her. What a mess you made of her."

"Milord!" Aggie's back was up now. "Unfortunately, Cecilie's character was formed long before I came upon the scene. She lost her mother when she was two and her father doted upon her. All her short life she has been accustomed to getting things her own way. Try as I might I was unable to do much. After all, she had only to run to her papa to have everything as she wanted it." She gazed at him steadily, only half aware of the labored thudding of her heart. They stood quite close, as once they had stood on the ballroom floor, she thought, then pushed the thought away.

The Earl's chest rose with the force of his emotion and he replied curtly. "Those days are over! That miserable chit may pout and cry all she pleases. She will have to learn who is in charge here. And so will you." He swung on his heel and was about to stride away.

A wave of anger raced over Aggie. How dare he blame *her!* "Milord!" she cried, her voice rising. "Wait!"

He turned back in surprise and faced her, still glowering.

Aggie drew herself up with dignity. "I am well aware of my inferior position in this establishment," she said icily. "Nor am I likely to forget it. But nothing will be helped by your thundering about like this. I am doing the best I can to help with Cecilie. She is not an easy child to deal with."

"That is certainly an understatement," snorted his lordship. "You have spoiled her rotten."

Aggie, who had been about to advise him on the best way to handle Cecilie, suddenly changed her mind. "If it is not too much to ask," she said coldly, "I should like to be told what it is she has done." She fixed him steadily with her eyes. She could not allow him to browbeat her like this.

The Earl took a deep breath as though to steady himself. "While you were out here taking the fresh air," he said, sarcasm heavy in his voice, "Cecilie decided to take that monkey for a walk." He glared at her.

Aggie shook her head. "Milord, what is so terrible about that?"

For a moment he looked so angry that she thought he might strike her. His chest swelled with his wrath and his face grew dark and stormy. "Life in the country has dulled your wits," he commented acidly. "Cecilie Winthrop is an heiress, with quite a portion, far too much to be cavorting about London's streets alone."

"Alone!" Aggie stared at him in horror.

"Quite alone," he replied. "If I had not been just returning and seen her, God knows where she would have strayed to." His eyes regarded her angrily. "I suppose that you have not forgotten that London's streets are not exactly safe for young heiresses. All my efforts to keep fortune hunters off will prove useless if one manages to make off with her to Gretna Green."

Aggie stood silent for a moment. "Cecilie would not run off with a stranger," she replied, much aware that this was not an adequate answer.

"I am not at all sure *what* Cecilie would or would not do," said the Earl coldly. "But that is beside the point. These men do not wait around for the woman's consent; they merely drag her into a carriage and take off. When they return from Scotland, the man

45

has the inheritance and the woman a miserable life." His eyes flashed at her. "Much as Cecilie provokes me, I should not like to wish such a fate on any woman. And besides," he seemed to be struggling to calm himself, "I have a duty to fulfill where she is concerned. Onerous as that duty is, I wish to discharge it properly." He shut his mouth with a snap.

"I will do what I can." Aggie strove to keep her voice even. "I will try to make Cecilie understand the dangers. She is not accustomed –"

The Earl gave her a look of disgust. "I do not care to hear any more excuses for that spoiled brat," he said flatly. "Nor for your part in this fiasco."

Aggie felt her anger rising again. Why must he always blame her? "I was not aware that I was offering excuses," she said coldly. "I was merely giving you information that I consider helpful."

The Earl's only acknowledgment was a fiercer frown.

"Now, if you are quite through bellowing" – she saw him wince slightly at her use of the word and was glad – "I shall go find Cecilie."

"You will find her in her room," he said stiffly, "where she is to remain until dinner." His eyes met hers squarely and Aggie knew he expected her to protest. Perversely, she contented herself with a nod. If he wanted to be so stubborn, let him. She had tried to tell him that this high-handed way of dealing with Cecilie could only have ill results, but he was too pigheaded to listen. Let him learn the hard way, she thought as she swept by him and into the house.

It was with some trepidation that she opened the door to their rooms. The thought of encountering Cecilie in a tantrum was not a pleasant one. But Cecilie was sitting by the window, playing with Dillydums. "There you are," she said in an aggrieved tone. "You'll never guess what that terrible man has done now! He refuses to let me take a walk!" She rose from her chair, her face flushing as she recalled her anger.

"His lordship is concerned for you." Aggie kept her voice calm, but it didn't help.

"Concerned?" said Cecilie. "The man is a monster! Imagine, there I was, taking a little stroll with Dillydums, quite enjoying myself. Nodding to the gentlemen and ladies that I passed. Then along comes the Earl, flies off the hooks, and begins bellowing at me. The grooms carry me forcibly into the carriage. Forcibly, Aggie! It was just too embarrassing."

"Cecilie, his lordship is very concerned.

Young ladies do not walk about London alone."

"I can't see why not," Cecilie declared. "It's just lovely."

"Cecilie, you *must* listen. There are men about, wicked men, who might spirit you away to Gretna Green."

Cecilie stared at her, eyes wide with wonder. "To Gretna Green?"

Aggie nodded. "Yes, and once married you would have no recourse."

"How very romantic," cried Cecilie. "An elopement."

Aggie shook her head in exasperation. "No, more like a kidnapping. There is nothing romantic about it. These are wicked men. To be married to one would be terrible." She called on her imagination to present her with images suitably terrifying to Cecilie's young mind. "You would have no fun, no new gowns, no pin money. You would not even get out of the house."

Cecilie considered this. "It does sound bad, Aggie. Don't worry. I won't consider it."

"Cecilie!" Aggie's patience was worn thin. "One does not *consider* being abducted. One does not reason with such men."

"All right, Aggie." Cecilie tossed her bright curls. "I'll be careful."

And with this Aggie had to be content. She knew that if she pressed any further she would only aggravate Cecilie and not serve her purpose at all.

"Did his lordship say anything about my come out?" asked Cecilie, their scuffle evidently forgotten.

Aggie shook her head. "This did not seem like a good time to raise the subject," she said with an irony completely lost on her charge.

"I have decided what sort of gown I want," said Cecilie, eyes aglow. "I want to get to the dressmaker and order it."

"What sort of gown have you in mind?" asked Aggie, fearing the worst.

Cecilie grinned. "It's to be a deep deep blue with a neck cut so." Her hands made a sweeping motion over her bosom.

Aggie stifled a sigh. "Deep blue is not a suitable color for a coming out ball," she said softly. "And if that neckline is to dip to where your hand indicated, his lordship will never agree."

Cecilie's pink lips settled into a pout. "He's so stuffy. Why did Papa have to give me such a guardian?"

"I'm sure he thought he had your welfare in mind. You know your papa always wanted the best for you."

Cecilie frowned. "Well, his lordship is

certainly not the best." A curious look came over her face and she tickled the monkey's ears absently. "But he has got an interesting chest. I wish that I might see it again."

"Cecilie!" This time Aggie could not contain her annoyance. "Young ladies should not even be aware of that portion of a gentleman's – anatomy."

"But, Aggie, you saw it. How could you *not* be aware? It was so – hairy. And the hair curled in the cutest little way."

"Cecilie! Stop that this instant." Aggie was aware that her face had flushed red and a quite disconcerting picture of the Earl's chest had flashed onto the screen of her memory. Vainly she tried to wipe it off. "Cecilie," she hoped her tone was firm, "young ladies never talk about such things."

"But why not? It's very interesting. I wonder why young ladies don't grow such hair."

"Cecilie! Well-bred young ladies should not see such things. At least until after they are married."

"But then," said Cecilie, with the in-exorable logic of the young, "it would be too late."

"Too late for what?" inquired Aggie, intrigued in spite of herself.

50

"Too late to know whether or not my husband had such a chest."

"Cecilie, one does not marry because of a man's chest."

Cecilie shrugged her shoulders. "Well, I am quite determined. My husband must be a good dancer, a crack horseman, and have a lot of hair on his chest."

Aggie, by now resigned to the fact that she could not end this conversation which was taking on unreal proportions, sighed. "Cecilie, one does not *see* one's intended's – body – until after the ceremony."

Cecilie tossed her curls. "Perhaps not. But I tell you I am resolved on this matter. I shall not marry a man unless he has a chest like that. I simply shall not."

Aggie could think of nothing more to say. She knew from experience that it was futile to try to change Cecilie's mind. She could only hope that this was some temporary whim of hers. As far as she was concerned, thought Aggie, it was not the chest itself, but the fact that it belonged to his lordship, that she found so disconcerting. She opened her mouth to caution Cecilie against informing the Earl of this new resolve, but she closed it again without doing so. It was dangerous to tell Cecilie that something might prove annoying to his lordship. For, should an occasion arise in which she *wished* to annoy him – as it well might – she would immediately revert to the use of such weapons. And in this case, at least, it could only work to her detriment. The Earl was a hard man, with a volatile temper, quite unused to dealing with temperamental young women. But the most important thing was that *he* held the power. And in any contest, no matter how uncomfortable Cecilie made him, the Earl was bound to best her.

Aggie sighed again. There was no way to make Cecilie realize this. The next days were going to prove very exasperating, Aggie thought. And she would be caught in the middle: between a willful recalcitrant child and a proud strongminded lord. It was not at all a pleasant prospect.

Chapter Four

The next several days passed without much incident, but Aggie did not really relax. How could she, when she had always to be alert so that Dillydums did not escape to roam the house or Cecilie to take to the sidewalks? Still, she appreciated the relative calm while she waited for the storm she knew was coming. And come it did.

They had been in London roughly a week when after luncheon one day Bates appeared. "His lordship wishes to see you both in the library," he announced.

Cecilie made a face, but kept silent and rose dutifully enough to follow her companion. Inside the library door Aggie paused. The Earl was at his desk, his gaze intent on a ledger. As the rustle of their gowns announced their presence he raised his head. "Good day."

It was impossible to detect anything from his tone and Aggie found herself scrutinizing his face for signs of his mood. "Good day, milord," she replied.

His lordship nodded toward some chairs. "Please be seated. We have a great deal to be discussed." He paused, awaiting a reply, but none came. "I have set the date for your come out," he continued. "Lady Bakiston has agreed to take the whole thing in hand. Who could ask for a better person to direct things?"

To this entirely rhetorical question Cecilie replied, "I could. I appreciate your putting yourself out for me," she continued with perfect composure. "But it is actually quite unnecessary. Aggie is quite capable of

53

handling the whole thing, so you may give Lady Bakiston my thanks and tell her we don't need her."

Denby's expression never wavered while Cecilie spoke. When she had finished, he merely smiled dryly. "I have already engaged Lady Bakison. She has her plans well underway."

"I do not want Lady Bakiston to plan anything," cried Cecilie. "This is *my* come out. Aggie and I have it all arranged."

The Earl regarded her soberly. "Lady Bakiston is most experienced in such matters. You and Miss Trimble are a couple of innocents in from the country. You don't know the situation. She does."

"That is unfair," cried Cecilie. "We have made plans already."

"You will have to forget them," said the Earl, fixing steely eyes upon her. "Lady Bakiston knows exactly what to do."

"No!" cried Cecilie, jumping to her feet. "You can't do this to me. I don't want some old dragonish dowager ruining my come out."

"Miss Winthrop!" The Earl's tone was not loud, but it was quite forceful. "Either Lady Bakiston manages the come out or there will be none. Do you understand?"

For a long moment Cecilie stared at him in amazement.

"Sit down, Miss Winthrop. Now."

Cecilie sat. Watching her, Aggie was not fooled. Cecilie was not beaten, she was merely biding her time.

"Lady Bakiston will handle all the arrangements," continued his lordship in a conversational tone. "This afternoon you are to go to Madame Dimond's on Bond Street to be measured for your gown."

Aggie waited for the explosion, but none came. "When can we talk to Lady Bakiston?" asked Cecilie with deceptive composure.

"It will not be necessary for you to be in contact with her at all. She is quite adept at planning such affairs."

Aggie sensed that his lordship desired to keep rumors about Cecilie's character from circulating among the *ton*. Once let that select group decide that she was eccentric and his task of finding her a suitable husband would be doubly difficult.

The Earl consulted his timepiece. "In an hour I shall accompany you to the dressmaker." He eyed them quizzically. "If you have any more questions, I shall answer them then. In the meantime I shall finish my accounts."

His eyes met Aggie's briefly, but she saw no warmth in them. Perhaps she had been fortunate, she told herself as she rose to her feet, not to have made an alliance with Denby. Who could have imagined that the tender glances and soft whispered words hid a man of such studied coldness?

It was not until they had reached the safety of their room that Cecilie spoke. "The man is insufferable!" she cried as the door closed behind them. "Who does he think he is?"

Aggie sighed. "I'm afraid he meant what he said. Things will be his way or not at all."

"It's so grossly unfair," Cecilie blurted out.

"Much of the world is unfair," commented Aggie. "Especially to women. Men have the power – political, economic, and legal. There is little you can do to fight that."

She was painfully aware that the tears in Cecilie's wide eyes were real ones. "You have led a very sheltered life, my dear. All men are not like your papa. They simply will not care about your feelings." She felt the tears rise to her own eyes at the thought of Denby's duplicity. "But perhaps things will not be so bad. After all, the Earl has his reputation to consider. If he gives a pinchpenny ball, it will only reflect on him. And this Lady Bakiston evidently knows exactly what to do. I'm sure things will run quite smoothly."

Cecilie considered this. "I suppose so," she finally conceded. "But he needn't be so top-lofty about everything. He acts like he was God Himself."

Though Aggie found this description of his lordship somewhat accurate, she did not think it fit to indicate so. "I expect we shall have to learn to live with his lordship," she said softly. "It seems unlikely that he will change."

Cecilie nodded absently. "No, I don't suppose he will. He seems far too stubborn for that. Well, at least we won't have to deal with this Lady Bakiston. She's probably an inferior type who gets paid for her efforts."

"There is nothing wrong with a gentle-woman being paid for her efforts," said Aggie softly. "We must live, too, you know."

Cecilie smiled. "Oh, I know that, Aggie. And anyway, you are not an inferior type."

Aggie accepted the statement in the spirit in which she was sure it was intended and smiled. "Well, we had best get ourselves in order. I doubt that his lordship is much of a man for waiting."

Cecilie giggled. "No, I don't suppose he is. My, how very fortunate for womankind that his lordship has elected to remain single. How terrible it would be to be leg-shackled to such an arrogant bully."

As she turned away to change her gown and redo her hair, Aggie smiled wryly. What would Cecilie say if she knew that once her companion had contemplated that very fate – and not with horror, but with delight!

When they descended the stairs at the appointed time, Cecilie seemed suitably subdued. Aggie, however, felt that she would not draw an easy breath until they had returned to the house on Grosvenor Square. It was most often when Cecilie was quiet like this that she suddenly erupted into a tantrum.

The Earl came out of the library and stood at the bottom of the stairs watching them. Aggie felt her breath quicken as his eyes slid over her. She must get over this foolish kind of reaction, she told herself firmly. The Earl's only relationship to her was as Cecilie's guardian. She would think of him in that light and no other. Still, as she reached the foot of the stairs and his eyes met hers, a strange quivering sensation ran down her spine. His eyes swung away before she could drop hers and she wondered momentarily at the warmth in them. But then he had turned to take his curly brimmed beaver and York tan riding gloves from the waiting Bates. "I've no idea how long we shall be," he said to the butler. "I have never before gone shopping for a gown for a come out."

Bates nodded and smiled, "Yes, milord."

Denby offered his arm to Cecilie and she took it with a slight but charming smile. Following behind them, Aggie was not at all fooled. When Cecilie turned on this much charm, it was always with some particular intent in mind; and today, Aggie knew, it was because of the gown. Cecilie had conceded in the matter of Lady Bakiston, but, precisely because she had, she would be less inclined to give in on the matter of the gown. Aggie foresaw a furious battle and more embarrassing and caustic comments from his lordship.

"Is Madame Dimond's a very fashionable establishment?" inquired Cecilie.

The Earl nodded. "Fashionable enough; I believe the Duchess of York patronizes this shop. But then, perhaps *you* know." His lordship sent a swift look in Aggie's direction, a look that she pretended not to see.

"No," replied Cecilie, just as evenly. "The last time I was at Oatlands we talked mostly of animals. The Duchess is quite fond of them, you know. It was she who told me where to buy Dillydums."

"I see." The Earl's tone revealed nothing, but Aggie could not help wondering. Did he think the child was lying to him? She herself had never accompanied Cecilie and her father to Oatlands. Indeed, she had been quite grateful for the brief periods of peace thus granted her. Life as Cecilie's companion left her little time for her own concerns. At first, of course, that had been good. It left her less time to brood over deceptive looks in smoky gray eyes and whispered words that had meant nothing to the whisperer.

She shook herself out of this mood of reverie. Only a fool would believe that Cecilie and his lordship were going to agree on a gown. And Aggie was no fool.

The ride was a short one. Now and then Cecilie exclaimed over some sight on the teeming streets, but mostly they rode in silence. As they neared Bond Street more and more fashionable ladies began to appear on the pavement. Aggie grew suddenly aware of bonnets and was soon convinced that theirs were rather out of style. In her case this was of little moment. She would, however, have to speak to Denby. Cecilie would need new things, not only for the ball, but for other occasions that would follow. "Milord?"

He turned to her and she felt herself coloring up. "Yes, Miss Trimble?"

"Since we are going to be at the dressmaker's, perhaps it would be wise to order more than one gown. If Cecilie is to be going about, she will need some new things."

The Earl regarded her gravely, then nodded. "That was also my thought," he said. "Since we are here, we might as well attend to it all." His eyes slid down over her gown, causing that strange quickening in her breast; and he seemed about to speak again. But he did not.

She watched him help Cecilie descend and then he offered her his hand. She did not want to touch him; she knew instinctively that to do so would be dangerous. But she could not very well ignore that outstretched hand, nor could she explain such rudeness on her part to the waiting Cecilie, who knew nothing at all concerning her previous acquaintance with his lordship. So Aggie laid her gloved hand in that which was offered her – and even through two pairs of gloves she felt the warmth of his fingers. As soon as her feet touched the ground she withdrew her hand with a mumbled, "Thank you, milord."

Cecilie was fairly trembling with eagerness and Aggie smiled as Denby led his ward into the shop. This was Cecilie's first visit to London, and one of her constant topics on the journey, and before, had been the gowns she was going to buy.

Madame Dimond herself met them inside the door, her round face beaming with delight. "Ahhhhh, Milord Denby. Such a long time I have not seen you. You are well, *n'est-ce pas?*"

The Earl nodded. "Quite well. This is my ward, Miss Cecilie Winthrop. And her companion Miss Agatha Trimble."

The little modiste, whose body was as round as her face, bobbed and nodded. "You will come this way, *s'il vous plaît*. We will sit in the comfort."

She led them into a small room furnished with comfortable chairs. Aggie meant to seat herself unobtrusively in the back, but somehow she ended up with the Earl on her left and Cecilie on her right.

"And now," said Madame Dimond from her place between the Earl and Cecilie, "you will tell me for what you want this gown?"

"Miss Winthrop is coming out," replied the Earl. "I think something in ivory satin. Not too décolleté. You understand."

"Ahhh yes," murmured the dressmaker.

"I have here the pattern book. Something like this. The little cap sleeves, the self-ruching at the neck and hem. It was a gown such as this that I made for Lady Alicia Temple, some few years back."

The Earl nodded, a strange look crossing his features. Aggie felt a shiver go over her. Denby knew this Lady Alicia, knew her in a very special way. That was instantly clear to her. But what else could she expect, she told herself severely. Long ago she had realized that she meant nothing to this man, that his whispered words of promise were nothing but lies. Naturally he had sought out other women; that was the way such men behaved.

She grew suddenly conscious that everyone was looking at her. "We are asking how you think about this pattern," said the dressmaker. "You see how the skirt flounces here." She pointed with a stubby forefinger.

Aggie nodded. "I think perhaps we should ask Cecilie," she replied. "She is the one who will wear it."

The three of them turned to Cecilie, who responded with another too-sweet smile. "Is that what girls are accustomed to wear?"

The dressmaker nodded. *"Oui.* Most *jeunes filles,* they wear such gowns."

Cecilie nodded. "Then I suppose it will
63

do. Now I'd like to see some stuff for other gowns."

Aggie found herself holding her breath, but the Earl merely nodded. "We'll see some stuffs for some day gowns and several for evening."

The choosing of these materials and patterns went so well that Aggie could scarcely believe it. Cecilie seemed entirely amenable to whatever his lordship suggested.

Aggie herself wished she already had the promised inheritance. Her own gowns were getting quite shabby and she did not have any idea what she could wear if they were to go to the theater, which seemed quite likely. In the country she had had no need for new gowns except as the old ones wore out. And even then she had not often replaced them. Consequently her wardrobe was not in very good condition.

She suppressed a sigh as she absently rubbed a pale peach silk between thumb and forefinger. If her purse had not been so empty, she would have a gown of this stuff and perhaps one of that pale, pale green lamé that the dressmaker now held. But such things were patently impossible.

She gave her attention to the materials that Cecilie and his lordship were discussing. Amazingly enough, it appeared that the two were on the most cordial of terms. And then Cecilie looked sweetly at the modiste and said, "Let me see your new French muslin, the very fine ones."

There was a moment of absolute silence while the dressmaker's eyes sought his lordship's. Evidently she read assent there for she clapped her hands and summoned a shop girl. "Bring the new French muslin."

"In blue-green," said Cecilie softly.

Again the dressmaker sought his lordship's eyes and so did the shop girl. His brief nod sent her scurrying away.

Silence lay heavy upon them as they waited. Aggie wondered if the Earl expected her to make some comment, but she had no idea what to say. Obviously there was something about this very fine muslin that she did not understand. There was nothing for it but to sit quietly and wait.

The girl returned with the bolt of material. Cecilie's eyes lit up. "Yes, that's it. That's the color!"

The Earl reached out and took the end of the swath between his fingers. As he held it up, Aggie bit back a cry. Fine? This muslin was so thin she could see through it clearly. "Ah yes," said his lordship dryly. "Very fine, indeed. And I collect you propose to damp your petticoat under it." His tone was so easily conversational that Cecilie's nod was automatic.

"You will not," said Denby in the same even tones. "Take that stuff away. It may be fit for cyprians or their like, but not for a ward of mine."

His eyes fastened on Aggie as he said this and immediately she felt the blood racing to her cheeks. Why must he always blame her?

"Mi-lo-rd!" Cecilie's wail ended in a shriek that stopped the shop girl in alarm. "I want a gown in that stuff. Pl-e-ase. I won't damp my petticoat. I promise." Tears stood out in Cecilie's wide eyes and her pink lips trembled as she begged again. "Please."

The Earl shook his head. "No, I am surprised that you should consider such a thing." His eyes raked over Aggie as though the whole episode had been her fault.

"You are a horrible, horrible man!" cried Cecilie. "I have done everything you wanted. Given in on every single thing. Now I want this gown."

The Earl looked at her sternly. "Miss Winthrop, kindly remember where you are."

Cecilie jumped to her feet and stood glaring down at him. "I don't *care* where I am," she yelled. "I – I want – that – gown!"

"Cecilie," Aggie began, but the Earl sent her such a look of disgust that she gave up trying to reason with the girl. Let his high and mighty lordship handle this himself. If he could! He would soon discover that Cecilie was not the type to cry off.

"Miss Winthrop," he began in tones obviously designed to placate, "you must be reasonable. A young woman such as yourself cannot afford to appear in public in such guise. It would give entirely the wrong impression."

"I don't care!" screamed Cecilie. "I want that gown!"

The Earl got to his feet, too, and Aggie, sitting between them, felt in imminent danger. Cecilie moved away, coming to a stop by a table that held patterns and sewing paraphernalia.

The Earl's face darkened almost imperceptibly. "That will be enough," he said sharply, so sharply that the shop girl cringed and Madame Dimond winced.

"It's not enough at all!" screamed Cecilie, by now thoroughly out of control. "I – want – that – gown!"

Aggie got to her feet and moved off to one side. The Earl could not know that the best thing would be to walk out and leave Cecilie without any audience for this performance. And she could hardly suggest it to him at the moment. She stood quietly, waiting to see what he would do.

For a long moment there was silence in the room; then Madame Dimond sent the shop girl a look and the two of them quietly departed, shutting the door behind them. Aggie considered following suit, but two things held her back. The first was recognition of the fact that her departure might be misconstrued by the Earl as an admission of defeat or a dereliction of duty. Strong as this motive for remaining was, however, even stronger was her desire to see what would happen in the ensuing battle. She was quite sure that Cecilie had never met such an opponent before and it seemed equally unlikely that his lordship had ever previously faced a screeching young woman.

"Cecilie," said the Earl, in tones of great authority. "You are disgracing yourself. You must stop this very instant." He paused as though waiting for a reply, but Cecilie's only response was to glare at him. "Such a gown would be unsuitable. Any decent person would tell you that." Again Aggie felt that the words were directed at her. "Now, we will just walk calmly out to the carriage and go home."

Cecilie's hand closed over a pincushion.

"I am not going anywhere until I get my gown!"

The Earl's back stiffened. "This is doing it up too brown!" he thundered. "You will come home and right now."

"No!" Cecilie emphasized this by throwing the pincushion with all her might. It bounced off his lordship's waistcoat and fell to the floor, scattering pins in every direction.

Aggie felt her knees begin to go weak. Cecilie had no idea what kind of opponent she had engaged with.

"That does it!" roared the Earl. "I am going to discuss some matters with Madame Dimond. I shall give you exactly ten minutes to compose yourself and get into the carriage. If you are not there by that time, I shall drive immediately home and dispose of that monkey!" He turned on his heel and stormed out, his brows drawn together in a terrible frown, his eyes blazing.

Aggie took one look at the girl, who stood mouth open in amazement. Then she did what should have been done long before. She, too, left the room, depriving Cecilie of her last spectator.

As she took her seat in the carriage, Aggie wondered if the Earl's ploy would work. Cecilie loved that monkey; it was her dearest

friend. For the Earl to threaten it like that –
Would he really follow through on such a
threat? Aggie wondered.

She settled herself on the squabs and tried
to stay calm. She would need all her wits
about her for the moment when his lordship
saw fit to discuss this matter. She was sure
he would read her a real scold; more than
likely he believed that she had been in
collusion with Cecilie. Wherever had the girl
learned about that French muslin? Aggie
wondered. Probably from one of the young
maidservants. They were usually quite
conversant on the latest fashions.

As the moments passed slowly by, Aggie
grew more anxious. She really did not doubt
that his lordship would get rid of the monkey
if Cecilie failed to obey. But it was not what
she thought that mattered; the important
thing was what Cecilie thought.

It seemed to the waiting Aggie that ten
minutes had long passed, but actually it was
only eight minutes later that Cecilie climbed
into the carriage and threw herself sullenly
on the seat. Aggie said nothing, prudently
keeping her eyes averted until some moments
later his lordship entered the carriage also.
His brows had returned to their normal
position and his eyes were cloudy rather than
blazing with anger. His mouth, however,

seemed grimly set and he said nothing as the carriage moved off.

The ride home was made in absolute silence, no one speaking a word. When the carriage stopped, the Earl addressed them both. "You will go directly to your rooms and stay there. I must have time to get my temper under control before I speak to you."

Cecilie did not even nod. She merely marched on up the stairs as though the Earl of Denby did not exist. He turned to Aggie and he was frowning again. "I have changed my mind. I want a word with you."

"Yes, milord." Aggie sighed. Perhaps it was just as well. If she bore the brunt of his anger, there would not be so much left to enrage Cecilie.

The Earl glared down at her. "How long has this kind of thing been going on?" he demanded.

"Since before I came into Cecilie's life," Aggie replied. "She has always gotten her way. She's used to it."

Denby scowled. "And if she does not, she throws these fits?"

Aggie nodded.

"I don't suppose you could have given me some warning," he said accusingly.

"I thought of it," admitted Aggie, wondering at the candor and honesty he

71

could wear and discard at will. Right now his eyes seemed to be pleading for her understanding and help. "But I couldn't tell you in front of Cecilie. As you have discovered, the best way to deal with her in this mood is simply to walk away." She risked a look into the eyes so close to her own. "I have never had any power over her. She could always go over my head to her papa. And she did."

Denby scowled. "The girl is spoiled rotten."

"I quite agree, milord," replied Aggie, wishing that he would not stand so close to her. It had been just like this so long ago, only then they had spoken of inconsequential things. Spoken, until they kissed. Her eyes widened and her lips softened at the memory. How very much she had loved him, she thought bitterly. And how very foolish that had been.

"Where did she learn about French muslin?" he demanded gruffly.

Aggie frowned. "I wonder myself, milord. I had no idea what it was until I saw it."

A strange look passed over his face and Aggie felt herself bristling up. Now he was going to read her a lecture. "If that is quite all," she said coldly, "I shall only give you one more piece of advice."

72

"And what might that be?" he asked softly, looking down at her with eyes that seemed warm and tender. She wanted to step back, to move further away from him, but she seemed rooted to the spot. For a long moment there was silence between them, then she managed to gather her wits. "Do not thwart Cecilie in public," she said, in what she hoped were even tones. "She has absolutely no sense of embarrassment. What you experienced today was actually quite minor."

The Earl nodded, but it did not appear that he really heard her. He gazed intently down at her, then asked, in a tone that was almost a caress, "Why have you never married?"

Aggie had been losing herself in the depths of those gray eyes, drawn backward in time to the days when tenderness had existed between them. His question caused a flood of scarlet to her cheeks and she drew back from him. "You go beyond the bounds, milord," she said stiffly. "That is no concern of yours." Holding her head high, she spun on her heel and quickly raced up the stairs. In her haste to escape his presence before the telltale tears fell, she did not see the look of pain that crossed his handsome features as he watched her retreating figure.

73

Chapter Five

Cecilie came out of her sulks, arrangements for the come out proceeded as planned, and Aggie tried her best to avoid his lordship. How dare he ask her such a personal question! She felt the heat of embarrassment spreading over her body whenever she thought of it. And what other answer could she have given him? Surely her pride would not allow her to tell him the truth – that she had delayed so long in waiting for his return that no other match had been possible.

Cecilie gave very little trouble. She watched Dillydums very carefully, she did not attempt to walk out alone, and she seemed reconciled to his lordship's control. Aggie was not sure how long this stage of affairs would last; but she welcomed the peace, regardless of its duration. She was having a difficult time with herself. She could not seem to think of the Earl merely as Cecilie's guardian. No matter how she tried she could not wipe out the memories of those long-ago days. Nor could she keep from seeing his lordship as he had been then

– with tenderness and warmth shining from his eyes.

All of this came to a focus several days before the come out when the new gowns arrived. Cecilie, in a gay, laughing mood, began to unpack them. "First, I shall lay them all out on the bed," she decided. "So we may admire them."

Aggie nodded. Certainly that was a harmless enough diversion. She turned back to her needlework, attending with only half an ear to Cecilie's squeals and comments. But suddenly Cecilie cried out, "Aggie, look here. We didn't order this." From the box she pulled a gown of pale peach silk, the very silk that Aggie had so admired that day at the shop. Obviously this gown was not Cecilie's. It was cut for a more womanly figure and the neckline was rather low for a young woman just come out.

"And here's another," announced Cecilie. Burrowing in the box, she pulled out a gown of palest green lamé. Aggie stared in surprise. How could such a mistake have been made? Two gowns of the very materials she had most admired. "Where is the bill?" she asked. "There has been some error."

Cecilie rummaged around through boxes and paper and finally emerged triumphant with the bill in her fist.

Aggie studied it. "The gowns are listed here," she said with a frown. "I do not understand. I will have to speak to the Earl."

Cecilie nodded absently. "Look, this gown is just the color for you. Why don't you try it on?"

Aggie was about to refuse, but the temptation was strong. After all, she had been a long time without pretty things. The gown was there; there would be no harm in just trying it on. She loved the shimmering peach color. "All right, but just for a moment. Then I must find his lordship and advise him of this mistake."

Cecilie insisted on helping with the gown, doing up the hooks and patting it into place, then backing off to see how it looked. "Oh, Aggie, it looks like it was made for you!" she squealed in delight, causing the monkey to forsake his perch on the bedpost and scramble into her arms.

Moving to the cheval glass, Aggie regarded herself almost with awe. The soft shade of the gown contrasted with the rich darkness of her hair. And it did fit perfectly. The décolletage was perhaps a little lower than she had ever worn, but it was not immodest. The long narrow sleeves edged in a delicate lace, and the similar lace edging the neckline, gave the gown a festive air.

"It's just the thing for you to wear to my come out," said Cecilie, clapping her hands.

Aggie shook her head. "I can't do that, dear. Besides, the gown is too young for me." She did not really believe that – she had the testimony of her eyes right before her – but she did not want to tell her charge that there was no money available for new clothes.

With Cecilie's help she carefully removed the gown and replaced it in the box. Then she put on her old one, a sprigged muslin faded by many washings. It looked more tired and lifeless than ever after the other. "Where is the bill?" Aggie asked.

Cecilie handed it to her. "I don't think you should tell him anything," she said with a gamine smile. "Just let him pay for them."

"Cecilie I can't do that."

Cecilie shrugged. "I should do it if I were you. He deserves it." And she made a small face.

"If we all got what we deserved," replied Aggie with a slight smile, "you and I might not like it either."

Cecilie made no reply to this; she just grinned and retreated to the bed with the monkey.

The bill firmly in hand, Aggie descended the staircase. She did not relish the idea of being alone with Denby, but to take Cecilie

77

along on such an interview was to court disaster. She approached the library door with something like fear. Most often his lordship spent the morning hours there, sequestered with his accounts. And she usually made it her business to avoid this area altogether. But now she would have to face him. She took a deep breath and rapped.

"Come in," called the Earl.

Mustering all her courage, she pushed open the door. As she had supposed, Denby sat at the great desk. For some moments he did not raise his head and as she looked at him sudden tears filled her eyes. Here was the man she had thought to spend her life beside.

"Yes, Ba –" He looked up, then got hurriedly to his feet, a pleased expression on his face. "Ag – Miss Trimble! Please sit down. How may I help you?" he came toward her and she barely kept herself from retreating.

"The dressmaker has made a mistake," she said, refusing the seat he gestured her to. "She has sent two gowns we did not order."

Something strange flickered in his eyes and he smiled warmly. "One is of peach satin. The other of pale green lamé."

Aggie stared at him. "How did you know that?"

Denby took another step closer. "I know because I ordered them. For you."

Color flooded Aggie's face. "Milord! You cannot."

His mouth tightened slightly. "You must have clothes for Cecilie's come out." He smiled a little. "I thought I handled it very well. I had the maid spirit out one of your old gowns so Madame Dimond could take your measurements from it. I hope they fit well."

More color flooded her face at the thought that she had tried the gown on. Aggie shook her head. "I cannot accept –"

The Earl's brows began to draw together. "Aggie," he said in a voice from the past, "you're not giving me a chance."

She wanted to scream at him then, her heart contracting with the pain of hearing him speak her given name. *You had your chance and you threw it away,* she wanted to scream. But she did not. Instead, she forced herself to speak calmly, "Milord, I cannot accept clothing from you. It is unseemly."

His mouth tightened further. "Miss Trimble," he said formally, "you forget your position here. As the companion of my ward you cannot appear at the ball in rags."

Aggie was struck silent. She was acutely conscious of the truth of his words. But how could she accept anything from him? The situation was impossible.

He moved closer, until only a few inches separated them. She wanted desperately to back away; his presence was overpowering. But she seemed rooted to the spot as his eyes searched hers. She felt the pulse throbbing in her throat and she swayed slightly from the weakness that was creeping over her. "Aggie," he said softly, and the word itself was a caress. "You're driving me mad like this. Can you never forget the past?"

His eyes burned into hers and she felt herself growing still weaker. Those eyes seemed to be hungrily seeking something and she was overcome with such a welling up of affection for him that she swayed involuntarily in his direction. She felt a moment of terror as the full realization of her feelings hit and then his arms encircled her and his lips descended on hers. There was one moment of startled awareness, one moment when she might conceivably have withdrawn, but she let it pass, still awash as she was with intense feeling.

And then it was too late. He drew her close against him; she felt the heat of his body, his mouth moving on hers, seeking, caressing. She ceased to be aware of individual things and was swept away on a great tide of emotion. It seemed that for the last five years she had been in some kind of half-sleep – not dead, but not alive. And now the touch of his lips had wakened her again, to an ecstasy that could not be denied.

She knew that she should not respond, that her best defense lay in being cold and lifeless. But there was no way she could keep her body from reacting to his touch, no way to close her lips against this tender onslaught.

When finally he released her, she could scarcely stand, so overpowered was she by the torrents of emotion that he had released in her. For a long moment she stood, forehead bowed against his chest. Then he put one hand under her chin and gently tilted back her head until she was forced to meet his eyes. It was almost as though the intervening years had never been – as though there still existed between them that wonderful bond of long ago.

"Aggie," he said softly, "you must accept the gowns." His eyes moved over her face. "There's so much I can do for you now. You'll see."

It took awhile for the meaning of his words to sink into her dazed mind, but when they did, Aggie wrenched herself free of his arms. He had not offered for her in marriage as he had said he would, not even told her why he had left so abruptly. But now, because of that one kiss, he thought she would be willing to – Rage rushed through her at the degrading thought. If he had not wanted to marry her before, when she was a good catch with a substantial dowry, he certainly did not have that in mind now. What he did have in mind was – unspeakable.

She drew herself up and stared at him from eyes gone icy. "You go beyond the bounds, milord. The past is dead. And with it any connection there may have been between us." She half expected him to argue, to tell her that the kiss proved her wrong. But he only stood, staring at her silently, his black brows drawn together. "I will wear the gowns because I must," she continued. "But I will reimburse you for them after Cecilie is wed and I come into what Lord Winthrop left me. I may be poor, but I do not need charity."

His expression changed then and he cried out, "Aggie! Please!" and took a step toward her, but this time she did not hesitate to back away.

"The only matter between us is Cecilie's future. And, since Lady Bakiston has everything in hand for the come out, I believe there is nothing more to discuss at the moment."

Denby's face, which seconds before had shown tenderness and desire, was now set in stony impassivity. His eyes, which had been warm and glowing, were now the cold gray of fieldstone.

"You make your position very clear, Miss Trimble. I shall try to remember it in the future. As for now, you are quite right; there is nothing more to be discussed."

Aggie nodded as she turned, fighting to keep back the telltale tears. "Good day, milord."

She was almost to the door when he spoke again. "I ordered the peach gown for the come out. I expect you to wear it then." The words sounded strange in the coldly formal tone that he used and Aggie choked back a sob, not daring to turn and look at him.

She swallowed twice before she could answer. "Very well, milord. I shall obey your command."

She did not see the spasm of pain that crossed his face or the half step he took toward her. Her eyes blinded with tears, she made her way out the door and down the hall to the little courtyard. She needed a few minutes alone before she could face Cecilie.

Sinking down on a stone bench, she stared unseeing at a deep red rose. How could she have let him kiss her like that? He had been gone for five long years, with never a word during that time. And not a word now as to his reasons for leaving so suddenly. And yet he had kissed her and looked at her as he had in the old days. She choked back another sob. What a fool she had been to give in to her treacherous body. Now the Earl knew he had some power over her. He knew. That was why he had made such a dishonorable remark. She felt the heat flooding her body at the thought of it. Oh yes, he could do so much for her. And all he wanted in return was – her honor!

She wiped futilely at her wet eyes. Yes, fate had been doubly cruel to her. Not only had it forced her back into contact with the man who had broken her heart, it had also constrained her to admit the painful truth – more painful than ever now that she saw his dishonorable motives – broken as her heart was, the pieces still yearned for him.

Chapter Six

The day of Cecilie's come out finally arrived. Aggie, surveying the great ballroom that occupied the entire fourth floor of the house, had to give the invisible Lady Bakiston credit. The masses of fresh flowers gave the room a festive appearance and the delicacies being prepared in the kitchen should please any palate.

Cecilie was suddenly rather nervous, begging Aggie to go have a look and be assured that the great barren room had been made presentable. Actually, the flowers and palms made a great deal of difference. Aggie sighed; it was in just such a ballroom that she had whirled in blissful joy in the arms of the then Viscount Acton. Hurriedly she pushed the memory aside. Those days were over. All she could expect from the Earl now were possible attacks on her virtue, such as that which had occurred a few days ago. She felt herself grow warm at the thought. She would have to be very careful. Now that she knew that his attraction for her was as strong as ever she must keep herself under control.

Thankfully he had not spoken to her about the matter again. Perhaps he had taken her icy words to heart. But it was quite disconcerting to feel his eyes upon her. She tried to avoid meeting those eyes that had once been the instruments of her betrayal, but she could not always do so. And when, perforce, her eyes met his, what she discovered there left her bewildered. If she had not known that it was entirely illogical and impossible, she would have sworn that his eyes spoke of hurt and pain.

She shook her head. The Earl had been quite formally polite and businesslike, and under the circumstances that was quite the best thing. It made life easier for all of them. The question was: how long would he remain that way? The terrible yearning inside herself... If there was anything like that inside him...

She turned away and hurried back down the stairs to reassure Cecilie and supervise her dressing. One could never tell what madcap stunt the girl might decide upon. And this night was crucial to her future. This was her first public appearance in the world of the *ton*. Nothing must spoil it – for Cecilie's sake and her own.

When she entered their rooms, Cecilie swung around from the bed where she was playing with Dillydums. "Does it look all right, Aggie? Really?" she asked anxiously.

"It looks very nice. Lady Bakiston has done a good job."

Cecilie made a face, but said nothing.

"I believe we should start dressing soon. It will take some time for Millie to do your hair."

"Yours, too," said Cecilie.

Aggie frowned. "I'll wear mine in its usual knot."

Cecilie sprang from the bed, causing the monkey to jump up and swing from the hangings in agitation. "Oh, Aggie, you mustn't. You'll spoil the whole thing. You're to wear the peach silk, of course. And it needs your hair done in a softer way. Maybe in the antique Roman style. Please, for me?" she begged.

Wearily, Aggie nodded. The strain of the last few days was beginning to tell on her; she simply did not have the energy to argue about unimportant things. "All right, but you must dress first."

Cecilie sighed. "I'm getting scared, Aggie. Why do people have to go through all this?"

Aggie smiled. "It's the custom, dear. The young men get a chance to see you and you get a chance to see them."

A glimmer of mischief lit Cecilie's eyes. "My husband will have to be a young man," she said. "Not old like the Earl."

"The Earl is hardly *old*," Aggie found herself replying, and was dismayed by the fact that her mind had just presented her with a picture of his lordship's bare chest.

Cecilie began to tease the monkey, tickling his nose with a feather from the pillow. "I know," she cried. "I shall take Dillydums along. He can sit on my shoulder. That way I shan't be lonely."

"Oh, Cecilie!" Aggie dropped into a chair. "You cannot take a monkey to a come out. Aside from the fact that his lordship might well have an attack of apoplexy –" The light in Cecilie's eyes warned her that this was not the right approach. "But even disregarding that – think of your own future. A man cannot be expected to court a woman *and* a monkey. And you *do* want to find a husband."

"Yes," agreed Cecilie with another sigh. "And at a ball I can find the good dancers. I suppose we shall need to go to Hyde Park to discover who's a good horseman."

Aggie nodded. "But now you must get dressed." Hopefully Cecilie had forgotten her third requirement for a husband. It would certainly be impossible for her to discover what a man's chest looked like before the wedding night unless . . .

The thought was so appalling that Aggie resisted it. But it would not be silenced. Suppose Cecilie found a man who was a good dancer *and* a crack horseman? Then suppose that she took matters into her own hands, as she was quite wont to do, and asked him outright about the hirsute quality of his chest! About to caution her charge against such a dangerous action – for surely such a request could be interpreted in many ways – Aggie shut her mouth sharply. It might be wiser not to mention the matter at all. Perhaps Cecilie had forgotten it. And even if she hadn't, warning her would not at all guarantee her compliance. It might even induce her to go ahead! Cecilie, having so little experience of the *ton*, had no idea of the complicity and wickedness of some men. It was impossible for her to imagine anyone taking advantage of her, especially as she knew so little of the opposite sex.

Aggie crossed to the wardrobe and withdrew the dress of ivory satin that Cecilie was to wear.

"You must put your gown on, too," said Cecilie. "I want Millie to do your hair right after mine."

Aggie nodded. It was easier just to go along with Cecilie's wishes. After all, what did it matter? No one would be paying attention to her anyway.

Cecilie looked quite ravishing in her gown. Its round neckline and little puffed sleeves accented the creaminess of her complexion. While Millie labored over the tousled curls, making sure each one looked adequately "natural," Aggie took the gown of peach silk from its hanger. Her fingers trembled as they touched the fine soft material. It had been a long time since she'd had a gown for the evening. And this one was so beautiful. How had he known that she liked this material and that pale green lamé? She had not thought her preference was so obvious. But somehow he had discovered it.

She must be very careful now – for if he had discovered her preference for materials, and with so little to work on – might he not also discover her preference for *him?* Especially after that revealing kiss. Then he would have an additional weapon at his disposal, a weapon to use in persuading her to become his mis – Her mind balked at the offending word and she shoved the thought aside. Her only dealings with his lordship now were those relating to Cecilie. Between the two of them there was nothing – nothing at all.

Another maid stepped forward and silently helped her off with her old gown. Her fingers felt all thumbs and she was aware of a growing nervousness. Of course, at any time she would be apprehensive about Cecilie's behavior and this was a most important occasion. But this nervousness was more than that. It was somehow related to the peach silk gown that was, in reality, a gift from Denby. No matter what she had said about reimbursing him, the truth was that he had paid for it. The gown, she decided, had become something more than a gown to her. She was being ridiculous, she thought, as the soft folds of silk fell around her. This was a gown and nothing more. Wearing it was a part of her job and did not in any way indicate her true feelings for Denby.

She stood silent while the maid arranged the rich folds of silk. This was perhaps the most beautiful gown she had ever owned – worn, she corrected herself. It clung to her body in all the right places, dipping low in the neck, but not too low, and falling to the floor in graceful folds.

By this time Millie had finished with Cecilie and, while she stood by, the maid released Aggie's hair from its restraining knot. It fell in a great cloud around her shoulders, making her face softer and younger.

"You should wear it like that, Aggie."

"I can't, dear." Aggie was careful not to reveal the dismay she felt at this suggestion, one advanced by the Earl long ago. "I'm far too old for that." And so Cecilie had to be content with Millie's bringing the tresses together at the back of the head and then coaxing them into two hanging ringlets.

91

"Oh Aggie," cried her ward. "You look absolutely lovely."

Aggie was not at all sure she wished to hear this, but looking in the cheval glass, she saw that a transformation had certainly been made. This creature, dazzling in shimmering silk, was not the drab, rather washed-out young woman she habitually saw in her glass. Her cheeks were rosy with excitement and her eyes sparkled.

"You look capital!" said Cecilie. "Why, it might be *your* come out."

Aggie managed not to wince. Cecilie could not know how painful such remembrances of the past were, remembrances that included a future alliance with the Earl. She found herself wishing that she did not look so well; it could not help her now to be attractive. Poor companions were far better off to be ugly or nondescript; then they were not so apt to be put in the way of temptation. A shiver passed over her as she remembered the feel of Denby's arms around her, the touch of his lips on hers. She must never allow such a situation to develop again. Never. For she knew quite clearly that once in his arms she could not keep from surrendering to his kisses. Character, honor, duty – nothing meant anything when he held her close.

92

She knew that now. And she must act accordingly.

In the ballroom later that evening as she stood flushing before Denby's gaze, Aggie reminded herself of her resolve. It was feather-brained to believe that she saw pain in his eyes. No one had hurt *him*.

He looked her over carefully, then smiled gravely. "You are looking quite well this evening, Miss Trimble. The gown was a fortunate choice. Do you approve of the design?"

Aggie nodded, her cheeks turning scarlet as she grew conscious of Cecilie's curious gaze.

"I particularly like the effect of the lace," he said, letting his eyes fall to where it lay against her bosom. It was impossible for Aggie to flush any deeper, but she felt the heat of embarrassment flooding her whole body.

"You are looking very good yourself," said Cecilie, surveying his black silk florentine breeches, black stockings, and slippers. Above the black waistcoat and full dress coat shimmered a gleaming white cravat.

The Earl inclined his head and turned his gaze to Cecilie. "That gown is most becoming to you. Lady Bakiston assures me that the crowd will be large."

"I wish we might waltz," said Cecilie, her mouth forming the beginning of a pout.

The Earl swallowed a sigh. He was obviously determined to be patient. "I'm sure Miss Trimble has explained to you. Until you have been to Almack's you cannot waltz. And until you have come out you cannot be invited to Almack's."

Cecilie shrugged. "I know all that. I just think it's unfair. Why should seven old women have all that power?"

His lordship coughed suddenly, almost, thought Aggie, as though he were concealing a laugh, but his face was suitably stern. "Do not let the Jersey hear you call *her* old," he warned. "She can ruin your reputation in ten seconds flat."

Cecilie tossed her curls, but she asked, "How shall I recognize Lady Jersey?"

Denby smiled. "She's small and dark, piquant. With great dark eyes. And she likes men." His gaze flicked toward Aggie and away again, and once more she felt that she was supposed to hear more than the words actually said.

It was then that the guests began arriving and it seemed to Aggie that they stood for hours, nodding and smiling, hearing names that she, at least, would never be able to recall.

However, she had no problem in recognizing or remembering Lady Jersey. Although no longer young, Jersey obviously took good care of herself. Her gown of pale lavender was constructed of the "fine" French muslin and revealed the lady's form in all its delights. From a small heart-shaped face two great dark eyes under long black lashes gazed at Aggie and she felt a sudden chill. The Jersey might like men; it was obvious that she did not care much for women. Aggie deliberately looked away as the lady smiled up at Denby from eyes gone suddenly very warm.

But finally the main task of greeting was over. Then Aggie was free to stand by the great banks of flowers, behind the line of dowagers in their chairs, and watch Cecilie being led through the steps of the dance. Every man who partnered her was catalogued and filed in Aggie's mind. None of them seemed particularly appealing to her, but she was aware that no man held much attraction for her but the unattainable Denby himself. She tried to think as Cecilie would. Consequently it was upon the best dancers that she bent her most intent gaze.

She was thus occupied when a sudden

95

commotion by the door caught her attention. Curious, she looked to see what latecomer had caused such a furor. Framed in the doorway stood a tall blond woman. She did not wear the French muslin; her gown was of silk, a deep and vibrant blue that seemed to draw all eyes. But perhaps it was not the gown itself, thought Aggie with a twinge of envy, but the way it fit, that caught one's attention. It looked like the lady had been poured into it, and with some caution, too, for fear the seams might split. The bodice was cut low, so low that it almost seemed as though at any moment her barely restrained bosom might escape its confines altogether. There was a decided rustle as the dowagers leaned toward each other.

"The woman's a fool," said one in red and white striped silk that reminded Aggie of an awning at the fair. "Denby's too sensible to be lured by such display."

The other matron, whose gown of bright yellow satin was in glaring contrast to a deep purple turban trimmed in green-dyed ostrich plumes, giggled in falsetto tones before replying in a hoarse whisper. "Denby's a man, ain't he? And you've got to admit Lady Alicia's got the looks for it. Her bosom's not as good as mine was, but it'll do. It'll do."

Her face crimson, Aggie moved silently

away. So this was the fabled Lady Alicia Temple. She paused beside a palm to take another look. Lady Alicia still stood in the doorway, surveying the crowd before her with imperious eyes. Certainly she did not lack confidence. Now Aggie wished she had stayed where she was. She might have heard more about Denby and Lady Alicia – heard, for instance, if they were already engaged in some sort of illicit – liaison.

As she watched, heart in mouth, Denby crossed the room to welcome the newcomer. Her gloved hands reached out to grab his and the kiss she gave him was hardly a mere salute of greeting. In fact, it might have become embarrassing if Denby had not extricated himself from her embrace and led the lady to the dance floor.

Lady Alicia trod the measures of the quadrille with grace, her blue-green eyes laughing warmly up at the Earl. Aggie felt a lump rising in her throat. Just so had he once looked down at her. For a terrible second she found herself wishing that some misfortune might befall the golden Lady Alicia. If only someone would step on that too-tight gown, causing the seams to part and leaving the lady exposed in her petticoat – if she were wearing one.

Aggie stopped her wandering imagination

in dismay. It was surely not the lady's fault the way Denby chose to behave. To be thinking such evil thoughts was very unlike her; Aggie felt a trifle ashamed.

She turned her attention determinedly from the Earl and sought among the throng for Cecilie's small form. Finally she found her, pacing off the measures of the quadrille with a sober-faced gentleman of middle age. He seemed quite attentive, but even at this distance Aggie could tell that Cecilie was bored. Unfortunately, the girl was not trying very hard to hide it from her partner. She returned little perfunctory nods to his remarks, remarks which from the earnest expression on his face might well have been compliments. Cecilie's behavior, however, did not seem to daunt her admirer, who amiably escorted her back to Aggie's side, paid her another compliment, and departed, still smiling.

"Who is that gentleman?" inquired Aggie casually.

Cecilie frowned. "He's the Marquess Connors. Quite fatiguing."

"He seemed to dance well," commented Aggie half aloud, as though to herself.

Cecilie shrugged. "Yes, he does. But when I asked about his cattle –" She sent Aggie a sidelong glance. "To find, you know, if he is a good rider."

Aggie nodded.

"Well, he isn't." Cecilie's small mouth formed a moue of disgust. "And then he read me the most dreadful lecture on the folly of keeping a big stable. All about the horrible expense of so many cattle, with figures and all. And then he went off scolding me about racing. He's quite a disagreeable creature. I hope he keeps his distance." Her eyes began to search out over the throng, but the expression on her face was not hopeful. "There's not a real out and outer in the whole room," she complained. "Lady Bakiston's guest list *stinks.*"

This last was far too loud for Aggie's peace of mind. "Please, Cecilie. You must not carry on so. Someone may hear you."

"I don't care," said Cecilie stubbornly, but she lowered her tone and cast a furtive glance around to see where the Earl might be. Thus it was that she discovered him dancing. "Aggie, who is that woman?" she asked curiously. "She simply hangs on his lordship."

"That," said Aggie in a voice she tried to strip of emotion, "is Lady Alicia Temple. She is a friend of the Earl's."

"An old, old friend from the looks of things," said Cecilie bluntly.

Aggie was about to reprimand her and then thought better of it. Sometimes the information learned from servants was very useful.

"I don't like her," said Cecilie definitely. "She's far too obvious about it. A woman should wait to be chased. Or," she added with a mischievous smile, "at least let the man *think* so."

"Cecil –" Aggie began, but her charge was already gone in a swirl of satin skirts. Aggie sighed. Life was not getting any easier. Not at all. And getting Cecilie safely married was not going to be a simple matter.

She sank down on a nearby chair. Thankfully there were no more dragonish dowagers nearby to tell her that they remembered *her* come out. Several had already done so, to her great embarrassment. And then there were the several older ladies, not yet dowagers but obviously obsessed with the fading of their charms, who had congratulated her on her entry into Denby's establishment. It was not until after the third of these creatures had dropped something about "so many advantages and the Earl such a prime article," that her dazed mind accepted the facts. These women clearly believed that she meant to parlay her position as Cecilie's companion into some kind of alliance with Denby. And from their sly looks and the way they rolled their eyes it was clear that they were not thinking of any honorable connection. This had become clear to her as she was speaking to this last woman and Aggie flushed scarlet to the roots of her hair and started to move away. But the offender had grabbed her arm. "I didn't mean to put you to the blush, my dear. But at your age – After all, we must take advantage of our opportunities."

Aggie had only been able to nod. Finally, spying a friend, the other woman had released her and trotted off.

Now, remembering, Aggie took a deep breath. She had to accept this as she accepted the rest. She had nowhere to run – no hiding place, no comforter, no partner in life. The man who had been supposed to take that place in her life had not done so. She must fend for herself. She tried to wrench her mind away from those terrible women and concentrate on Cecilie and what was happening to her.

As she stood looking out over the dance floor, she felt a presence behind her. Without turning, she knew instantly that Denby stood there, his eyes fastened upon her. She forced herself to remain still. She did not want to get into any contention with him; or to have him argue with Cecilie. So far things had been going along quite well. Aggie wanted them to continue to do so.

Denby took the step that brought him up beside her. He stood so close that the arm of his coat brushed the sleeve of her gown. "It seems to be going well, does it not?" he said conversationally.

"Very well, milord," replied Aggie, her eyes still on the floor.

"Do you think Cecilie has seen anyone she finds suitable?"

Aggie shook her head. "I think not." She forced herself to turn and face him. "You must understand Cecilie. She is very young. She wants a young man. Someone to have fun with." Her eyes pleaded with him to understand.

"Fun?" said the Earl in a tone of disbelief, his eyes clouding over. "My acquaintance with the institution of matrimony is limited and is not of a firsthand nature," he said somewhat dryly. "But never have I heard of anyone who was leg-shackled merely for the fun of it!"

"Cecilie is young," Aggie repeated. "Her mother died when she was still a babe. She has little idea of the reality of marriage."

"Have you considered informing her?" asked the Earl in the same dry tones.

"Of course I have. But Cecilie only learns from experience; words of advice have very little effect on her."

The Earl sighed. "I must have been daft or in my cups to take on the guardianship of such a creature. Thank God I have no daughters of my own who will someday reach this obnoxious condition."

"If you had daughters, milord," replied Aggie over the lump in her throat, "I am confident you'd do better at raising them than Cecilie's papa did."

His eyes reflected amazement. "You are? I should have thought you'd pity the poor things for having a tyrant for a papa."

Aggie allowed herself a small smile. "A tyrant, if he be consistent in his tyranny, can be lived with," she declared. "When a man is swayed by tears and pouts, a young person becomes quite spoiled and self-indulgent. And if he runs now hot, now cold – first persuadable and then not – his children may be very disturbed; for there is no consistency in their lives."

The Earl's eyes were suddenly warm. "You have a great knowledge of children," he said in a voice of admiration.

"It is a necessary prerequisite for a

governess-companion," replied Aggie, losing herself in the warm depths of his gaze.

And then, just as he leaned toward her confidentially, just as he seemed about to say something very important, there was the rustle of satin and the sound of a deep husky voice. "There you are, Denby, you bad boy. Come. Since you refuse to let them play any waltzes, you must dance this quadrille with me."

Before she turned, Aggie knew that the voice belonged to Lady Alicia Temple. For one long moment his lordship's eyes still held hers. Then he turned and she did the same. Up close, Lady Alicia was even more stunning. Her complexion was flawless, her hair the hue of burnished gold, and the cut of her gown... Aggie averted her eyes.

"Lady Temple," said the Earl, evidently wishing to preserve the amenities, "this is Miss Trimble, Miss Winthrop's companion."

The two women stared at each other. Aggie endeavored to keep her face blankly polite, but Lady Alicia evidently felt no such constraint. Her glance was direct and derogatory, as though she had no time to waste on lowly companions. Her aristocratic nose wrinkled in what could only be called distaste and her nod was as imperceptible as possible.

Aggie returned the nod, wishing again that someone would give this high-and-mighty lady the set-down she needed. But the Earl obeyed the tug on his arm and followed to the dance floor where Lady Alicia's execution of the intricate measures of the quadrille still did not burst the gown's strained seams. Like a sausage casing, thought Aggie angrily, that's what the lady looked like – a blue stuffed sausage. But for some reason the ridiculous image did not serve to cheer her up. How like the man to be taken by some overblown creature like that, who exposed her charms to public viewing.

Aggie turned away. This kind of thinking was stupid – and futile. The Earl was Cecilie's guardian; that was all. As long as he conducted himself properly on that score, what he did with his private life was no concern of hers. No concern at all.

Chapter Seven

For a few days after the ball, things went quite well in Denby's establishment. Cecilie moved about, keeping Dillydums always with her. The monkey seemed very contented and at home except that whenever Denby entered the room the little creature ran gibbering into Cecilie's arms and hid his face in her shoulder. No wonder, thought Aggie, the poor thing no doubt remembered his ill-treatment at the hands of the Earl. A dry smile twisted Aggie's mouth at such thoughts. The Earl had a great deal of ill-treatment to account for!

The days passed slowly. Aggie tried to teach Cecilie the fundamentals of needle-point. She made an amusing picture, peering intently down at her work while the monkey on her shoulder mimicked her expression of concentration. But soon Cecilie would fling the work aside and jump up to do something more active.

"Aggie," she cried one morning, "I am going absolutely mad shut up here."

"We'll be going to the theater in several

days," Aggie reminded her. "You'll get to see a lot of people then."

"I know. But I want to do something *now*. I'm so dreadfully, dreadfully bored."

"I know, dear." Aggie put aside her sewing. "But that's natural. We were all so excited about your ball. Now that it's over we are naturally feeling a little lost and let down. That will pass as soon as we begin to go out." For some unaccountable reason her mind presented her with a picture of herself in Denby's arms, being whirled around the floor to the pulsating rhythm of the waltz. "I'll tell you what. It's such a lovely day out. Why don't we take Dillydums and go out in the courtyard for a while? But be sure to put him on his leash."

Cecilie nodded. "All right. I'm awfully tired of sitting up here. I wish there were an easier way of getting a husband."

Aggie allowed herself a small smile. "After all, my dear, you will be spending the rest of your life with this man. A person should take her time in making such a decision."

"I suppose so," said Cecilie, her eyes widening with mischief. "But think how much simpler it would be if we could just go to a market, or a fair, like Papa did to buy horses!" Her eyes lit up with merriment. "Just think, all the men could line up and we

107

could go along and inspect their looks." She giggled. "Even their teeth as Papa used to do with the horses."

"But men cannot be bought and sold," protested Aggie, trying to stop a little smile that insisted on tugging at the corners of her mouth.

"Oh, I know that." Cecilie brushed the objection aside. "And they could have a big card suspended behind them that told important things, like 'good dancer,' 'crack horseman,' and the like." She burst into a sudden fit of laugher and Aggie could not forbear laughing, too.

"What is it now, you little minx?" she asked. "What has your imagination been conjuring up?"

Cecilie resumed a straight face. "I was just thinking how very ideal such a situation would be for me." And she burst into laughter again.

Aggie waited patiently. It was good to see Cecilie merry once more.

When she stopped laughing, Cecilie wiped at her eyes. "Shut your eyes, Aggie. Just keep them shut and imagine what I tell you."

Aggie nodded and obediently closed her eyes.

"First, it's a great building, built in a big circle, sort of like the amphitheater. And all around the edges are little cubbyholes, sort of like stalls. Over each one hangs the sign."

Aggie's imagination built such a building for her and furnished it as Cecilie described. Then it stopped in front of one of the cubbyholes.

"The men stand or walk about, showing themselves off," continued Cecilie. "Can you see his lordship among them?"

Without opening her eyes, Aggie nodded again. She could see him quite plainly.

"He's wearing riding boots," Cecilie went on. "And inexpressibles of tan Bedford cord."

Aggie nodded again. She could see him as clearly as if he stood before her.

"And," said Cecilie in triumphant tones, "every man's chest is bare!"

Aggie's eyes flew open with the shock, but not before her mind had presented her with a very clear picture of the Earl's unclad chest, the shadowy mat of hair. "Cecilie! You must not say such things! They are not proper for young ladies to discuss."

"But, Aggie, wouldn't it be a good idea?" persisted Cecilie. "Think how nice it would be. We could walk up and down the aisles, admiring all the gentlemen."

By now Aggie's shock had somewhat abated. She shook her head. "Oh, Cecilie.

But what if the tables were turned and we were on display? I collect you would not like that so much."

Cecilie tossed her blond head and wrinkled her nose. "Oh, I don't know. It wouldn't be too bad. I could look at the gentlemen while they looked at me. And you know, Aggie," she said in sudden seriousness, "all this is really not so far from the truth."

Aggie gazed at her in astonishment. "What do you mean?"

"Well, that's sort of what the come out was for – to exhibit me. And when we go to the theater, we are on display. So are the gentlemen."

Aggie considered this. "I suppose you're right," she conceded. "But certainly society would not look with much favor on your plan."

Cecilie's sigh was only partly exaggerated. "I suppose not. The *ton* is very dishonest. Always hiding the truth from itself."

"Perhaps it would be more accurate to say that it is *polite*," commented Aggie.

Cecilie shrugged. "Everyone knows that the marriage business is exactly that – a business. I don't know what they hope to achieve by deceiving themselves."

Privately, Aggie thought that her ward had reached quite a mature understanding on the subject. But, knowing Cecilie's characteristic honesty, she thought it wiser not to tell her so. It would obviously not do her any good to advance such opinions among the *ton*, and it might do her a good deal of harm.

"Shall we go down to the garden now?" said Aggie, and Cecilie, snapping the monkey's leash, nodded.

At the bottom of the front stairs they were met by Bates. "His lordship wishes to see you in the library," he said.

Aggie nodded. "Very well, Bates. We shall go directly there." She glanced at the monkey. "Perhaps you should call a footman to return Dillydums to the room. He does not do so well when his – when we are having a discussion." It might be common knowledge that Dillydums couldn't stand his lordship, but she did not intend to mention the matter to his servants.

"Yes, miss," said Bates, taking the monkey from Cecilie.

"What do you suppose he wants?" asked Cecilie as they moved off down the hall.

"I've no idea," replied Aggie. "But we shall soon know."

She paused at the door to draw a deep breath. As always, the thought of seeing Denby was disturbing to her. She followed Cecilie into the room.

111

The Earl looked up from his desk. "Come in, ladies. Be seated. We have a matter to discuss."

Aggie and Cecilie took the proffered seats and turned to the Earl in expectation. He drew up a chair facing them. "The come out was quite successful," he said, "and has resulted in Cecilie receiving several offers."

Cecilie caught her breath. "Wh-who?" she stammered.

The Earl did not seem to hear her. "So far you have received three offers. Two of them need no discussion. The men are not suitable and I dismissed them. The third, however, seems quite an eligible connection."

"Who?" repeated Cecilie, by how having regained her breath.

"I am coming to that," said the Earl patiently. "This man is eminently suitable. He has quite a lot of property. He has agreed to very favorable terms on the jointure in the event you are made a widow. He seems genuinely fond of you. I advise you to accept him."

"His name!" cried Cecilie impatiently. "Tell me his name."

"The Marquess Connors," announced the Earl.

"No! No! No! I'll never marry that – that –"

Aggie had expected some such outburst; still, she was startled by its vehemence. Could Cecilie never do things in an ordinary, reasonable way? Why couldn't she say a simple no and let it go at that?

By now Cecilie was on her feet, dramatically clutching her handkerchief. "I'll never marry such a man," she declared again.

The Earl's face clouded and his brows began to draw together. "Sit down, Cecilie. There is no need to give me a Cheltenham tragedy. Why don't you like Connors?"

Cecilie resumed her seat with an aggrieved air of martyrdom. "He's a stuffy old man," she pouted. "All he did was lecture and scold about horses and the cost of racing."

The Earl nodded. "He recently lost a bundle and swore off racing."

"That's hardly my fault," said an affronted Cecilie. "Besides that, he's an old, old man. Older even than you."

A certain tightening around Denby's mouth told Aggie that this hit had scored. "The man is not that old," said his lordship. "I can't send you off with some little lordling still tied to his papa's purse strings."

Cecilie stared at him defiantly. "I will not be married to some dreadful old man," she cried angrily. "And you shall not make me.

113

Not even if you lock me in the attic and feed me only bread and water!"

Aggie felt a giggle bubbling up in her throat; sometimes Cecilie's dramatics were quite amusing. One look at his lordship's face, however, caused her to swallow the giggle immediately.

"You are being quite ridiculous," he said sternly. "I should do no such thing." He paused and seemed to be contemplating even worse atrocities.

"Who were the other two?" asked Aggie in an effort to ease the strain.

"It doesn't matter," replied the Earl. "They were not at all suitable."

Aggie nodded and was surprised to hear Cecilie say, "I think I have the right to decide that."

"Cecilie. Really. The Earl knows best about such things." Couldn't the girl tell his lordship was near to exploding? The way his dark brows drew together, the stiff erect way he sat in his chair, and the grim tightening of his mouth, certainly indicated as much.

"It's my life," insisted Cecilie. "And I have a right to know."

The Earl shrugged. "So far as I know I am in charge here. As your guardian I am empowered to turn away anyone I please. The final decision is mine."

"That's not fair," screamed Cecilie, again jumping to her feet and beginning to pace around the room in a distracted fashion. "I am the one who has to live with the man, aren't I?" she demanded angrily.

"I have not overlooked that." The Earl was obviously doing his best to keep his temper in hand. "But I know these two. They are both fortune hunters of the worst stripe. There is no way that I would let you marry either of them." His black brows met in the line that indicated his anger. "The matter is closed. We will not discuss it further." He glared at her until she resumed her seat.

But Cecilie was not cowed. Even as she sat there, she returned his glare defiantly.

The Earl spoke slowly, evenly, and his tones carried the greatest authority. "The Marquess is an honorable man. It ill behooves you to dismiss his suit so lightly." He paused, fixing his eyes on her sternly. "The Marquess has requested permission to call. I have given it to him. You may expect him this afternoon."

Cecilie's chin jutted out stubbornly. "I won't see him," she declared angrily. "I despise the man."

"You *will* see him," the Earl replied harshly. "And behave civilly. Otherwise

115

you will no longer have a monkey for a pet."

Cecilie jumped to her feet, her face gone white at the threat. "You – you wouldn't!" she cried in a voice that broke.

Aggie felt real concern for the girl. It was not Cecilie's fault that she had always gotten her own way. This was quite a painful awakening for her. And his lordship was not helping at all with his tyrannical, high-handed ways.

"You mistake your man," he said curtly, "if you think I make empty threats. I shall do anything necessary to getting you safely wed. Anything!"

The threat was quite real. Even Cecilie saw that. She faced him for one long moment while the tears rolled unheeded down her cheeks. When finally she spoke, her voice was strained. "You are a despicable man," she declared. "Quite the most depraved and cruel person that I have ever had the misfortune to know." And holding herself in wounded dignity she marched slowly from the room.

Aggie got to her feet to follow. Cecilie needed her now as she had never needed her before.

"Miss Trimble!" The Earl's words rolled

through the room like thunder. Automatically Aggie fell back into the chair, her heart pounding in her throat. This was ridiculous, she told herself, her annoyance growing. Just because he had bungled the thing, he thought he could yell at *her*.

She raised her eyes to his. "Yes, milord?" She deliberately kept her voice low and even in the hope that he would take a rebuke from it.

Whether he took the hint was impossible to say. He did, however, modulate his tone somewhat. "I wish to speak to you. You can go to Cecilie later."

Aggie cast a look toward the door. In her present mood it was difficult to say what Cecilie might do. "I really should go to her –" she began.

Denby's mask of composure slipped. "Later!" he snapped, his eyes flashing with pent-up anger. "I want to talk to you. Now."

Aggie's expression was not one of agreement, but she forced herself to nod. "Very well, milord. What do you want to talk about?"

He flashed her a look of pure rage. "About that idiot charge of yours! What else?"

Aggie felt her hackles rising. All this was his own fault. If he weren't such a bully – "Cecilie is not an idiot," she said.

The Earl grimaced as though in pain. "She certainly behaves like one! She's impossible."

He stared at her for several minutes while she searched her mind for some reply, but decided to make none. Rational discussion with a person in such a rage was well nigh impossible.

"Well, have you nothing to say?" he demanded crossly. "I don't know why you obstruct me like this. Surely the girl's marriage will benefit you, too!"

Now Aggie's hackles were really up. She rose quite steadily to her feet and returned his angry glare with one of her own. "You mistake yourself, milord. *I* do not obstruct your plans. You do that quite well yourself." She continued to gaze into his blazing gray eyes; she had no other choice. She would not behave like some abject hireling.

He took a step toward her, but she held her ground. "What are you talking about?" he growled.

"Your tyrannical ways. It's quite clear that you've never dealt with anyone like Cecilie before. But do you ask for advice or even try to figure out the best way to deal with her?" She had not thought his face could darken any further, but it did. She had never seen him so angry before, but suddenly she didn't care. "Of course not," she continued. "You merely go on in the same bullying manner, riding roughshod over everything in your way. Well," she said, giving him a look of pity, "you've made a terrible mess of things. And it's all your own conceited fault!" By the time she had finished this impassioned speech her bosom was heaving under the thin fabric gown and their eyes were locked in deadly combat.

It was with some surprise that Aggie realized the effect of her words, but it was too late now to take them back. Best just to leave him to his rage.

She turned toward the door, but he was there instantly, his hands gripping her upper arms cruelly. "Just a minute. You're not going anywhere. Since you think you know so much, *you* tell me. How can Cecilie be handled?"

For some insane reason a picture of Lady Alicia sprang to life in Aggie's head. "Surely a man like yourself," she said caustically, "a man who's been on the town these many years, knows that soft words and persuasion work better with young women than angry avowals of authority." His face was very close to hers now and she felt her knees trembling with something akin to fear. But in spite of the fact that his fingers dug painfully into her arms, she was not physically afraid of him. This fear was of a different nature.

He stared at her for long seconds, his anger reflected in his eyes, his anger and something else she could not quite distinguish. When finally he spoke, there was a strained quality to his voice. "Soft words and persuasion," he said gruffly. "And yet there are some women who reject even that."

There is was again – that strange look in his eyes – of hurt. Yet how could that be? She had not hurt him. *He* was the one who had run away, left her without a word of explanation.

"You speak in riddles, milord," she replied, making her voice as brisk as possible.

"Riddles, is it?" he snarled, pulling her sharply against his chest. "Soft words," he repeated, his mouth against her hair. "And persuasion. They have gotten me nowhere at all."

Her mind was a mass of confusion. He sounded almost as though he were speaking of the two of them. And he couldn't be. She tried to wriggle free of his arms; the heat of his body, the male smell of him, the feel of his arms around her, all were causing her body to respond.

"Aggie!" he said, and the word was plea and groan combined. In her surprise she raised her eyes to his. There was only a brief moment when their gazes locked, but it was enough for Aggie to see what blazed there – desire. A shudder ran through her trembling body as she stood helpless in his arms. And then he bent his head and took her lips. Here was no softness, no persuasion. His mouth was hard and demanding, its pressure on hers insistent. She tried to fight him, to remain cold and impassive – a woman's best defense in such a situation.

But she could not do it. Her own body rebelled against the constraints she tried to impose on it. There was no way she could fight both Denby and herself. It took all her effort to keep herself from throwing all judgment to the wind and giving herself up completely to him. She could not keep her lips from softening and opening under his, or her body from melting against his hardness. She did manage not to throw her arms around his neck in utter abandon. When finally he released her mouth, she felt drained of all resistance.

But then he looked down at her and a cruel smile twisted the lips that had just left hers. "It seems that there is more than one kind of persuasion," he said sardonically.

Aggie was wrenched suddenly out of her ecstasy into a world of harsh reality. She drew herself up to her full height. "Release me," she said in broken tones. "You have had your revenge. That should be sufficient."

For a moment the anger in his eyes dissolved and she glimpsed again that look of pain. Then his eyes clouded over. It seemed that he was about to say something to her, something important, but a sudden knocking on the door caused him to drop his hands and abruptly back away. "Yes?" he barked.

The door opened to disclose a distraught Bates. "It's the young lady, milord."

The Earl frowned darkly. "What about her?"

"She's gone, milord." Bates made no attempt to hide his apprehension.

"Gone!" echoed Denby stupidly. "What do you mean – gone?"

Bates seemed about to wring his hands. "She came out of the library, milord. And she seemed quite angry. She swept up the stairs and came down again with the monkey. And then, milord," he paused in obvious distress.

"Yes?"

The Earl's tone was not encouraging, but Bates plunged on. "Then she went out."

"Just like that – she went out," bellowed the Earl. "And you didn't stop her?"

Bates looked slightly affronted. "It was not my place to put hands on the young lady, milord." He hesitated. "I sent Dunner after her, milord. He won't let her come to harm. And Franklin went along, so he could come back and report where she went."

Since his lordship seemed to have lapsed into a stunned silence, Aggie spoke. "You did well, Bates. Especially in such trying circumstances."

The old butler sent her a grateful look. "Thank you, miss. I did the best I could." His gaze returned to Denby, almost furtively.

His lordship seemed to gather his wits. "Yes, Bates. Well done. As soon as Franklin returns let me know."

"Yes, milord." Bates made his retreat.

Aggie turned her gaze on Denby. He was still frowning, his fine features distorted by his rage. "Well," he said angrily, "what do I do now?"

Aggie considered. "You might send out and scour the streets," she said, restraining herself from reminding him that all this could have been averted if he had not insisted on her staying with him. "Or you might sit here and wait for Franklin's report." She paused as a sudden thought struck her. "She might even come back herself. She could have just gone for a walk."

It was obvious from the contortions of his handsome features that the Earl was fighting a battle with his anger. Finally he seemed to have conquered it enough to permit him to speak. "Do you really think that is possible?" He was unable to keep complete incredulity from his voice, but he was at least clearly sincere in his desire for her opinion.

Aggie felt herself suddenly very weary and sank into a chair. "I can't really say. But it seems entirely possible. After all, where has she to go? She knows no one in the city. She has no funds. Perhaps after her anger fades she will realize that and return." Wearily she leaned her head on her hand. Would they never get Cecilie well married so that she could escape this terrible round of frustration and pain?

The Earl spent some time in silence before he spoke again. "I hope to God you're right. This city is full of the most wicked men. If she should fall into their hands –" He shuddered and sank into a chair.

"Don't worry, milord." Aggie found herself taking the role of comforter. "No one can hurt her with Dunner there."

He shook his head. "I suppose not. Still,

it's hard work waiting." He consulted his timepiece. "I'll give her another hour, then I go to Bow Street."

Aggie nodded. She was trying not to think of that, but to concentrate on the moment when Cecilie would be found. She must be found.

Some thirty minutes passed slowly by – so slowly that to Aggie they seemed like years. And then there was the sound of the door knocker. They looked at each other, but neither made a sound as they waited for whatever noises should reach them from the hall.

Finally Bates knocked discreetly.

"Come in," said the Earl, his voice still gruff.

Bates entered beaming. "The young lady has returned, milord. I have prevailed upon her to wait in the hall."

Denby nodded. "Send her in."

Aggie sent him a quick glance. "Milord," she began, but he cut her off with a look of utter outrage. Then Cecilie came in, wearing the peaceful smile of innocence.

"My, Aggie, are you and his lordship still talking?" She did not wait for a reply, and Aggie, at least, was clearly aware of the mischief in her eyes. "I took Dillydums for a walk. It's the nicest kind of day out. I'm sorry I didn't wear my bonnet. I do hope my nose won't freckle, but I was rather in a blue funk and I wanted to escape before I did any damage to his lordship's establishment." She gave the Earl a quick glance, but did not pause for comment. "The weather was just beautiful and I walked out all my rage. In fact," she said, smiling sweetly at the Earl, apparently oblivious to his fiercely frowning brows and the angry set of his mouth, "the walk cleared my mind. I see the error of my ways. You were quite right, milord. The poor Marquess deserves another chance. So if you've nothing more to discuss, I'll just go up to my room and rest a little. Walking does tire one so." And still wearing that sweet smile of innocence, she cast them each a quizzical glance, turned, and walked cheerfully from the room.

The Earl took one step after her and opened his mouth. But he closed it again with a sudden snap and stood silent until the sound of her footsteps had retreated down the hall. Then he threw Aggie a look of utter disgust. "I shall be out for dinner," he said, his voice betraying the struggle it caused him to speak evenly. "Pray God I shall not have to see either of you until night after next when we go to Drury Lane."

And then, while Aggie still stood stunned,

he stormed from the room, yelling for Bates as he went.

Aggie sighed heavily. Incredible as it seemed, Cecilie had won this round. But she could not continue to do so. And the brash way in which she had covered her infraction of the rules... The Earl would not take well to being gulled by a woman, especially one not yet full grown. With another sigh Aggie turned toward the door. She must go and talk to her ward, but what she would say was beyond imagining.

Chapter Eight

The next hours were difficult ones for Aggie. Part of her could not help rejoicing in the fact that a mere chit like Cecilie should have managed to thwart his lordship as she had, but another part of her could not help but sympathize with Denby. She, too, had had her moments of frustration and anger over Cecilie's behavior. But eventually she had learned the best ways to manage the girl. It could not be expected, however, that Denby would take such a subtle approach. His lordship seemed to feel that he knew how to handle everything.

From time to time Cecilie would giggle and remark about the stupid look on his lordship's face when she returned. To all this Aggie turned a deaf ear, merely keeping her attention on her needlework. Only once did she comment. "The Earl is not a man to be trifled with. You should not antagonize him deliberately."

Cecilie's eyes widened with that look of innocence she did so well. "But Aggie, I only spoke the truth. I was really hipped. You wouldn't want me to throw things, would you?"

"Of course not. Such behavior is extremely unladylike."

"Well then," said Cecilie as though that settled it, "you must see that I had to go for a walk."

Aggie did not see this. However, it seemed rather useless to say so. "You could at least have worn your bonnet and gloves."

"Oh, Aggie, I was too hipped to think of things like that! You know, you should have seen the expression on Bates's face. He knew he couldn't stop me." Her eyes gleamed at the memory. "I just sailed past him big as life."

Aggie did not smile. "You will not make

yourself popular with the servants by putting them in such delicate positions."

"Oh pooh!" said Cecilie, tickling the monkey with a feather from the comforter and giggling at the antics this inspired in the little beast. "You are becoming stuffy. If the Earl yells at his servants because they can't stop me from taking a walk, that's not my fault. He's just mean." And she made a face. "One of these days I shall be married and then the Earl won't be able to tell me what to do. And if he comes anywhere near me, I shall cut him dead. Papa taught me how." And she stared through the imaginary Denby with an iciness that made Aggie smile.

"In order to be married you must find a husband," Aggie reminded her charge. "Are you quite sure the Marquess is unsuitable?" She asked the question very quietly, trying not to drive the girl further into her antagonism.

Cecilie sighed. "I know you are being patient with me, Aggie, but truly the man is dreadful bore. The only thing he can do well is dance." She turned to Aggie with a mischievous smile. "And didn't you tell me that marriage must be based on something more than the ability to dance well?"

"Of course I did," replied Aggie. "But you
129

well know I had in mind something a little more important than dancing – or riding."

Cecilie's smile broadened and a giggle bubbled from her throat. "You also told me it would be impossible to find out about chests."

Aggie's smile faded. The vision of Denby's bare chest appeared far too often in her mind as it was. "Cecilie! I know that you think this whole matter quite amusing. But you must consider that marriage is a serious business. You are deciding on a partner for life."

"That is precisely why I cannot be leg-shackled to a perfect block like the Marquess," replied Cecilie. Then, seeing Aggie's expression, she hurried on. "But I will receive him. And I'll be polite. Surely that will satisfy his lordship."

Aggie was not too sure of this, but she did not think it wise to say so. Let Cecilie make whatever conciliatory amends she could. In his present mood the Earl was not going to be easy to placate. She swallowed a sigh. How differently she had once planned her future. Back in those beautiful days she had envisioned a life of love and happiness with Denby beside her. Well, she told herself, perhaps she should consider herself lucky. Denby was not the man she had thought him. He was arrogant and tyrannical; witness his behavior with Cecilie.

Yet, angry as she was with him, Aggie knew that in all fairness he could not be blamed for flying up in the boughs over Cecilie's behavior. She had certainly been frustrated, irritated, and driven almost to distraction by her charge's waywardness, especially during her early days as companion when she had not yet discovered the best way of subtly guiding her. And the Earl was a man – and a lord. He was used to everyone doing his bidding. He must find Cecilie's pranks particularly galling.

It was only thirty minutes later that Bates announced the Marquess. Cecilie gave her curls a quick brush and turned to her companion. "At least we won't have to worry much about conversation. The Marquess talks enough for ten."

Moments later they entered the drawing room. The Marquess rose and bowed stiffly over Cecilie's fingers. "Ahhhhh, Miss Winthrop. What a pleasure to see you again. You are looking extraordinarily well."

Cecilie acknowledged this with a small nod. "Please be seated, milord."

Aggie, watching everything, suppressed another sigh. When she wanted to, Cecilie could play the grand lady quite well. She was not at all sure, however, how long Cecilie would *want* to.

"I hope you have had a pleasant several days since your gala occasion," said the Marquess.

Cecilie nodded, but did not reply. The Marquess seemed a little perturbed by her lack of response. Evidently he saw drawing room conversation as a very set form, in which one made a remark and then the other. Rather like a game of ball between two children, thought Aggie.

There were some moments of silence during which Aggie devoted herself to her needlework, Cecilie considered her finger-nails, and the Marquess grew increasingly ill at ease.

Finally the Marquess cleared his throat. "Ahhhh, Miss Winthrop, is there anything you wish to know? That is – about me?" He concluded this by putting his gloved fingertips together in a tentlike shape and looking rather smug, as though anything she might wish to know was sure to redound to his credit.

The question caught Aggie by surprise and she pricked her finger and swallowed a silent ouch. Surely Cecilie would not ask – not of the Marquess, a man she had already decided against.

132

Demurely Cecilie raised wide eyes. "Yes, milord, there is one thing I should like to know."

"Speak, my dear, speak." The Marquess positively beamed, the expression sitting rather incongruously on his usually sober face.

"I should like to know if you have –"

Aggie bit her bottom lip to keep back a cry.

"Many animals," continued Cecilie sweetly.

Aggie let her breath out slowly.

"Animals?" The Marquess seemed puzzled.

"Animals," repeated Cecilie. "Dogs, cats, monkeys." Her eyes widened even further. "I am quite fond of animals, you see. Have you a country estate? I believe I should like that best – to live on an estate like Oatlands. How wonderful it must be – to live as the Duchess of York, surrounded by dogs, cats, monkeys, birds; all sorts of rare beasts. I'm sure you would never complain as the Duke does, though good-naturedly to be sure, that all the chairs are filled with animals. After all, what does a little shedding hair matter? Your valet can be sure that it doesn't stick to your clothes."

The Marquess sat through this monologue with the stunned expression of a man who has just seen a vision of loveliness turn into a monster. It was clearly apparent to Aggie that no amount of blunt or beauty would ever persuade the Marquess to ally himself with a woman who expected such an establishment.

"I know!" said Cecilie, jumping to her feet. "I shall go get Dillydums, so you can see him. He's just an adorable little thing."

The Marquess suddenly found his tongue. "Really, Miss Winthrop, that is not at all necessary."

"I'm sure you will just love him," prattled Cecilie. "I know you will," she said with a smile. "I'm sure you'll make an excellent husband, loving animals as you do. We shall deal so well together. You do like animals, don't you, milord?"

A dazed Marquess got to his feet and nodded. "Yes, yes, of course. You must excuse me, Miss Winthrop. I have just remembered a most important engagement. Can't imagine how it slipped my mind." And he kissed her fingertips and departed as hastily as dignity and decorum would permit.

The two women stood in silence until they heard the sound of the massive front door closing. Then Cecilie broke into whoops of laugher. "Oh Aggie, did you see his face? Did you? Oh, the poor, poor man. I must

134

have given him a terrible fright." And she began to laugh so hard that for a time she could not speak.

Aggie fought to hold back her own laughter. The Marquess had been amusing, but it would not be at all funny when news of this reached the Earl, as inevitably it would. She said as much to Cecilie.

"But Aggie," the girl replied, wiping hastily at her eyes, "I did everything I said I would. I received the Marquess. I was polite and attentive." A mischievous smile lit her face. "I answered all his questions."

"And you frightened the poor man nearly to death," commented Aggie dryly.

Cecilie grinned. "He did seem rather disturbed. But I only told him the truth." Her smile softened and she closed her eyes as though to better envision her dream. "You know, Aggie, I've always loved animals. It would be so wonderful to have as many as I want. All kinds." A blissful smile lit her face as she slid further into her dream.

"That makes a nice dream," Aggie replied, realizing that her charge spoke the truth. "But you must think, dear. Animals are nice, but they must be fed and cared for. And they do cause a certain amount of confusion."

"Yes, yes. I know." Cecilie brushed this aside. "But that is nothing if one has money.

And, after all," her eyes danced merrily, "why else should one marry?"

"There is such a thing as love," Aggie remarked quietly, aware suddenly that a great lump had risen in her throat as she spoke.

"Love." Cecilie said the word as she might have said fever or grief, as though it signified an experience entirely unknown to her. "I don't know that I want to feel love. From what I have read it may be a terrible nuisance." Cecilie's small nose wrinkled at the thought. "I really think that it's much more sensible to love animals. In the first place, they are just about sure to return your love. And they don't go about picking and pecking at everything one does. They are always there when you need them. Not gallivanting about at a hunt or rushing off to some gaming club." Cecilie's face darkened in a frown. "If only Papa had left my funds to my own management. Then I might never have married. But now..." She sighed deeply. "With his lordship the way he is, I suppose I really have no choice in the matter."

"Even if his lordship were not – your guardian," said Aggie, "you should still want a husband. The world is not a good place for a woman alone."

136

Miss Winthrop's eyes grew concerned. "Why did you never marry, Aggie?" she asked softly.

The question caught Aggie by surprise and for a moment she was unable to answer. Finally she mustered her wits enough to mumble, "I had only one Season."

"One is enough, Aggie. You're still very beautiful. You must have been a real stunner then. There must have been many men making offers for you."

Aggie smiled slightly, her composure regained. Obviously Cecilie knew nothing of what had occurred between his lordship and her companion. "Not many, but some," she replied.

"Then why didn't you choose one?" asked Cecilie.

"There were none that I could love," Aggie said. "And I knew that I could marry for no other reason. Also, at that time I thought my papa well off. I believed I would have another Season to find a husband in. But then my papa died. And there were no more young men."

Cecilie's white forehead wrinkled in a frown. "See? When you had no substance, they all deserted you."

Aggie looked at her charge thoughtfully.

"That is the way of the world, Cecilie. There is nothing unusual about it."

"I don't know about love," said Cecilie. "What made you think you must have that?"

Aggie made no answer. She could not tell Cecilie the truth, but, as the girl's keen eyes focused on her, she felt the scarlet flooding her face. For a long moment there was silence in the room. Then Cecilie's face took on an expression of awe. "Oh, Aggie," she whispered, "I see it all now. *You* loved someone. Do not deny it. It's written on your face. Oh, Aggie, what happened?"

Aggie tried to collect her chaotic thoughts. Clearly she couldn't tell Cecilie the truth; it would be unwise for her to know about the Earl. It could do nothing but make her more outraged at him. But it was obvious that she expected her companion to say something. "I – I did love someone, Cecilie, but it is very painful to talk about. I – the man I chose did not deserve my love." A vision of Denby's dark brooding face rose to haunt her. What she said was true. Of course, his treatment of Cecilie did not really damage him in her eyes. He was a strong-minded man and used to running things. It was his disappearance that had made him unworthy of her regard. How many long and sleepless nights she had spent puzzling over it. Even now she found it incomprehensible; to have spoken to her as he had, to have led her on in that cruel fashion. But no matter. The past was over – finished. Denby had no place in her future except as Cecilie's guardian.

A soft hand enclosed her own. "I'm sorry, Aggie," the girl whispered. "I see that it still hurts. I'm very sorry."

Blinking rapidly, Aggie held back the tears. "It's all right, my dear. I managed to survive it."

Cecilie shook her head vehemently, almost dislodging a pink bow perched among her curls. "It's just not fair. I don't think I shall want to be in love. It looks entirely too painful. I shall just look for someone I can like. A good dancer, a crack horseman, someone who likes animals –"

She paused as though about to continue, but Aggie interrupted. "It seems sensible to follow such a course, my dear. Quite possibly you are right. As long as you have some affection for the man of your choice. After all, he is to be the father of your children."

This caused Cecilie to pause. "Children! Of course. Oh dear, my list of requirements is getting rather long, I fear. But surely a man who like animals will like children, shouldn't you think?"

"Perhaps," said Aggie. "But I should not

139

like to depend upon it. Men can be quite strange creat –"

The door to the drawing room opened suddenly. The Earl stood in the doorway and he did not appear at all pleased. He was wearing a blue coat with brass buttons, breeches of cream kerseymere, top boots, and a deep stiff cravat. He paused a moment, raking them over with his eyes.

Aggie saw clearly that he was angry, quite angry. His brows already met in the dark line that portended trouble and the set of his jaw was grim. "So..." he said and the word hung in the air like the most ominous of threats.

"Good day, milord," Aggie forced herself to say.

"It has not been a good day for me," he snapped. "I do not know why I had to be chosen for such a task." He swung on them, his frown deepening. "I had thought someone here might have at least a modicum of sense." His eyes pinned Aggie.

She forced herself to remain calm. "Milord," she replied, "what has happened to anger you so?"

"I was returning home to change for my dinner engagement," he said, fighting to control himself. "And as we turned the corner at the Square, Connors came by in an open carriage. The man looked positively ill. His face was almost green." He paused to glare at Cecilie. "I stopped my rig to inquire about his health. And I heard such a tale that my blood ran cold. The man was gibbering almost insanely and in such shock that it took me some time to calm him. Finally, I succeeded in prying from him some nonsense about Cecilie's multitudes of animals and the fact that he was not York and could not allow his wife to set up to rival Wombwell's Menagerie. At first, I couldn't make head nor tail of any of it, but finally I got the sense of the thing. Cecilie was up to her old tricks." He paused before the culprit and glared down at her.

Aggie had to give her ward credit; Cecilie did not quiver under the intensity of those blazing eyes. She faced the Earl calmly.

There was a moment of silence, the room quiet except for the sound of the Earl's heavy breathing. "Well?" he snapped. "What have you to say for yourself?"

Cecilie's back was stiffly erect, but her tone was quiet. "The Marquess is a strange man, milord. I treated him quite politely, I assure you. You can ask Aggie."

"The Marquess is not that strange," the Earl declared hotly, not at all placated. "Exactly what did you say to the man?"

"He asked if I had any questions," Cecilie replied. "And so I asked him if he liked animals."

Denby scowled. "There was more to it than that. What's this about York and Wombwell's?"

Cecilie's face wore an expression of aggrieved innocence. "I only told him how much I enjoyed Oatlands and the Duchess's animals. We did not mention Wombwell's at all. Though I should like to see it. Did we, Aggie?"

As the Earl's eyes swung round to her, Aggie wished devoutly that she were somewhere else, anywhere else. "There was no discussion of Wombwell's," she said. "And Cecilie's account is essentially correct. The Marquess did ask her if she had any questions and she did ask him if he liked animals."

"I see." Denby glowered at her, but she refused to drop her eyes, though her heart thudded painfully.

"Well, you certainly did a job on the man!" He paused for a moment as though to control himself. "He withdrew his offer of marriage. Said he didn't want a wife after all. He's going back to his country estate, which is remarkably free of animals!"

Denby paused again in front of Cecilie's

chair and regarded her angrily. "I suppose you think yourself quite smart to have so easily shed an unwanted suitor."

Cecilie made no answer to this and Aggie thanked God for it. It was best not to trifle with the Earl when he was in such a rage.

"Well," he continued bitterly, "you are quite mistaken. First, you could have reported to me that your impressions of the man had not changed and then I should have conveyed that to the Marquess, as diplomatically as possible – with little pain or embarrassment on either side. Now the idiot is apt to go babbling all round London about Denby's ward who has a screw loose upstairs."

"There is nothing wrong with my understanding," Cecilie said crisply. "And I can hardly be blamed if the Marquess is so enamored of his blunt that the thought of spending a little of it throws him into hysteria. He left here so fast one would have thought that we were after his life's blood."

The Earl did not find this amusing. "You might have considered that having your name bandied about as an eccentric is not likely to enhance your chances in the marriage mart."

"I am not eccentric," said Cecilie. "I merely prefer loving animals to loving

143

money-hungry humans. There is certainly nothing strange about that."

The Earl regarded her grimly. "I am not convinced that you were not rude to the man. I have known Connors for a long time and I have never known him to be in such a state."

Aggie felt that the time had come for her to speak. She much doubted that he would listen, but she had her responsibility in the matter. "Cecilie was not rude," she said quietly. Her first words drew his eyes, but she managed to return his gaze. "She was perhaps a little overly enthusiastic concerning the quantity of animals she would like to have, but she was also truthful. She has always wished for a large estate and a great number of pets." With every word she spoke the Earl's face darkened further, but she persisted. "I must agree with you that her behavior was unfortunate. However, this *was* a moment for truth. And since the opinion of her future husband on this subject is of obvious concern to her, and, since he invited her questions, I believe she was within her rights to respond. She need not, however, have frightened him." Here she directed a severe look at Cecilie, whose demure expression could not quite hide the triumph in her eyes.

For a long moment the Earl glared at them both. Then he shrugged his broad shoulders eloquently. "You have won this round," he said to Cecilie. "Just take care that you do not scare away *all* the eligible connections. For that, I would remind you, would result in your spending the rest of your days in my establishment – a prospect which I fear would greatly shorten my life span!" Then, with one more glare at each of them, he stamped off, obviously in high dudgeon.

Aggie felt her shoulders sagging. All her energy seemed to have drained away. More than anything in this world she longed to find Cecilie a suitable husband. She must do so, she told herself wearily as they started up the stairs, because she did not know how much longer she could bear the strain of living in the same household with a man who alternated between fits of rage and attacks on her honor.

Chapter Nine

The next day passed very quietly. Aggie felt listless and tired: the aftermath, she knew, of the turmoil over Cecilie's behavior to the

Marquess. Cecilie herself was subdued, moving about quietly and speaking softly to the monkey. But gradually her spirits seemed to revive and she grew more cheerful.

Considering the Earl's last outburst, Aggie was unsure if they would even be going to Drury Lane as planned. She thought about asking Bates if he knew. Since her intervention for him with Denby the old butler had been greeting her with friendly smiles. Still, she did not like to ask such questions. Fortunately, however, Bates came to her late in the day to announce, "His lordship asked me to remind you of your theater engagement for tomorrow evening. He asks that you be ready early because he dislikes missing the first act."

Aggie nodded. She had a feeling that the message had been considerably softened in the transition. "Thank you, Bates. Do you happen to know what the play is?"

"I believe Mr. Kean is appearing as Iago in *Othello*," replied Bates with a small smile. "A capital performer, Mr. Kean. He has taken the city by storm. I see him myself whenever I can."

"Thank you, Bates. I am sure we'll enjoy it."

So before they went to bed that night she and Cecilie spent some time before the wardrobe. Aggie's choice was simple. She had already worn the peach silk, now she would wear the green lamé. But Cecilie had so many new gowns that the choice was difficult. Finally she chose one of pale lavender net over a darker satin slip. Watching, Aggie was grateful that Denby had been present at the ordering of these gowns. At least she was spared any worry over the propriety of Cecilie's dress. Idly, she wondered what sort of mood he would be in the next evening.

She had not seen him since he had stomped off after confronting Cecilie and she was just as glad. When he was angry, he was very difficult to deal with. And when he was not, when he looked at her with tenderness in his eyes ... She pushed the thought away. There could be no tenderness between herself and the Earl; he had destroyed that possibility long ago.

The next evening, as she helped Cecilie into the lavender gown, Aggie tried not to think that soon she would be greeting the Earl. She meant to keep her full attention on Cecilie's toilette. The lavender gown fit well. Its V-shaped neck was sufficiently high to please the Earl and yet low enough to make Cecilie feel grown-up. Bands of black velvet ribbon crisscrossed the high bodice and trimmed the little cap sleeves. Cecilie looked enchanting.

"Hurry, Aggie. I want to see you in your new gown."

As one of the silent maids stepped forward to help her, Aggie wished the evening well over. She was no longer accustomed to the quizzing of the beaux and exquisites and, not only that, she would probably also have to face the stares of a great many ladies who envied her her position in his lordship's household. It was clear enough by now that the Earl was considered a very good catch – whether by a wife or a lightskirt.

The light-green dress fell in soft folds around her. She stood in front of the cheval glass and suddenly she started. This gown! She had had a gown like this then, almost the identical color and of a very similar cut. It had had the same rounded décolletage *à l'enfant*, the short fitted sleeves embroidered in thread of the same shade, the close-fitting bodice with a high waist, and a short train behind. This gown was practically identical to one she had worn as she whirled round the ballrooms in his arms. Could he have remembered the gown so completely? It seemed incredible.

As the maid Millie led her to a seat and began to coax her hair into the style now called *à la Madonna,* with a center part and loose curls flowing from the crown of the head, Aggie fought to regain her composure. It must simply be coincidence. That was the only way to account for it. She would give it no more thought.

But that was easier said than done and when Millie pronounced herself satisfied with the effect of miss's hair and Aggie rose to take out her mama's opals, the only jewels she had managed to save, she saw that her hands trembled. What could he mean by ordering her such a gown? It seemed to make no sense. Why should he want to remind her of the awful thing he had done?

She finally managed to fasten the necklace and fix the earbobs in place. Then she turned to pick up her best cashmere and her white kid gloves. They were old now, but still quite good. She had not worn them much in the last years.

She took one more look at Cecilie. "You look very nice, my dear. That color suits you."

"I feel quite elegant," replied Cecilie, her eyes sparkling. "If only I could waltz tonight."

Since they were going to the theater, Aggie ignored this. Cecilie knew quite well that until she was offered a cherished voucher for

Almack's she could not waltz in public; there was no need to remind her.

They reached the bottom of the great stairs just as Denby emerged from the library. In his coat of black superfine with covered buttons, white marcella waistcoat, black silk breeches and stockings, and black pumps, he made an imposing figure. But Aggie's gaze did not linger on his clothes; it was the expression on his face that most concerned her. She looked directly at his eyebrows; they were separated by a respectable distance and his eyes were not cloudy with anger. Indeed, they seemed to regard her with considerable warmth. She found this almost as disconcerting as his rage.

"Good evening, ladies." His tone was certainly mellow enough, and there was no trace of dissatisfaction on his face as he surveyed them.

"Good evening, milord." Cecilie's tone was even, but Aggie feared that her own seemed rather timid.

"I see that the gown fits admirably," said Denby. His eyes met hers quickly and it seemed to her as though they held a question.

"Yes," she replied. "It's a lovely color. And I like the pattern." She did not know why she added that last; perhaps to see if his eyes would change. And they seemed to. Did he want to know if *she* remembered the other gown? She hoped he would not ask her in front of Cecilie. If the girl ever learned that Denby had jilted her companion ... A shiver ran over Aggie as she realized how implacably such information would turn Cecilie against her guardian.

Denby turned to Cecilie. "Perhaps we shall get some offers after tonight," he said. "You look quite lovely."

Cecilie nodded demurely. "Thank you, milord. I look forward to seeing Mr. Kean."

Denby smiled. "He is quite the rage these days. Everyone throngs to see him." He turned again to Aggie. "I'm sure you will enjoy Kean. His talent is considerable." His eyes were warm as he smiled down upon her.

"I have always liked *Othello*," she heard herself saying.

"Good." Without further words Denby took the cashmere from over her arm and shawled her. As he did so his gloved fingers brushed the back of her neck ever so lightly. A sensation like liquid fire ran down her spine. Fortunately he could not see her face and by the time he had come round to shawl Cecilie she had regained her composure. Then with a smile at each he offered them his arms and escorted them to the carriage.

Soon they were comfortably seated. "Are

you aware of the story of *Othello?*" Denby asked Cecilie. His tone was quite pleasant and Aggie hoped that Cecilie would not take objection to it.

"Yes, milord, I am." Cecilie's smile indicated that she forgave him for asking such a question. "Aggie and I read most of the plays of Shakespeare." She twisted the blond curl that lay on her shoulder. "But the story of Othello is so sad. I like the comedies better, where things come to a good end and people are happy."

Denby sighed, his eyes clouding over suddenly. "At times the world *is* sad and things do not come to the good ends that we wish for." Here he gave Aggie such a look of longing that the blood rushed to her cheeks and she turned hastily away lest Cecilie see and guess the truth.

But the girl was deep in her own thoughts and took no notice. "Why was Othello so stupidly suspicious?" she asked. "Why couldn't he believe Desdemona?"

Denby sighed again. "Where love is concerned," he said, "men are often stupid. And women, too."

Aggie felt these last words were directed to her, but she steadfastly refused to turn back from the window, though she saw little of the London streets, blurred as they were by her tears. How could he talk this way? Almost as though she, and not *he*, had been the one to destroy their happiness. It was terribly unfair and if Cecilie had not been there, she might have been tempted by her unhappiness to tell him so. But she kept her tongue firmly between her teeth. Her business now was to get Cecilie safely married, not to be raking over old wounds.

Cecilie sighed, too. "I think what I have decided is right," she said, causing Aggie to forget her resolve and turn from the window. "Love sounds far too painful a business for me," she continued with a quaint seriousness that Aggie might have found amusing if the conversation had been about some other topic. "I believe I shall just avoid it altogether."

Denby laughed, the bitter sound of a man in pain. "A commendable decision, Cecilie. Let us hope you stick by it."

Aggie saw Cecilie glance at him curiously. *Dear God, if she guessed something from his remarks –*

"You sound like a man who has loved," said Cecilie, her eyes on his face.

"The Earl has been on the town for some time now," Aggie interjected quickly. "It is the fashion for the beaux to speak critically of love. Is it not, milord?" Her eyes pleaded with him to understand, not to let Cecilie know the truth.

For a moment he hesitated and then he summoned a smile. It was not reflected in his eyes, but perhaps Cecilie would not see that. "Miss Trimble is right," he said in a cheerful tone. "You must not pay attention to our cynicism. Besides, we will find you a man for whom you have some partiality. Then you will learn, after the marriage, to love him."

"I do not recall any of Shakespeare's stories like that," Cecilie said.

Aggie was momentarily grateful that they had not read *The Taming of the Shrew*. They were approaching Drury Lane by this time and so the Earl did not need to answer.

Cecilie, eager to see the crowds, had to be physically restrained from hanging out the window. "But Aggie," she said, "just look at all the people! And all dressed in their best. Just look at them! Gems are shining everywhere."

"Yes, Cecilie, I know. It is always like this," Aggie replied. "Remember what I told you. People go to the theater to see and be seen."

The smile on Cecilie's face told her companion that she was also remembering their conversation about having a place to go to choose a husband, but thankfully Cecilie did not mention that.

"Some people," added his lordship dryly, "still go to the theater for the purpose of seeing the play. But they are a definite minority and need not be considered."

"I suppose not," agreed Cecilie, completely missing the irony of his statement. "Still, I shall rather enjoy seeing what I have read being acted out."

The coachman had finally worked his way close to the porticoes. The Earl preceded them out and turned to give them assistance in descending. "Stay close to me," he said as Cecilie reached the ground.

Moments later Aggie, too, had descended and he led them through the crowds into the rotunda. Cecilie's eyes grew wide as she surveyed the two stories, the circular gallery that separated them, and the rich cupola with the chandelier dangling from it. Aggie smiled. Certainly the theater was a lovely sight, dazzling with its gilt and rich furnishings. She saw Cecilie's glance go from the eight columns of the peristyle done in rich Siena marble, which supported the highly decorated entablature, to the right and left doorways flanked by Ionic columns of dark-colored porphyry.

The Earl's box was one of the best in the

theater, giving an excellent view of the stage. It also gave an excellent view of its occupants to the other patrons of the theater, but Aggie had no time to think of that. She turned to share Cecilie's exclamations of wonder and surprise at the great size of the gilt-encrusted theater. This was made somewhat awkward by the fact that the Earl had put himself between the two women. This made him far closer than Aggie liked, but there was little she could do about it. If the Earl wanted to sit between them, he would. And if it made her uncomfortable to lean across him – as it most assuredly did – then she would simply have to bear it.

"Look! Look! Over there!" cried Cecilie. "See the fat lady with the tiara. And there, I see Lady Jersey."

Aggie was glad to see that the Jersey was deep in conversation and did not seem to notice Denby. But then, a box just across the way was entered by several well-clad gentlemen, and among them, resplendent in emerald green silk and blazing with diamonds, came Lady Alicia Temple. The neck of her gown was cut so low that Aggie almost gasped when she saw it. It did not, however, seem to disturb the gentlemen flocking round, some of whom Aggie recognized as the scions of England's best families. There was no other woman in the box. Was one of the men Lady Temple's husband?

Cecilie, too, had noticed the commotion. "Look, Aggie," she said, "there is Lady Alicia."

Aggie nodded, finding the conversation rather trying, especially as the lady chose that moment to wave gaily and blow Denby a kiss.

Cecilie turned to him with curious eyes. "Which of the gentlemen is Lady Alicia's husband?"

The Earl looked a trifle startled. "The lady has no husband," he replied.

Cecilie's delicate eyebrow rose. "No husband, milord? Then why has she no companion?"

Denby began to look uncomfortable and Aggie realized that her conception of Lady Alicia's reputation had been rather accurate.

"The lady is a widow," the Earl explained in discomfort. "She needs no companion."

"And her guardian?" asked Cecilie in a tone that made Aggie somewhat edgy.

"She has no guardian." Now Denby was definitely ill at ease. "Her husband doted on her, the old fool. And he left all her substance in her hands."

"Really?" The look on Cecilie's face

increased Aggie's nervousness. The girl seemed lost in thought for some minutes. Then she turned to the Earl. "I have decided – I want to be a widow."

Denby, whose mind was not yet accustomed to the devious twistings of Cecilie's thought, started as though pricked by a pin. "A widow?"

"Yes," declared Cecilie. "Then I can manage my own affairs without interference from a husband."

The Earl coughed suddenly, almost as though hiding a laugh. "There is a slight problem here. One must be a wife before one becomes a widow."

"Can't you find me a very old husband?" Cecilie asked innocently.

"Cecilie!" Aggie cried. "How can you? You must live with this man."

Cecilie looked surprised. "But only for a while, Aggie. Then I should have everything my way."

Aggie shook her head, but Denby burst into laughter. "Well, Cecilie, you are honest at least. Which many women are not."

Aggie thought this, too, was directed at her, but, as he went right on, perhaps it was not.

"You may just put the idea from your mind," his lordship said to Cecilie firmly.

"You need a husband to keep you from utter disaster and as your guardian I should never consent to a marriage contract that would put you in the perilous position of managing your own funds, even as a widow."

Cecilie began to pout at this, but Aggie could not help but agree, though silently, with Denby. Cecilie, left to run her own affairs, would go broke in a fortnight!

"Besides," said the Earl, "you may find it nice to have a husband. And no doubt you will want children. It is far better for your sons to have a father to guide them. So you should have a younger man."

"I suppose so," agreed Cecilie, her eyes slipping down to the Earl's white waistcoat. For once Aggie was grateful for Cecilie's scatterbrained ways. At least, this thing about chests could be used to keep her from becoming an old man's toy.

The curtain rose then and Aggie and Denby were spared any more discussion on the subject. By the time intermission came, Cecilie had quite forgotten the matter as she launched into an enthusiastic discussion of the play. "What a wicked, wicked man Iago is." She said the words softly, almost as if she feared that someone might overhear her.

"Kean plays him very villainously," agreed his lordship. He turned to Aggie. "I find that I have several matters to discuss with friends. I trust that you and Cecilie can manage till I return?"

Cecilie scarcely heard him, engrossed as she was with the great crowd below, but Aggie nodded. "Yes, milord."

He rose and bowed, then made his way out of the box, to seek out Lady Alicia, no doubt, thought Aggie bitterly. Then she was called back to the present by Cecilie's squeal as some new sight presented itself to her fascinated eyes.

Some few minutes passed, the two of them trying to recognize faces they knew. Suddenly from behind them came a voice. "Such lovely ladies."

Aggie swung around, ready to oust the intruder, but Cecilie had already leaped to her feet. "Lord Parrington! How good to see you again. Do come in and take a chair. Perhaps you can help us put names to all these faces."

"Anything to please you, lovely lady," said Parrington, and Aggie decided immediately that she did not like the man. There was something about him that made her uneasy, though she could not put a finger on it. He seemed well enough dressed and Cecilie evidently recalled him from the come out, but Aggie simply did not like him. It was nothing physically visible. He was an attractive enough man, of medium height with fair hair and dark eyes. There was nothing suspicious about his manner either. It was all open blunt honesty, all "hail-fellow-well-met." And then the thought hit Aggie with a terrifying jolt. Just so did Mr. Kean play the terrible Iago!

As the two continued to discuss the play and the crowd, Aggie watched in silence. There was nothing she could do to rid them of the man; obviously Cecilie was enjoying his company. If only the Earl would return. He would know what to do. She looked out over the theater, searching for him. Perhaps she could attract his attention.

Almost of their own volition her eyes came to rest on the box that held Lady Alicia. And there he was, sitting beside her in a place obviously vacated precisely for him. Lady Alicia was leaning attentively toward him, leaning far too much, thought Aggie angrily, considering the neckline of her gown. She stared at them fixedly, hoping to get his attention to the situation that now existed in his box. But the Earl seemed oblivious of her concentrated looks. Lady Temple elicited all his attention.

Aggie found her hands tightening into fists. Why wasn't the man here where he belonged instead of dangling after that widow? In pained silence she watched Cecilie giggle and flirt with Parrington. For one dreadful moment she thought the girl might even ask him about his chest, but evidently she had decided that that and the question of children could wait for a later day, perhaps after she had seen him ride and explored the question of animals.

The latter seemed already decided in Parrington's favor, for the scattered words and phrases that reached Aggie's ears often had to do with the antics of Dillydums. And, since Parrington sat enthralled through the whole recital, Aggie could only conclude that he very much liked animals or he was a consummate actor.

Finally, to her intense relief, the man rose and made his good-byes. Aggie had a definite feeling that he wanted to leave before the Earl returned, but again it was only a feeling.

Lord Parrington had only been gone a few seconds when the door opened to admit the Earl. The shadows in the back of the box prevented her from seeing his face clearly, but as soon as he spoke Aggie knew their pleasant evening was at an end. "Was that Parrington leaving here?" he asked.

He attempted to keep his tone even and Cecilie was deceived into answering. "Oh yes, milord. He's the most amusing man. An excellent dancer. And a great lover of animals."

"Indeed!" replied his lordship and this time Cecilie, too, caught his mood. "His dancing I can have no quarrel with, but his love for animals clearly does not extend to his horses."

"Whatever do you mean?" Cecilie's pink lips made a pout.

"I mean that Parrington's beasts are ill-treated. And anyone can see it."

"Oh dear!" cried Cecilie. "And he seemed an excellent choice."

"That's no matter," replied the Earl flatly. "I have already refused him."

"Already!" By now Cecilie was quite agitated.

"Yes," replied the Earl grimly. "He was one of those I told you about – a fortune hunter."

Cecilie said no more and the Earl seemed satisfied, but Aggie was not. Cecilie never gave up this easily. And just because the Earl said Parrington ill-treated his animals that did not mean that Cecilie would believe him. Aggie did, however, and she wondered curiously if the evil in men gave off some subtle kind of vibrations to those around them. Was it the bad treatment of his animals

163

that Aggie had sensed or was it some future evil centering around Cecilie? She found herself very grateful that the Earl had refused Parrington's offer. But a small niggling fear would not be silenced.

Obviously the Earl's refusal had not made Parrington give up. He was trying to get to Cecilie in spite of it. And, knowing Denby's determination, Aggie saw the only recourse left to Parrington if he wanted to marry Cecilie – as he must see it too – Gretna Green! Ordinarily, this would not be too frightening. Parrington was forbidden the house and she was usually on hand when Cecilie went out. But given her charge's fits of anger and decisions to rush out and walk them off... Aggie decided to speak privately to Bates. He might not be able to stop Cecilie from leaving the house, but he could at least send footmen with her – and with private instructions to prevent her from entering any carriages.

Considerably relieved by this decision, she relaxed a little and turned her attention back to the play. She would very much like to see Mr. Kean as Othello, she thought. The man had a great deal of talent.

Through the remainder of the play and even the afterpiece the Earl and Cecilie both remained silent. It was not an uncomfortable silence. Cecilie appeared to have accepted his lordship's evaluation of Parrington and the Earl seemed content that the matter was closed. Aggie, however, was not at all sure. Cecilie's silence need indicate only thought, not compliance. She had seen such behavior before. Indeed, she had been the chief victim of it. And she resolved to be especially on guard.

The ride home was given over to idle chatter about clothes and the play and passed pleasantly enough. The Earl left them at the foot of the stairs. "Good night, Cecilie. Good night, Miss Trimble." His eyes seemed to look overlong into her and Aggie felt her heart contracting. Then his gaze slid over the gown, almost as though he were trying to retain a picture of it in his memory – or compare it with one already there. "I am glad the gown pleased you," he said softly. "It pleased me. Very much."

Then, before she could do more than murmur a thank you, he was gone, disappearing into the library with Bates at his heels. With a sigh Aggie turned and followed Cecilie up the stairs to their beds. She would think about his words later. Tonight she must sleep.

Chapter Ten

No mention was made of Lord Parrington in the days that followed. Aggie dared to hope that Cecilie had forgotten him. Perhaps the Earl's comment about the man's horses *had* changed her mind. Where animals were concerned, she would stand for no cruelty. Any man, once condemned on that score, would never be able to worm his way back into her good graces.

Several gentlemen came to call, but Cecilie pronounced them all perfect blocks and the Earl did not press any of them upon her. His lordship, it seemed, was being very polite. Between the two of them, Cecilie and the Earl, Aggie felt sometimes like she was watching a play. It was almost as though they were each playing a part – determined to convince the other that the roles were the real people. To Aggie, who knew them both rather well, such behavior was more than a little peculiar.

To see the Earl, whom she had more than once observed in a towering rage with his ward, behave to her with such extreme politeness gave Aggie a feeling of unreality. And Cecilie's behavior did nothing to alleviate that feeling. She was so utterly charming and pliable, so deferring to the Earl's every opinion, that Aggie felt almost nauseated by it. If it hadn't been so sickening, it might almost have been amusing. And still the two of them persisted in playing out their farce. And there was nothing Aggie could do about it.

After all, she told herself somewhat petulantly, which actually wasn't like her at all, she had enough trouble keeping in check her feelings for the Earl. He spent most of the days away from the house on Grosvenor Square, but he dined with them almost every evening. When his eyes met hers or lingered on her person, when she was anywhere near him, she was again overpowered by the force of her feelings for him. They were stupid feelings, of course – even dangerous, considering her vulnerable position in his household, but they were also feelings that could not be denied. His simple presence in a room caused her breath to quicken and her heart to flutter strangely in her breast. The warmth in those smoky gray eyes completely unnerved her. Thank heaven, she need not be alone with him! Cecilie's presence forced her to keep a tight rein on her emotions.

Otherwise she might well have been tempted to give way to the terrible longing that consumed her – a longing to feel the strength of his arms around her and the pressure of his mouth on hers. Such thoughts troubled her mind a great deal and, indeed, occupied it much of the time.

It was such thoughts that she was thinking one morning about a week after their excursion to the theater as she and Cecilie sat at breakfast. "Aggie!"

She could tell from Cecilie's tone that this was not the first time her ward had called her name. She shook herself slightly. "Yes, my dear? I'm afraid I was woolgathering."

"You do that a great deal lately," said Cecilie thoughtfully, but before Aggie could prepare herself for an attack of questions, Cecilie grinned and shook the *Morning Chronicle* she was holding. "Look, Aggie! Mr. Sadler, the aeronaut, is going up in his balloon. It sounds like great fun."

Aggie shook her head. "That doesn't sound like fun to me."

Cecilie's eyes widened. "Why not?"

"Such ascents can be rather dangerous, as I recall."

"Oh, marvelously exciting!" cried Cecilie.

Aggie sighed. "I doubt if it is much fun to be half frozen or to be forced to slash a

168

hole in one's balloon in order not to be landed in the river. Such accidents often happen to aeronauts."

"But the weather is warm," said Cecilie.

Aggie shook her head slightly. "I understand it is quite cold up high."

Cecilie's face took on a bemused expression. "Just imagine. Floating up above all the housetops. Almost like a bird."

Aggie eyed her charge sharply. "Cecilie, be sensible. Balloon ascension is a very dangerous occupation! Not an amusement for young ladies."

"Yes, Aggie, I know." Cecilie's face wore an expression of contrition. "But don't you think it might be educational to watch?" She consulted the paper again. "It says here that Mr. Sadler will make an ascension this afternoon at three from Hyde Park."

Aggie smiled. "Well, at least he should be out of the way before the fashionables arrive for their ride at five."

"Oh, Aggie, I should very much like to see the balloon go up. Mayn't we go?" Her wide eyes pleaded with Aggie. "I've been most awfully good," she continued as Aggie offered no response. "You know I have."

Aggie had to agree to that. "I know it, Cecilie. But I cannot take you to such a thing without the Earl's permission."

She expected a pout and an exclamation of anger, but Cecilie merely smiled. "I'll just go now and ask him myself." And she rose from the table.

Aggie was somewhat taken aback by the suddenness of the thing, but Cecilie was gone before she could muster her arguments. Aggie sighed again. She was probably upsetting herself over nothing. Surely the Earl would forbid such a junket. She attempted to lose herself in reading the latest theater reviews, but she could not concentrate. Then she decided she had best be prepared to deal with Cecilie's disappointment.

But when Cecilie returned some moments later, her face was wreathed in smiles. "His lordship says it's a capital idea, very educational." From the look of triumph in her eyes Aggie knew that this must have been one of Cecilie's arguments for the trip. "He says Winters will go along as well as the grooms. To keep an eye on us."

Aggie nodded. The ways of his lordship were past understanding.

"He even says I may take Dillydums," Cecilie chatted gaily on. "As long as I keep him on the leash." She clapped her hands together in excitement. "Oh, Aggie, it will be just capital. I can scarcely wait. I wish it were time already!"

In the next hours Aggie, too, wished for a way to speed time by. First they must decide on a gown for Cecilie, then on a bonnet and slippers. Then Aggie was plied with question after question about the nature of balloons and the miraculous gas that allowed them to rise, and their behavior after they had risen. To all of which Aggie had perforce to reply, "I'm sorry, Cecilie, I really don't know."

"But Aggie, it is all so interesting!"

The afternoon did finally arrive, in spite of Cecilie's protestations that it obviously was never going to, and Cecilie, her blond curls hidden by a straw gypsy hat tied by a wide blue scarf, looked very young and pretty in her blue-sprigged muslin. Aggie herself wore yellow-sprigged muslin and a more sedate bonnet of woven straw which was kept in place by two broad ribbons tied under the chin. Dillydums, attired in his usual blue trousers and red jacket, was perched on Cecilie's shoulder. His little black eyes seemed to take in everything he saw. Aggie would have really preferred not to bring along the monkey. Cecilie alone was more than enough to handle. But Dillydums was there and to insist that he stay behind might bring on a tantrum. And right now Aggie wished only for peace.

She wondered momentarily where this terrible tiredness she so often felt was coming from. She had never before been so utterly weary, except – She shook her head. She was not going to think about those days anymore. Or the grief she had felt. She would never feel such grief again. She had promised herself that. Yet –

"Aggie! You're woolgathering again," Cecilie eyed her curiously. "Whatever are you thinking about these days?"

Aggie managed a smile. "Nothing important. Shall we go?" And picking up her reticule and gloves, she followed Cecilie down the stairs and into the carriage.

The streets of the city were full of people and Cecilie's bright eyes darted everywhere. "Look, oh look!" she called repeatedly, until Aggie thought her neck would break from the constant motion. She turned down requests for baked apples, sticky buns, and tea, reminding Cecilie of the difficulty of eating anything with Dillydums perched on her shoulder, ready to reach out and pinch a piece.

"Oh, all right. But Aggie, you put such a damper on things. Smile a little. You're terribly glum these days."

Cecilie turned immediately back to the fascinating street and so did not see the color that rose to Aggie's cheeks at this accusation. She must get hold of herself. She could not bear having Cecilie after her with questions like this.

By this time they had reached the park, where a considerable number of people had gathered to see the brave aeronaut take to the skies. Off in the distance a small herd of deer and several cows could be seen grazing, on occasion raising their heads to contemplate with mild brown eyes the antics of these strange humans.

Winters threaded their carriage skillfully through the others until they were fairly close to the great balloon. Cecilie clapped her hands in glee. "Oh, this is wonderful. Just capital!"

Aggie had to admit that the balloon was rather exciting. It seemed quite large, hovering high in the sky above them, and decorated with bright designs in gay colors. A network of rope attached it to the colorfully decorated car below. And the whole was held to some sort of anchoring platform on the ground with more ropes. The bright and brilliant colors and the gay cheerful mood of the crowd gave the occasion a very festive appearance.

"See!" cried the excited Cecilie. "They are handing in things. Oh! It's so exciting!"

Then a rising tide of sound announced the approach of the intrepid Sadler, his youthful face wreathed in smiles. To Aggie's surprise, the young man actually looked happy.

"Isn't he handsome?" cried Cecilie. "So brave."

Aggie held back the question that had sprung to her lips. She dared not ask if Cecilie had just added aeronautical exploits to the list of prerequisites for a husband. Aggie did not at all like the look of this and she wished fervently that the Earl had denied Cecilie the trip, or at least had had sense enough to come along.

She watched in silence as the aeronaut mounted the car. "Oh!" cried Cecilie suddenly. "I must get closer." And before Aggie could stop her she had scrambled out of the carriage and was worming her way through the crowd.

"Cecilie! Stop!" Aggie hurried to follow, but the crowd was densely packed and passage was very difficult. She had never before been alone on foot in such a crowd, but her worry over Cecilie kept most of her own feelings in abeyance. She pushed and shoved, trying to get closer to the balloon. She must get to Cecilie.

She had almost reached the edge of the space that was cordoned off by ropes when an exclamation went up from the crowd of onlookers. Aggie shoved her way to the front just in time to see the balloon rising. The aeronaut stood gaily waving and beside him, her bonnet askew and Dillydums jumping up and down on her shoulder, stood Cecilie!

"Cecilie! No! You must not!" cried Aggie, hardly aware that she spoke.

A kindly-looking man next to her chuckled. "Ain't no yelling gonna bring that thing down now. No sirree. Mr. Sadler, he's going to Dover."

"Dover!" Aggie felt the ground begin to sink beneath her. "He can't!" She turned frantically back toward the carriage. She must find Winters. They had to do something. She began blindly pushing her way through the crowd.

"Miss! Miss!" Aggie finally realized that it was Winters who was impeding her progress. She tried to calm herself.

"It's Cecilie," she said. "She's gone with the aeronaut."

"Yes, miss. I seen." Winter's lined face was almost as pale as hers.

"Oh," cried Aggie, and the word was a wail. "What shall we do?"

"My guess is we'd better get back to the

Earl," he said after a moment's pause, and it was clear that the idea frightened him almost as much as it did her.

She nodded dumbly. "I suppose we'll have to."

As by a common thought their heads turned and their eyes moved to the sky. The balloon was now a small white speck to the south of them. "Well," said Winters, in an obvious attempt to cheer her, "he's got the right wind. That's Dover way."

Aggie nodded. As the people around them dispersed, she just stood there, too upset to know what she was doing.

"Miss," said Winters, "the quicker we finds his lordship, the quicker he can go after her."

Aggie allowed herself to be led back to the carriage and helped inside. As Winters guided the horses into the stream of conveyances leaving the park, she fought to keep back the tears. The Earl was going to be furious – and rightly so, she supposed – though she could not see how she could have avoided any of it. How could anyone be expected to know that Cecilie would do such a foolish thing? Her shoulders shook then with her efforts to hold back the sobs. Cecilie, up in that balloon, in a thin muslin gown. She had read that it got very cold up there. But even worse was what would happen when the balloon came down! Balloons could loose their gas and fall. She shuddered. Or when they were almost down, they could be suddenly seized by the wind and dragged through trees and against buildings. She must stop thinking like this, she told herself. It would do no one any good. She tried to force her mind to other scenes, to keep from seeing Cecilie's lively young body all bruised and bloodied.

They reached the house on Grosvenor Square and Aggie hurried up to the door. There was no time to think of her own feelings. She must get help for Cecilie. "The Earl?" she asked Bates. "Is he in?"

"He just got in, miss. He's in the library."

Bates seemed about to tell her something more, but she was already gone, hurrying down the hall as fast as her trembling legs would take her. She did not stop to knock on the door, but pushed hurriedly through. "Denby, it's –"

She stopped suddenly, frozen by what she saw. The Earl stood by his desk, and near him, in fact bare inches away, stood Lady Alicia. Her dress of coral sarcenet showed every voluptuous curve. For some strange reason Aggie felt a new strength come into her legs as the lady's cold green eyes swept over her disdainfully. Lady Alicia could have Denby later; right now *she* needed him. "I'm sorry to intrude, milord, but I must speak to you. Urgently."

Lady Alicia sniffed delicately. "Surely this can wai –"

"I must speak to you now," repeated Aggie. "Immediately, milord."

His eyes moved over her sharply once and then he turned to the woman who stood so close to him. "I'm sure you will excuse me, Lady Alicia. It shouldn't take me long. Miss Trimble." And putting a hand under Aggie's arm, he led her out into the hall and softly closed the door. "Now, what is it that causes you to come bursting in on me like this?"

Now that she was facing him, Aggie was almost unable to go on, but she knew she must. "C-Cecilie has gone up in a b-balloon," she stammered.

For a long moment he stared at her. Then he grabbed her by the shoulders and shook her. "She has *what?*"

Aggie didn't mind the pain of his grasp. It helped to clear her head. "She jumped out of the carriage," she explained. "And I followed her. Winters, too. But the crowd was too great. We couldn't catch her. And when I got to the balloon it was already going up. And Cecilie was in it."

178

She watched the anger gather in his eyes like thunder-clouds. "The little idiot. Where was it headed?"

"They said Dover." She did not seem able to move and in spite of the bite of his fingers in the soft flesh of her arms, she dreaded the moment he would let go of her. She did not know if she could stand alone.

Denby seemed to be glaring down at her, but she could tell from his eyes that he did not see her, that he was thinking. He dropped his hands suddenly and turned to shout. "Bates!"

Aggie leaned trembling against the wall.

"Have my rig readied. The bays, I think. Someone to drive it. And the stallion. Plenty of blankets. And tell Winters to come along."

"Yes, milord."

"I'll just get my cloak," said Aggie wearily.

The Earl turned on her, his eyes blazing. "You'll do no such thing. You'll stay right here till I fetch her back."

"But –"

"I haven't time to argue," he said harshly. "You're ready to collapse now. The last thing I need is *two* irresponsible women on my hands."

She was too exhausted even to answer this; the only thought in her mind was the hope that she would not disgrace herself by sinking to the floor while he still stood there.

His eyes seemed to hold a sudden tenderness. "Don't worry about her, Aggie. Providence sometimes protects such fools. She's probably enjoying herself." The sound of a carriage could be heard pulling up in front. "Listen, I've got to go. Give Lady Alicia my regrets. Tell her I was called away suddenly. Nothing more. There's no need for all of London to know." His eyes probed hers for one long moment, and then he was gone and she stood there shaking.

It took her several minutes to restore her features to some composure. She removed her bonnet and gloves and gave them to Bates; then, absentmindedly patting down her hair, she reentered the library.

Lady Alicia swung around. "Well, Den –"

"The Earl was called away on a matter of business," Aggie said smoothly, refusing to be dismayed by the look of pure hatred that came flashing from Lady Alicia's green eyes. "He asked me to give you his regrets and beg your forgiveness."

"Of course." Lady Alicia's eyes were veiled now as she let them slowly travel over the young woman who stood before her. Aggie was almost at the edge of her limits, but she did not waver. It was quite obvious that Lady Alicia saw the Earl as her exclusive property and disliked having anyone close to her territory.

Though she had seemed to accept Aggie's explanation, the lady made no move to leave. Aggie felt her small remaining store of strength fading. "If you'll excuse me," she began. "I have things to do."

"I'm sure," said Lady Alicia, "that your duties are not so onerous that you cannot spare me a few moments of your time."

Aggie forced herself to remain rigidly upright. She longed to say something vicious and nasty to Lady Alicia, but good manners – and common sense – forbade it. "I do not know what matters you might wish to speak to me about," she said quietly.

"Really?" Lady Alicia's voice was soft, but dangerously so. "I can think of at least one."

It was Aggie's turn to say, "Really?"

She saw Lady Alicia's eyebrows shoot up at such a reply and her ladyship's pale complexion turned somewhat rosier. "Arrogance will get you nowhere," said the lady.

"I was not aware of being arrogant," Aggie replied, keeping her voice even.

Lady Alicia tossed her glistening hair. "I should think that a woman in your delicate position would be more careful about whom she offended."

Suddenly Aggie was tired of this cat and mouse game. "Lady Alicia," she said crisply, "if you have something to say to me, kindly spit it out. I have other things to do."

The lady's green eyes sparked dangerously. "I doubt that the Earl would care to have you insult his guests."

But this threat had little effect on Aggie. The way she felt at the moment she did not care if the Earl dismissed her. "What is it you wish to say?" she repeated.

"The Earl is a very handsome man." Her ladyship smiled rather maliciously. "I suppose it is only natural that a woman like you should set out lures for him." She tossed her head haughtily. "Just be aware that it will do you no good. The Earl is not about to marry a penniless companion."

Aggie felt new waves of strength pouring into her. She did not have to bear such outrage quietly. She looked directly into Lady Alicia's cold green eyes. "I never supposed that the Earl intends to marry – anyone," she replied calmly.

Lady Alicia flushed at the implication of the last word, and, casting Aggie one last look of hatred, flounced angrily from the room.

Aggie forced herself to stand there until she heard the carriage pull away, and then, no longer having anything it was necessary to do, she sank slowly to the floor in a swoon of sweet forgetfulness.

It was Bates who found her there and had her carried to her room by a strong young footman. She wakened in her bed some moments later to see Millie's anxious face bending over her. "You give us all a turn, miss, you did." She was busily undoing Aggie's gown.

"No, no. I must get up," Aggie protested weakly.

Millie shook her head. "Now, miss, Bates says it's best you rest awhile. His lordship ain't even got to Dover yet. It'll be a long while afore we get any word."

Aggie had to concede the truth of this and she fell back among the pillows and surrendered to Millie's ministrations.

"Now you just close your eyes and rest, miss," soothed Millie. "Bates, he says his lordship took along a couple grooms. One of them'll get back to us soon as he can. Don't you go worrying now. Miss Cecilie, she's game as a pebble, she is. No little balloon flight ain't gonna hurt her." And with a last solicitous look, Millie turned down the lamp and went out, closing the door softly behind her.

In the darkness Aggie lay trembling. She could still feel his piercing gaze, the grip of his hands on her bruised flesh. Of course he blamed her. What else was there for him to do? And truthfully, how could he have supposed that Cecilie would behave in such a foolhardy fashion? How could anyone have supposed?

Aggie tossed restlessly in the bed. Where was Cecilie now? And where was Denby? For a moment she had a mental image of him, riding at top speed along the Dover Road, the carriage and mounted grooms trailing behind. She tried to hold her thoughts on him. He would find an abashed Cecilie and read her a terrific scold. Then the two of them would come on home. It had to be that way, she told herself. It simply had to. She could not let herself think of Cecilie fallen from the balloon car, of Cecilie lying still and bleeding somewhere between London and Dover. And then her control broke and she fell to weeping in great choking sobs until finally exhaustion and sleep overtook her.

Chapter Eleven

The early morning sun streaming through the window woke Aggie from a sleep of pure exhaustion. For one moment she wondered why she felt so tired. Then memory came flooding back. She was on her feet instantly, reaching for the bellpull. How could she have slept? How could she have possibly slept when Cecilie was in danger? She dragged on her dressing gown and was hunting for her slippers when the door opened and Millie appeared.

"Yes, miss?"

"Is there news?" asked Aggie, trying to keep her voice calm.

Millie nodded enthusiastically. "Oh yes, miss. Everything's all right. One of the grooms come riding in at first light. The balloon come down in a hay field afore dark. Miss Cecilie and the monkey was both fine. They'll be home with his lordship later in the day – toward evening maybe."

"You're sure she's all right?" Aggie was finding it hard to believe such good news.

Millie nodded briskly. "Oh, yes, miss. I

know this groom." Here Millie flushed a little. "He says Miss Cecilie looked just as perky as ever and that monkey, too. He says they both looked like they enjoyed it."

Aggie shook her head wearily. "What *will* she think of next?"

A little smile tugged at Millie's lips. "I wouldn't worry none about Miss Cecilie for a while. She's got to ride all the way from Dover while his lordship gives her a royal scold. That oughta make her think twice."

Aggie nodded. There was little sense in telling the maid that Cecilie's proclivity for seeking out mischief could not be squashed, even by the Earl's fury. She knew his lordship's servants stood in awe of him, as she herself did, but Cecilie would not be abashed by a scold, no matter how vehemently delivered. The child did not seem to realize the seriousness of her situation.

Aggie put a trembling hand to her throbbing head. How would she ever manage to get out of this bumble broth? And what would the Earl have to say when he returned? He seemed determined to believe that Cecilie's wrongdoing was always her companion's fault and she dreaded having him glare at her in that ferocious way and shout. She shut her eyes wearily.

"Now, miss." Millie tugged at her sleeve. "You still ain't looking too well. Whyn't you lie abed awhile longer?"

Aggie shook her head. "No, no. I can't. Maybe I'll walk in the garden a little."

Millie nodded. "That sounds nice, miss. The roses is all abloom. So pretty. I'll just help you get into your clothes, then you can have a little breakfast afore your walk."

Aggie shook her head. "I'm not hungry."

"Now, miss." Millie looked pained. "You'll only be making yourself sick like that. You got to eat for strength."

Aggie nodded feebly. She knew the maid was right, but still she resisted the idea. How was she to eat when her stomach was in such turmoil, when her mind was filled with the most vivid pictures of the Earl in anger? Still, she allowed herself to be gowned and combed and, almost like a little child, led to the breakfast room. She managed to get a little of the food down, enough to satisfy Bates and the watching Millie, both of whom were treating her with the utmost solicitude.

Then she rose and made her way out into the courtyard. Her head was a whirl of mad thoughts and she knew she must settle it. She could not go on like this; the strain was too much. Perhaps she should ask Denby to release her from her position as Cecilie's companion, tell him to find someone else to act as watchdog. She needed to get away from him. Sharp-tongued women like Lady Alicia were already bandying her name about in malicious whispers. If she stayed much longer in such a situation, she would have no good name left. And without that her chances of securing another position were very small – or of opening her school.

Slowly she paced among the roses, their fragrant sweetness unnoticed by her senses. What was she to do? Life here was becoming intolerable. If she was not waiting for Cecilie to do some mad thing, she was fearful of what his lordship would say to her, or, even worse, how he would look at her. She was still unable to drive the idea from her mind that she had seen hurt in his eyes – hurt and pain. Yet how could that be? She had had nothing to do with his abrupt departure five years ago. *She* was the one who had been abandoned. *She* was the one in pain.

The day wore slowly on. As the sun rose higher Aggie left the garden for the coolness of the library. Her head still throbbed painfully, but she moved restlessly around the room. Bates had drawn the heavy velvet drapes and the room was dim. Aggie tried to settle in a chair and rest peacefully, to eat a little of the lunch they brought her; but every fresh sound caused her to start up and she wanted to sob with utter frustration. Why couldn't they just get back and get it over with?

It was the waiting, she knew, that kept her nerves so taut – the waiting for his angry looks and shouts. And, from deep within her came the disquieting awareness that her mind was all too full of the memory that it was after his anger that he had laid hands on her. It was after his anger that he had pulled her so swiftly into his arms and claimed her lips with an ardor that entirely vanquished all her resolutions to no longer allow him a place of regard in her heart. She knew what her head said: that such a man was unworthy of her love. But when he held her in his arms, when his lips devoured hers, her head was helpless. Then her body took control, her traitorous body that insisted on belonging to him! Aggie dropped her aching head into her hands. Dear God, why had she been so unfortunate as to develop a partiality for such a man?

Finally, sitting there in the dimness, her eyelids fluttered shut and she fell into a light doze. Sometime later sounds in the hall roused her and for a moment she could not get her bearings. Then she realized where she was and leaped hastily to her feet. Perhaps it was them!

Hurriedly she made her way to the door. Peering out, she saw that Cecilie and his lordship stood in the front hall. "Cecilie!" Aggie hurried toward her. "Are you all right? You're sure?"

Cecilie smiled. Aside from being a little mussed, she looked quite well. "Really, Aggie, I am fine. It was a wonderful trip. A bit chilly, perhaps, but Mr. Sadler gave me his jacket." Here she cast a patronizing glance at his lordship. "And it was just marvelous looking down on everything. The houses were so very tiny."

Suddenly Aggie realized that Cecilie was without the monkey. "Where is Dillydums?" she asked.

Cecilie's white forehead puckered in a frown. "One of the grooms has him. He didn't like it in the carriage. But he loved it up in the balloon. You should go up sometime, Aggie, you really should."

The Earl, whose face had grown increasingly more baleful through this recital, now broke in. "Miss Trimble will do no such thing," he said gruffly. "The journey home has been long and tiring. I suggest you go to your room and rest before dinner."

Cecilie's face took on a strange expression,

but her tone was demure enough. "Yes, milord," she said and moved toward the stairs.

As Aggie turned to follow her, she felt a warm hand on her arm. The shivers that sped over her caused her to flush. "Just a minute, Miss Trimble," said the Earl. "I wish a word with you." He waited until Cecilie had disappeared from view. "We have got to do something," he said harshly, "before this girl either kills herself or ruins her reputation completely."

Aggie could only nod.

The Earl frowned and she felt her heart contracting. "If only she had not refused Connors. He could keep her in line."

"I doubt that, milord." Aggie spoke without thinking and was distressed to see his frown deepen.

"The girl needs a strong hand," he said sternly. "She must be mastered."

Sudden waves of fury poured over Aggie. How pigheaded could the man be? "Cecilie is not a horse," she snapped. "She cannot be broken like one."

"Neither can she be permitted to run loose through the city, leaving havoc in her wake," he replied gruffly.

Aggie felt her anger rising. "I did not permit her to run loose," she cried. "I did my very best to keep her in hand. *You* were the one who said she could go. Balloon flights indeed! You might know that Cecilie would get into mischief at such an event. And anyway, if you knew more about her, you would know that it was *you* who prevented her from accepting the Marquess."

The Earl glared at her, his brows making the straight line that denoted his anger and his eyes flashing. "You're talking nonsense," he said harshly. "Utter nonsense. The girl was dead set against the man before he ever offered."

Aggie was quivering with rage now. She was tired of taking the blame for everything. And, inexplicably, just at that moment, her mind presented her with a vivid picture of Lady Alicia gazing up at Denby with flattering eyes. "If you did not have such a good opinion of yourself as a man who can handle women," she said boldly, "you might have considered asking for advice. Cecilie, thank God, is not deceived by your charming manners or your good looks. She cannot be flattered into acceding to your wishes."

His frown deepened and he took a step closer. "Nor can she be bullied," Aggie hurried to add, her heart rising up into her throat.

The Earl grabbed her arms and gazed
192

down intently into her eyes. "Then Aggie, in the name of heaven, will you tell me how the girl *can* be handled – guided into a decent marriage?"

His eyes bored into hers and Aggie felt herself sinking into their depths. She almost forgot that they were quarreling. Suddenly she wanted to help him. "Sometimes..." Her voice faltered with the intensity of her emotions. "Sometimes I have gotten her to do what I wished by – by absolutely forbidding it. If you had a likely candidate, a *young* man," she added, "you might get her to form a partiality for him by being very unkind to him and forbidding him to call."

For more long moments he stared at her, his fingers biting into her arms, and then he laughed. It was not a pleasant sound. "Do you mean that in attempting to drive her *from* Parrington, I may have been driving her *to* him?"

She nodded.

Anger flared into his eyes again and he shook her slightly. "Why didn't you tell me this before?"

His anger caused hers to return. "You have not asked for the benefit of my experience," she reminded him icily. "Instead you have chosen to blame me for everything that goes wrong."

His dark face hardened. "Perhaps I have," he admitted, his voice in no way apologetic. "But then, perhaps I have had good cause."

"You are absolutely hopeless," Aggie cried, fanning her anger higher. That could not be hurt she had seen in his eyes just then. "You are so puffed up with your own importance that it is sickening."

She almost cried aloud as he shook her again, more harshly. But still she glared at him defiantly. "I have spoken the truth," she insisted. "And I am not sorry. You can't bully me into submission."

Something strange flickered momentarily in his eyes and to her surprise he relaxed his grip on her. She stepped quickly away from him, her hand seeking the banister for support. "Perhaps, milord, I should seek another position." She regretted the words as soon as they left her mouth, yet she knew the rightness of such an action.

The Earl's face darkened further. His mouth settled into a line of grim determination and his eyes turned cold and hard as stone. "Perhaps you are right. After all, I *can* dismiss you any time I please, can't I?" And his eyes raked her coldly.

Aggie fought the panic that threatened her as the idea of never seeing him again pressed itself sharply into her consciousness, but she managed to remain calm. "You needn't bother to dismiss me," she said curtly. "I'll begin looking for another place tomorrow."

"You may find it rather difficult," he said harshly, his eyes veiled.

She looked at him sharply. "I don't see why. I am a competent companion."

The Earl's mouth tightened cruelly. "I doubt that some indulgent papas would think so. After all, your charge has done some rather scatterbrained things, hasn't she? That is hardly good advertisement for your proficiency."

Aggie felt the scarlet flooding her cheeks. "I did not know that Cecilie's escapades were public knowledge." She managed to get the words out without stammering, but the threat behind his words was apparent.

His smile did nothing to put her at ease. "Perhaps they are not." He grimaced. "I have certainly done everything humanly possible to prevent the wagging of tongues." His eyes grew even colder. "However, it will be difficult to hush up the last matter. And besides that, there is the small matter of references."

Aggie gasped as though she had been struck and her hand went unconsciously to her breast. "Do you mean to say –"

His lordship nodded. His mouth set in a

stubborn line, he shrugged his broad shoulders eloquently. "I must tell the truth, must I not?"

"You know very well –" Aggie began, but he silenced her with a hard look.

"Listen, Aggie –" He saw her wince in pain at the use of her given name and his eyes grew darker. "I will put the matter to you quite plainly. You are Cecilie's companion. You will remain so until the girl is married and you collect your inheritance. I have decided that it will be this way." His eyes moved over her angrily, leaving her trembling like an aspen in a storm. "I believe you know enough of the *ton* to understand the efficacy of a well-placed whisper."

Aggie felt as though she had been slapped. "This..." she faltered. "This is blackmail, clear and simple. How dare you!" Her breasts heaved in indignation under the thin muslin gown. "How dare you do such a thing!"

"I am the Earl of Denby." He said the words clearly, spacing them for effect. "I do as I please." His eyes glinted cruelly. "The sooner you realize this, the better we shall deal together."

She knew he was right. He had all the power, all the force of society was behind him. She was nothing – a poverty-stricken little companion, indebted to him for the very food she ate. "You would really ruin my life?"

A muscle twitched in the side of his jaw, but his tone was steady and his eyes remained hard and cold. "The choice is yours, Miss Trimble. Nothing need be ruined. Nothing at all."

She dug her nails into her palms; the pain of it – clean physical pain – might help clear her head. "I seem to have no choice," she said finally. "No choice at all."

His eyes softened for a moment and he took a step toward her. "Aggie, it doesn't have to be like this. I could –"

"No thank you, milord." She cut him off before he could finish his dishonorable offer. "Understand this. I will remain as Cecilie's companion because I must. But I will run into the street penniless – and – and naked, before I consent to become anything to you!"

She saw the pain in his eyes before he could veil it, sharp and bitter as her pain had been, and she wondered again how he could imagine himself the injured party.

"I quite understand you," he replied harshly, his eyes smoldering down at her. "My reasons for keeping you here have to do with Cecilie – nothing more."

With the memory of his searing kisses still

imprinted on her memory, she could not believe this. But it was safer to let it pass, safer not to discuss the thing further. "If that is all," she said, her head still proudly high, "then I shall go up to Cecilie."

Denby nodded. "That will do. I suppose it is futile to ask, but you might use whatever wiles you possess to convince the girl that young Sadler is not an eligible connection." He ran his hand wearily through his hair and for the first time she noticed the dark shadows of fatigue under his eyes.

"I will do what I can," she said. "Cecilie is a very romantic young woman. Logic does not have much effect on her."

His lordship laughed, loud and harshly. "As far as I can tell nothing sensible has much effect on her. She is a complete enigma to me."

He bowed his head wearily and she was aware that he had probably not slept all night. "I'll go to Cecilie and you can get some rest." The words were out before she realized their implication.

His head snapped up and he looked at her sharply, as though surprised by her concern for him. "I'll go to bed at bedtime," he said. "I have an important dinner engagement." He looked down at his soiled and dusty clothes. "And I have just time to wash and change."

The little sympathy she had felt for him because of his fatigue vanished completely. She had a clear vision of Lady Alicia waiting somewhere in a little room, the small intimate table lit by candles, the scent of expensive perfume in the air, the lady in a gown that revealed all her charms. "I hope you enjoy your dinner," she said sharply and marched out so swiftly that she did not see the look of startled curiosity on his face nor the way he stroked his dark chin speculatively, as though her words revealed to him something of infinite interest.

Chapter Twelve

The next day found them more or less settled back into their routine. Neither Cecilie nor Dillydums seemed any the worse for their flight. Indeed, Cecilie kept insisting that it had been great fun, a capital adventure. She took every opportunity to extol the pleasures of balloon flight to her companion.

Aggie nodded absently. Being very much a ground kind of person, she could not wax enthusiastic about hanging high above the city. Descriptions of tiny houses and people the size of ants left her cold. Besides, she found it difficult to erase from her mind that last scene with the Earl. If only there were some way she could leave this place. But he had made it clear that she could not, that to do so would mean being penniless and ruining any chance of her finding another position. She also puzzled over that look of pain in his eyes. It could not be accounted for; it seemed too deep and genuine to be caused merely by disappointed desire. But she could find nothing else to account for it.

She pondered over his strange behavior, trying not to recall the sinking sensation of submission that had overcome her in his arms. She must fight that with all her strength, she knew. For her mind insisted that to surrender to the Earl would mean eventual disaster. It was clear that he wanted her – as he had wanted her before, she told herself, yet more circumspectly then. But if he had suffered no qualms at leaving her then, when their love had been legitimate, how much easier it would be for him to dissolve an illegitimate union. Aggie knew well the ways of London's bucks. They went from woman to woman as a bee goes from flower to flower, sipping the nectar and caring nothing for what they left behind. And she did not think she could stand having once known his love – no, she amended, his passion – and then being deserted. That would be the end of her reputation, her pride, her very life.

Somehow she must cling to her resolves; she must refuse his advances, keep herself aloof until Cecilie was married. Then she at least would have the inheritance. There was nothing to do but hold on. No other answer.

She was still going over and over events in her mind, looking for a way out when there was none, when Bates appeared at the door of the sitting room. He looked just a trifle dismayed. Aggie rose to her feet as he said, "If I might have a word with you, Miss Trimble."

"Of course, Bates." She joined him by the door. "What is it?"

"There's a caller, miss." Bates lowered his voice. "A Lord Parrington."

"Parrington!" Dismay made Aggie's voice rise.

"Yes, miss. He's come to call on Miss Cecilie."

"Oh dear, Bates. Did his lordship leave no instructions?"

"No, miss. I only know the last time he

201

was here, the Earl looked rather angry when he left."

Aggie tried to think. "I wish we could send him away."

"I can't do that, miss. Not without the Earl's orders."

Aggie stood thinking. How could she tell what Denby wanted done? True, he had turned down Parrington's offer, but he had not left any orders about Parrington himself. While she stood there, trying to decide, she heard footsteps in the hall.

"Ahhh, here you are." Lord Parrington's voice was bright and cheerful. "My, how lovely you ladies look."

Cecilie, who had been gazing out the window, turned to greet him, a stern expression on her face. "Good day," she said sharply, so sharply that Aggie, already agonizing about Denby's reaction to such a call, was quite startled. Bates chose that moment to fade discreetly away.

Even Lord Parrington seemed taken aback by Cecilie's sharpness, but he quickly marshaled his wits and forced a smile. "Good day to you, Miss Winthrop." He nodded to Aggie. "Miss Trimble."

"What do you want?" demanded Cecilie truculently.

This time Parrington had more difficulty

in appearing unmoved. "Why, I have come to pay a social call. To inquire after your health since your exposure in the balloon."

"My health is fine, thank you," Cecilie replied flatly. There was something very wrong here, Aggie could see. Cecilie was being almost rude.

"And your little friend Dillydums?" continued Parrington, ignoring her tone.

Cecilie fastened him with a bellicose eye. "You needn't inquire after Dillydums," she said crossly.

Lord Parrington settled himself somewhat uneasily on the edge of a chair. Clearly this call was not going as he had expected. "But my dear Miss Winthrop, I must. I was extremely upset by the thought of the poor thing's plight. Shivering up there in the cold."

Aggie found that she was staring at them and resolutely picked up her needlework which was lying nearby. It was clear that Cecilie was going to handle this. She would need no help.

Cecilie did not take a chair. She drew herself up to her full height and glared at the offending Parrington. "The game is up, milord," she declared hotly.

Parrington looked confused. And no

wonder, thought Aggie. She herself did not fully understand what was occurring.

"I said," repeated Cecilie icily, "the game is up. There is no use in your trying to pull the wool over my eyes."

"But, Miss Winthr –" Parrington began.

"Milord Parrington," Cecilie said in her haughtiest tones. "You are quite wasting your time. I may be a young woman, and a trifle foolish about animals, but there is nothing wrong with my understanding – or my eyes."

"I don't understand –" Parrington began.

"The matter is quite apparent," continued Cecilie coldly. "Your concern for animals is faked." She held up a slim hand to halt his protest. "I have seen your horses, milord. I looked at them closely. They were not the cattle of a man who cares for his beasts. They were ill-fed and ill-treated."

Parrington was on his feet now. "Those were new horses, just bought," he explained suavely. "The poor things need feeding up."

It was a palpable lie, thought Aggie, but really a rather good one under the circumstances. Cecilie was not convinced. "Good day, Milord Parrington. Kindly do not bother to call again. I shall not be in."

"But –"

Calmly Cecilie turned her back on the

man. For the merest fraction of a second Aggie saw the anger in his eyes, then he masked it and bade her good day. "I shall endeavor with all my might to change your harsh opinion of me," he said to Cecilie's rigid back; but she stiffly ignored him, as with one last ingratiating smile toward Aggie, he left the room.

Moments later Cecilie turned from the window. Tears of rage stood out in her eyes as she faced Aggie. "That impossible man. I hate him!"

"But, Cecilie," Aggie could not help asking, "I thought you liked the man."

Cecilie frowned. "I did – before."

"Before?"

"Before his lordship told me about Parrington's horses."

"You believed his lordship?" The words were out before Aggie could stop them.

"No," said Cecilie with a little smile. "Not when he said it." Her smile widened. "I do not believe much of what the Earl says." She settled herself comfortably in a chair. "But it did give me cause to think. So I decided to find out."

"And how did you do that?" asked Aggie curiously.

Cecilie smiled again, a little wickedly. "Millie has a certain groom for a friend,

Waters. And she asked him. When he was waiting for the Earl one night at White's, he had the opportunity. So he looked over Lord Parrington's cattle – and spoke to his grooms. They were quick to tell him that Parrington is not good to his beasts at all. They complained of him bitterly." She gave Aggie a smug look. "Waters brought the word back to Millie and Millie to me. And I determined if ever I saw Lord Parrington again to give him a good piece of my mind." She smiled with obvious satisfaction. "And I did, didn't I, Aggie?"

Aggie nodded. "You did indeed, my dear. But do you think you might have been a trifle rude?"

"I hope so," replied Cecilie complacently. "His lordship said Lord Parrington was nothing but a fortune hunter. And he was right. The man deserves to be dealt with sharply."

Aggie did not at all deny this; what did disturb her was the flash of malevolent hatred that she had seen in Parrington's eyes during that one unguarded second. She felt that the man was evil and very much to be feared. But surely Cecilie had given him such a set-down that he would not call again. And, since the Earl would never listen to his offer, Cecilie ought to be safe enough. Aggie pushed the fear to the back of her mind. Aside from spreading malicious rumors, there seemed very little that Lord Parrington could do.

With a sigh, Cecilie rose from the chair. "This business of looking for a husband is rather dreary." She turned to Aggie with a little grin. "I still think my idea of a kind of marketplace is a good one."

Aggie shook her head. "Good idea or not, it is not feasible. You know it."

Cecilie's grin widened. "But, Aggie, think of all those bare chest –"

"Cecilie! That is enough!" Aggie felt that she simply could not stand any more such talk. It inevitably brought to her mind a picture of the Earl's unclothed chest. And the resultant warmth and longing that rose in her breast completely unnerved her. She wondered sometimes that she could speak to him at all. His very presence in a room gave her such an intense feeling that she could scarcely function properly. And there seemed no way to change her feelings. It was entirely useless to think of not having such feelings. No matter what she told herself about their unsuitability, she could not make them go away. She could not regard the Earl as an ordinary man; it was just impossible.

As Cecilie rose and moved toward the window, Aggie returned her attention to her needlework. "Have you seen no one that you could form a partiality for?" she asked idly.

"There is young Mr. Sadler." Cecilie's eyes glowed. "He's such a courageous man. We did a deal of talking on the way to Dover. And I thought at first..." She sighed. "But no, he won't do. You see, he won't take a woman along with him generally. It was an accident yesterday, you know. I bumped a rope climbing in. I thought it would be glorious fun, but he said he wouldn't want his wife floating about in a balloon. And he hasn't much money, nor much time for animals. So I decided not to set my cap for him."

Aggie found she had been holding her breath and slowly let it out. She made no comment. Sometimes silence was the best way to deal with Cecilie.

"But I am getting tired of waiting, Aggie." Cecilie took a turn around the room. "I want to have a husband; to be a grown-up lady who can do as she pleases."

Aggie smiled. "Grown-up ladies seldom get to do as they please."

"Of course they do," said Cecilie. "Why else should they grow up? Look at Lady Alicia. And Lady Jersey. Why, Jersey can

208

keep anyone she wants in or out of Almack's. Certainly she can do as she pleases."

Aggie sighed. Cecilie was right, but only to a degree. "Lady Alicia is a fashionable widow," she reminded her charge. "And Lady Jersey is a leader of the *ton*. You are neither. Nor are you likely to be for some time."

"I know, but still – if I had a husband – certainly he would be more amenable than the Earl." She smiled impishly. "Especially if I were good to him."

"Cecilie! Wherever have you heard such things?" Aggie's outrage was in part assumed, but it was not necessary to let her know it. The girl was getting far too forward in her remarks.

Cecilie shrugged. "Millie tells me all about the great ladies. How the men flock to attend them. How they buy new gowns every week. Why, Lady Alicia never wears the same gown twice. Never. Millie says the lady has dozens of beaux."

Aggie found this whole discussion uncomfortable, but she dared not show it.

Cecilie's voice fell to a hushed tone. "Millie says Lady Alicia can have any man in London, but she wants his lordship." The girl's eyes gleamed with mischief. "Do you suppose she's seen his chest?"

Aggie was too disturbed to scold Cecilie for this unladylike talk. A small voice inside her told her that the lady in question had undoubtedly seen the Earl's unclothed chest, not once but many times. And the thought made Aggie quite wretched.

"Oh," cried Cecilie, "if only some wonderful man would come along and sweep me off my feet." She hugged herself. "I want to be mistress of my own establishment."

The door to the sitting room opened quite suddenly and the Earl stood there. He was wearing Bedford cords, a coat of brown nankeen, and a striped twill waistcoat. Though he had obviously just come in from the street, his boots gleamed brightly.

"Good day, milord." Cecilie's tone was quite cheerful and Aggie knew that the girl was thinking that this time, at least, the Earl would find her actions acceptable. To Cecilie's surprise the Earl did not return her greeting.

Instead, he strode into the room and took up a stand before the hearth. Cecilie was still too lost in her feelings of virtue to notice, but Aggie sensed immediately that something was angering him. For several long moments he stared at the two of them. Cecilie did not seem to mind, but Aggie felt her breath quicken and she knew they were in for a scold. She tried to think of the reason for his anger, but she could think of nothing else that Cecilie had done wrong. Nor she herself.

Then Denby turned directly to face her. "You had callers today." It was a statement, not a question.

Aggie nodded. "Yes, milord."

"I see." His frown darkened. "And did you not think it ill-advised to receive a fortune hunter?"

So this was it. Aggie took a deep breath. "I did not receive Lord Parrington," she replied quietly. "Nor did Cecilie. He came into the room while I was trying to discover from Bates if you had left any orders concerning him."

"And you let him stay? A fortune hunter!" The Earl's tone was caustic and Aggie flushed in spite of herself. She was about to continue her explanation when Cecilie broke in.

Her expression of complacency had fled and she glared at Denby with the righteous indignation of one who has been terribly wronged. "Just a minute, milord." Her voice was so sharp that the Earl's head came up in surprise and his gray eyes focused on her.

Spellbound, Aggie watched the two glare at each other. "There was no need for Aggie to send Lord Parrington away," Cecilie said

211

icily. "And if you were not so intent on bullying everyone, you would give us a chance to explain." She faced the Earl bravely, her back rigid and her eyes blazing.

His lordship's chin went jutting out even further and Aggie saw him take a deep breath as though to control his anger. "Very well," he said finally in a voice that clearly betrayed his efforts at restraint. "Since I suspect that this may take some time I suggest we all be seated." As he spoke he drew up a lyre-back chair and sat down. His position was certainly not a relaxed one and when Cecilie settled herself, she took a position of equal rigidity. Denby looked at her coldly. "You may begin."

Cecilie nodded. "As I was telling you, Lord Parrington practically forced his way in. He was very cordial and friendly."

The Earl seemed about to say something, then curbed himself. Aggie, watching the two, felt admiration for Cecilie. She might be young and naive, but when Cecilie believed she was right and when she got her back up about it, there was no withstanding her.

"Yes, Lord Parrington was very friendly," Cecilie continued while the Earl grappled with his rage. "I'm afraid, though, that I rather ruined his day."

She paused, seeming to invite comment, and his lordship inquired in a choked voice, "How so?"

Cecilie smiled smugly. "He inquired about my health after the balloon flight and about Dillydums." She paused dramatically. "Imagine! A man who treats his cattle so poorly! I told him I wanted nothing to do with a man who is unkind to animals."

His lordship's eyebrows grew closer with each sentence, but the expression of surprise that crept over his features was startling.

"Then," said Cecilie in the same indignant tone, "he tried to feed me some Banbury tale about having new-bought his team. But I knew better and I sent him packing. I assure you, milord" – Cecilie concluded her story with obvious satisfaction – "that I would never have anything to do with such a man. Please inform Bates that in the future I am not to be at home to him."

"Very well," replied his lordship in a strangely strangled tone. Aggie wondered for a moment if he might be choking back a laugh. Cecilie's attitude *was* rather amusing.

Denby got to his feet. "May I offer you my apologies, Miss Winthrop? You handled a difficult situation with finesse. I con-gratulate you."

Cecilie rose, too, assuming an air of gravity

213

that almost made the relieved Aggie giggle. "Thank you, milord. I appreciate your approval. And now, if we have nothing further to discuss, I believe I shall release Dillydums from his imprisonment in my chamber and take him for a stroll in the garden."

The Earl nodded. "An excellent idea."

As Cecilie turned toward the door, Aggie rose to follow her. She was acutely aware of the heart pounding in her breast and the blood pulsing in her veins. She did not want to be left alone with his lordship, but as she moved to pass him, he laid a detaining hand on her arm. The flesh under his warm fingers seemed to quiver with a life of its own and she stopped as he said, "Go ahead to the garden, Cecilie. I shall detain Miss Trimble for a few moments."

Cecilie nodded. "Keep Aggie as long as you please, milord. I don't need her right now." And Cecilie passed from the room like some great dowager.

If the Earl's hand had not still been on her arm, Aggie would have seen the humor in Cecilie's actions. But Denby's touch drove everything else from her mind. All her body seemed to be concentrating on the spot that he was touching.

He waited until the door closed behind

Cecilie and Aggie stood there, her head bowed. They were too close for her to dare look up at him; she could not chance betraying her feelings. His hand seemed to burn into her flesh as he spoke. "I kept you behind because I owe you an apology."

Aggie nodded, keeping her eyes on his buff waistcoat. She took a step to move away, but his hand restrained her.

"Being Cecilie's guardian has unnerved me," he said softly. "Never have I been accustomed to – to bullying women." There was a pause as though he expected a reply, but Aggie could think of nothing to say. "I have been bullying you, have I not?"

This time Aggie's nod was more vigorous, but still she did not raise her head.

There was the sound of a deep sigh. Then, in a voice hoarse with emotion, Denby asked, "Am I so repugnant to you that you can't bear to look at me?"

Aggie's head snapped up in surprise. "Of course not." Moved by the pain in his voice, she answered without thinking. But then, as his eyes held hers, she realized what she had done. His eyes seemed to be drawing her into their smoky depths and she was powerless to prevent it. She did not know that her own eyes widened with fright and her lower lip trembled. His gaze held hers steadily and her knees began to tremble. Finally she wrenched her eyes away, but they fell on the lips so close to her own and her trembling increased. Fascinated, she gazed at the mouth that had driven her to such heights of joy and she knew with sinking heart that she wanted to feel those lips on hers again, wanted to be lost in his arms.

"Do you accept my apology?" he asked softly.

"Yes, milord." She managed to find her voice.

"Good." His eyes were warm and loving. Aggie fought their power. For what seemed an eternity, she stood there, waiting, her heart pounding in her throat.

Finally he spoke again. "I am glad you forgive me, Aggie. I want us to deal well together." And then, with a warm smile and a swift caress to her cheek, he left the sitting room.

Aggie had no idea how long she stood there, fighting to regain her sense. It was useless to remind herself of what he had done to her. When he looked at her like that, she wanted only one thing, the feel of his arms, the arms of a man who had once deserted her.

Aggie sank onto a divan and burst into tears.

Chapter Thirteen

Several days passed. Aggie and Cecilie received a few callers – more blocks, Cecilie averred. Gapeseeds, peageese, none of them even remotely husband material. This one was too fat, that one too thin. This too tall, that too short. This had no use for animals, that none for children. This danced like a stick, that sat on his horse like an old woman.

In spite of this, the Earl and Cecilie returned to a state of formal politeness, though now Aggie sensed a little more respect on Denby's part. This gave her a great deal of satisfaction. It was time he realized that Cecilie's understanding was actually quite good. She was not at all dense, just a little stubborn, and more than a little naive.

Their dinners were almost pleasant, Cecilie and the Earl vying to outdo each other in good manners. The only jarring note was caused by Aggie's feelings for Denby. She could not relax in his company. Even though he was unfailingly polite to her and there were no more incidents during which he made advances, she could not help but be torn by her longing for him, a longing that seemed to shake the very depths of her being.

It was nearly a week after Cecilie's unexpected balloon flight that the Earl announced that they would be attending Covent Garden two nights hence. "Kemble is doing Hamlet," he said, his eyes surveying them both. "It should be interesting."

Aggie nodded. She spoke very little in his presence these days. There seemed to be a strange constriction in her throat.

"That sounds capital," said Cecilie pleasantly. "Though it is another tragedy. Perhaps someday soon we may see a comedy."

Denby nodded. "I will keep that in mind." He smiled slightly. "Indeed, I had not forgotten your preference. It is only that Kemble is getting on and one never knows how much longer we shall be able to see him."

Cecilie nodded. "I understand."

"I believe you still have some gowns you have not yet worn," his lordship said.

"Yes, milord. Several."

"Good. I don't want anyone to think that I am a nip-farthing. On the other hand, we don't want to waste your substance."

"You're quite right, milord," agreed

Cecilie. There was something in her tone that caused Aggie to look at her sharply. Even with her new composure it was not like Cecilie to agree so sweetly. Unless... Then, as Cecilie smiled at his lordship and went on talking, she knew she had guessed right. "I have more than enough gowns, but Aggie has not."

Aggie felt the blood rush to her face, but Cecilie did not pause.

"She has only the two new ones we purchased before. Her morning gowns are all quite faded, too. I should like for us to order her some new gowns. Charged to my account, of course."

Finally Aggie found her tongue. "Really, Cecilie, what I have are fine. You must not waste your money on me."

Cecilie turned to the Earl. "Look at the gown she is wearing now, milord. It is quite old. I swear she was wearing it when she came to me five years ago."

As Denby's eyes swept over her, Aggie flushed even more. The gown was old – and shabby, but she had not minded. Now, however, under the scrutiny of the Earl's eyes, she had a sudden picture of the charming, well-dressed Lady Alicia and she felt herself dowdy and plain.

It seemed a very long time before the Earl

spoke, but when he did, his voice was soft. "You are quite right. Miss Trimble needs some new gowns. We shall see to it."

Genuine joy shown on Cecilie's face. "Capital, milord. You know, you are really not such a bad fellow after all."

Denby's eyes held amusement, but he did not smile as he answered gravely, "I hoped that time and proximity would convince you of that." He shot a quick glance at Aggie. "It does most people."

"You are both very kind," said Aggie, ignoring this last thrust. "But my gowns are just fine."

"Nonsense." The Earl leaned over and fingered the material of her gown. "This stuff is about to disintegrate. Besides, you must consider Miss Winthrop's reputation – and mine. You do not want us branded as clutch-fisted, now do you?"

Of course she didn't, but neither did she want to be the recipient of the Earl's charity, which she very much suspected was what he intended. There seemed little she could do to stop him, however, and so she resigned herself.

"Good," said Cecilie to his lordship. "Do you suppose we can get one made before Covent Garden?"

The Earl smiled. "Of course. You can go to Bond Street tomorrow."

"We can't go tomorrow," said Aggie. "We have other things to do."

Denby continued to smile at Cecilie. "Never fear. Miss Trimble will have a new gown for Covent Garden whether she will or no. I shall see to it in the morning. First thing."

Cecilie clapped her hands. "Very good, milord. Thank you."

True to the Earl's word, Aggie's new gown arrived early on the day of their trip to the theater. Accompanying it was a message that the morning gowns and walking dresses he had also ordered would soon follow. Aggie shook her head. This expense was too much.

But Cecilie unpacked the gown with childish glee. "Oh, Aggie, do look! It's just lovely!"

Uncomfortable as she was with the whole thing, Aggie was forced to agree. The gown was of cream-colored satin embroidered with seed pearls. Its deep-cut neckline was surrounded by a delicate lace-edged ruffle – Brussels lace, thought Aggie, shuddering at the cost. The ruffle extended over the shoulders to make little sleeves and the skirt terminated in a row of the same lace which

221

also formed the belt and dangled in two long ribbons down the back of the gown. It was an absolutely beautiful gown – very like the one in which she had made her own come out. But that gown and all her other good ones had been sold long ago to pay her father's creditors. "It is far too costly a gown for a companion," she said, her heart in her throat.

"Nonsense," said Cecilie. "It is just the thing for you. And we shall have Millie put your hair up on top of your head – in all those little curls – and twist a string of pearls through it. Yes, that will be perfect. Just perfect."

As she stood before her cheval glass that evening Aggie felt like a different woman. The gown enhanced her rosy complexion and the rich sheen of her dark hair. She stifled an exclamation as she saw how deep the neckline delved, much more than that in the gown for her come out had. But of course she was now a mature woman; and, after all, this gown was not indecent. It certainly did not give her the look of a poverty-stricken companion, however, and for a moment she flushed as she considered what the whispering tongues would say. Her father's affairs had been bruited about the *ton* and everyone was well aware that his daughter had little income. They knew she could not afford such a rich gown. People would say that she was putting herself forward. Well, there was little she could do about it. Denby was not a man to be gainsaid and it was clear that he intended her to have this gown.

Her eyes moved to where her dark hair was piled high in shining ringlets and threaded through with strands of gleaming pearls. The effect was quite beautiful, she thought, and spoke admiringly to Millie, whose smile reflected her joy in the praise.

Cecilie, who had been slipping into her gown, turned as Aggie entered her room. "Oh my!" she breathed. "It's an absolute stopper!"

Aggie halted in embarrassment, wondering for the hundredth time where Cecilie acquired these additions to her vocabulary.

"Oh, Aggie, if only someone could see you now!" Cecilie cried.

The color fled Aggie's cheeks immediately and she sent Cecilie a warning glance. She did not want her story circulated among the help, but her pallor was not entirely caused by that. In a few moments, the person Cecilie was speaking of *would* see her. She would be facing the Earl. And how would this gown affect him?

She turned her attention to Cecilie. Of pale blue silk with long narrow sleeves and a fashionably high bodice, her gown emphasized Cecilie's fair coloring. "You look quite beautiful," Aggie said.

Cecilie shrugged, but her eyes reflected excitement. "One never knows. Perhaps tonight we will see my future husband."

"Perhaps," agreed Aggie. She looked Cecilie over carefully. Her fair hair cascaded in a fall of curls from high on the back of her head – what Millie called the antique Roman style. It was very becoming and Cecilie, with her flushed face and sparkling eyes, made a very attractive picture.

Aggie smiled. "I expect we'd better get downstairs. His lordship doesn't like to be late, you know. And besides, Kemble is a great actor. I should hate to miss any of the performance myself."

Cecilie nodded and, accepting her shawl and gloves from the waiting maid, gave one last pat to Dillydums and followed Aggie to the stairs.

Aggie paused at the top to let Cecilie precede her. She had no wish to feel the Earl's gray eyes surveying her as she descended the great stairs. She might do something ridiculous like trip on her gown and she didn't want that to happen. Tonight she felt very regal and she wanted to preserve the feeling as long as possible.

The Earl emerged from the library just as they reached the bottom of the stairs. His *corbeau*-colored coat fit snugly across his broad shoulders and his inexpressibles molded a perfect pair of legs. His waistcoat was white satin and his intricately tied cravat was a thing of beauty. His eyes swept over them both and Aggie felt the blood racing to her cheeks. "Well, Miss Winthrop," he said to Cecilie, "what do you think of Miss Trimble's gown?"

Cecilie gave him a broad smile. "I think it's a real stunner," she proclaimed enthusiastically. "You must have had a lot of experience in choosing gowns."

Aggie's flush deepened. Of course Denby had had his share of innamoratas. What lord hadn't? And probably, as was the custom, he had bought them gowns. But Cecilie was not supposed to know about such things.

For the briefest moment Denby's eyes darkened, then his brows relaxed and .he spoke to Cecilie in a very even tone, as though he had realized that her remark was truly innocent. "Actually, this is my first excursion into the business of dressmaking." He flashed a look at Aggie, but she evaded it. "Madame Dimond was very helpful."

Aggie kept her eyes averted. She knew very well that there was no coincidence in the fact that the dresses he had bought her resembled those she had once owned and danced in with him, but she did not intend to let that change her mind about him.

The Earl offered them each an arm and soon they were settled in the carriage, Aggie still slightly breathless from that brief contact with him.

The drive to Covent Garden was occupied with small talk between the Earl and Cecilie. Occasionally Aggie was asked for her opinion on some matter, but the rest of the time she sat silent, contemplating the look in his eyes as he had gazed down at her. But soon they were at the theater and she had no time for remembering. The street was busy, coaches and horses everywhere, orange girls and playbill sellers hawking their wares. The crush was perhaps not so great as it had been at Drury Lane. Still, there were a great many people and Aggie again bethought herself of the clacking of vicious tongues. But it was far too late to worry about that kind of thing and with her head high she took the arm the Earl offered and went forward through the crowd.

The street was full, but very shortly he had succeeded in guiding them through the throng and into the building. Once inside it was a matter of a few minutes to reach his box, obviously one of the best in the house.

Again Denby stationed himself between her and Cecilie and again Aggie wished he had not. With him so near she was having trouble maintaining her pose of cool calmness. In truth, she felt like the greenest of girls, a chit barely out of the schoolroom. It was ridiculous for a woman of her age to behave like such a ninny. Very foolish.

She set herself to looking out over the pit. Here and there a fop raised a quizzing glass, but Aggie coldly stared him down. She smiled wryly. Anyone who had been examined by the Earl's stony gray eyes could withstand the worst kind of quizzing.

The curtain soon rose and Aggie watched the great Kemble in admiration. He did not seem to have changed much in the five years since she had last seen him, though some of his gestures did seem a little too theatrically dramatic. But that, perhaps, was the effect of having seen Mr. Kean. Aggie tried to remember what the latest reviews had said. There was some kind of rivalry between the two men – with Kean representing Nature and Kemble representing Art. Aggie was not sure which actor she most enjoyed, but she did wish she might see Mr. Kean do Hamelt so as to have a clearer ground of comparison.

The Earl watched in silence, his face set in expressionless lines; and when, from time to time, she glanced at him, he seemed lost in thought.

As the intermission neared, Aggie found she was growing uncomfortable. And when the curtain fell, she realized why. She did not want the Earl to leave the box and seek our Lady Alicia, as he had done at Drury Lane. But of course she had no way to stop him and no right to do so. She forced her features to remain set in calmness.

But the Earl did not seem inclined to move. He sat quite still, chatting politely with Cecilie, his former somber expression no longer in evidence. Perhaps, thought Aggie, Lady Alicia was not in the theater. She had not seen her before the curtain went up, but of course she could have come in late, as the fashionables so often did. Quite casually Aggie allowed her eyes to roam over the boxes filled with richly dressed nobility. But she did not find Lady Alicia in any of them. Slowly Aggie let herself relax. It looked like tonight, at least, she would be spared the lady's insults.

At that moment the door in the back of the box opened and a gay feminine voice called out, "Denby, my love, how good to see you!"

Aggie fought the panic that threatened her

as Lady Alicia swept into the box. She was wearing a gown of silver lamé. Like all her gowns it fit like a second skin and its deep neckline revealed an ample expanse of white bosom where diamonds flashed. Aggie swallowed hastily, thinking that this gown made her own seem maidenly demure. The barest little straps of sleeves lying carelessly over Lady Alicia's white shoulders supported the bodice rather precariously and the gown fell from it in a clinging way that emphasized every one of Lady Alicia's numerous curves. Aggie felt like the dullest of creatures beside this sparkling gem.

"Good evening, Lady Alicia." Denby's voice was quite bland, but even in her agitation Aggie thought she detected a note of disapproval.

Lady Alicia wrinkled her aristocratic nose. "My, my, Denby, we *are* formal tonight." Her red lips outed kissably and Aggie found she was clenching her hands so tightly that the nails bit into her palms. How this woman could infuriate her!

The Earl smiled politely. "I believe you have met my ward, Miss Winthrop." He turned to Cecilie. "And her companion, Miss Trimble." He indicated Aggie.

Lady Alicia's eyes rested objectively on Cecilie for a brief moment, but when they swung toward Aggie, their greenness turned quite cold. The lady nodded. "Yes, we have met."

"Really, Alicia," drawled a male voice from behind her. "You are neglecting me most dreadfully."

Aggie looked up in surprise. So taken had she been with Lady Alicia's presence and the feelings it raised in her that she had not even noticed that a man had entered with her.

"Now, Henry." Lady Alicia turned her pouty smile on the newcomer. "Don't be a ninny." She extended a slim white bejeweled hand and the man advanced into the box. "You know Henry, Lord Gale," she said to Denby.

The Earl nodded. "We are acquainted." Again Aggie heard that strange tone in his voice, but she could not quite decide what it indicated.

The newcomer nodded briefly to Denby, let his eyes flick over Aggie with a kind of cool disinterest, and turned a dazzling smile on Cecilie. "So, this vision of loveliness is the celebrated Miss Winthrop. I declare, my dear one, who can see anyone else when you are present?"

Cecilie's eyes sparkled at the compliment, but Aggie saw the Earl's lips tighten in a grim line. As Lord Gale continued his effusive compliments, Aggie watched him covertly. It would not have taken the Earl's look of displeasure to convince her that this Bond Street fribble was not good husband material. His breeches of pale blue above white silk stockings were certainly not standard theater garb. But beyond that, this waistcoat of lemon yellow contrasted none too favorably with his pink coat. Aggie looked closely, but there was no denying it. Lord Gale's coat *was* pink. And Lord Gale's hair, hanging in pomaded ringlets that could not be other than artificially produced, was red – a bright vibrant red.

Aggie suppressed a grimace of distaste. This man was an exquisite who obviously thought he cast everyone else into the shade, one of those Bond Street beaux who misinterpreted Beau Brummell's advice on looking well-dressed. Aggie could remember her father saying more than once that the Beau's ideal was cleanliness and elegance, not the foppery which made this man a spectacle.

But her attention was diverted from the elegant Lord Gale by the sweetly coaxing tones of Lady Alicia. "Dear Denby, do come for a stroll with me in the lobby. It's so dull just sitting here."

Aggie found she was holding her breath, but she let it out slowly as the Earl shook his head. "No, Alicia, I don't wish to walk now."

"Oh, Denby." Lady Alicia pouted in that delicious way of hers and bent low, revealing a great deal of bosom. And not un-intentionally, thought Aggie, gritting her teeth. "Don't be so dull."

The Earl's tone was unfailingly polite. "Alicia, I do not wish to leave the box right now. Please understand that."

Lady Alicia flounced a little and drew back. "Very well, my love." Then she turned and smiled at Denby again. "I'll see you later."

The Earl made no answer to this and Lady Alicia moved out of the box, her hips in the tight lamé gown swaying provocatively.

Aggie's attention was now free to return to Cecilie, who was beaming up at Lord Gale and listening avidly to the extravagant compliments he was paying her. Aggie cast a sidelong glance at the Earl. His face was set in blank lines, but she detected a telltale quiver in the muscle by his jaw. Denby was no more pleased than she to have this male milliner lisping over Cecilie. Glancing down, she saw his hands, which were lying on top of his well-muscled legs, clench and unclench spasmodically. Plainly, Denby was disturbed by Lord Gale's advances to

Cecilie, but also, plainly, he was trying to contain his anger. Was he remembering, Aggie wondered, the information she had given him? Was he remembering that she had told him that the surest way to get Cecilie interested in a man was to forbid her to see him? Taking another glance at his face, Aggie wondered how long he could hold himself in check. She supposed that his lordship had not often had occasion to restrain himself. Men in positions of power such as his were frequently unused to having anyone obstruct their desires.

Finally, to her great relief, the curtain rose again. Lord Gale bowed low over Cecilie's outstretched fingers, his red curls bobbing in what seemed to Aggie a ludicrous fashion. "So, my adorable one. I must leave you now and return to my companions. Ah, if only I had known that tonight I would find my happiness, I would have come to the theater alone. Adieu, my sweet."

Aggie saw Denby's lip curl as he was forced to hear this affected farewell. She herself found it quite distasteful. But Cecilie seemed pleased by it. "Adieu, Lord Gale," she said and, as he left the box, she sent after him a radiant smile.

Dear God, Aggie thought. *Surely Cecilie could not have formed an affection for such a worthless popinjay?* She bit her bottom lip to keep from saying anything.

Cecilie turned back to them. "Well," she said enthusiastically, "the evening was not a total loss. What an entertaining man." As she spoke she turned to the Earl, seeming to invite his comment.

Aggie thought his eyes seemed a trifle glazed, almost as though the effort to curb his real opinion on the matter was too much for him, but when he spoke, his tone was even, though a trifle dry. "Yes, indeed, a very entertaining fellow."

When Cecilie would have followed this with more effusions on Lord Gale, Aggie interfered, whispering that since she very much wished to hear the rest of Mr. Kemble's performance, would Cecilie please, wait till later to discuss this new ac-quaintance.

Cecilie acquiesed quite nicely, returning her gaze to the stage, and Aggie sensed the tension slowly draining from the big man beside her. As it did, she herself relaxed and let herself enjoy the play. After all, Cecilie had just met this court card. Probably he would see someone else and quite forget about her. And with this consoling thought she devoted her attention to the play.

Fortunately, the afterpiece was such a

funny piece of foolishness that the journey home was devoted to discussing it. So when the Earl stopped at the bottom of the great stairs, he was still in a relaxed humor and he wished Cecilie a pleasant good night. Cecilie smiled blithely and with her best manners thanked him for an interesting evening at the theater before she tripped gaily up the stairs to see to her darling Dillydums.

Aggie offered her thanks quickly and turned to follow, but was detained by the Earl's, "A moment, Miss Trimble."

"Yes, milord." She did not want to look up into his eyes and yet she did.

"Do you suppose she could really form an attachment for that young fool?" he asked quietly.

Aggie shook her head. "I should like to say that it is impossible, milord, but I cannot. The only thing we can do now is wait. If we say nothing –" She shrugged. "Cecilie may well tire of him. Also, he may forget her."

Denby's jaw stiffened. "I doubt that," he said grimly. "I've heard of young Gale. He's in a bad way financially. He needs an heiress of Cecilie's caliber. Also, if he thinks he can bamboozle her later as he did tonight with all those nauseating compliments..." He shook his head. "If he offers for her, I'll have

235

to refuse him. I can't in good conscience let her marry such a wastrel."

Aggie's heart overflowed with compassion for him. Whatever had come between them, he was obviously doing his very best for Cecilie and that was not at all easy. Without thinking, Aggie laid a hand on his sleeve. "Don't get yourself upset yet, milord. It will all work out. And I will do what I can – indirectly, of course – to channel Cecilie's affections in some other direction." She sighed heavily. "If only some acceptable man would present himself." She smiled slightly. "Acceptable to you *and* to Cecilie."

The Earl smiled, too. "We shall just have to wait until he does." His fingers covered the hand that rested on his sleeve and Aggie, aware suddenly of the danger of touching him so familiarly, tried to draw it back. But he captured and kept it. "I want to thank you, Aggie, for your help." His eyes grew warm as he gazed down at her. "I have been ungrateful at times – and rather overbearing, I fear." He smiled ruefully. "But Cecilie *is* rather an unusual girl and I am new at the guardian business."

Aggie nodded, but her thoughts were not on his words. He was standing so close, she was so terribly conscious of his physical presence. Even worse, she was aware of a deep yearning within herself, a yearning to throw herself into the arms that were so close to her. She swayed slightly toward him and for a fraction of a second it seemed that he might reach out for her, but suddenly he dropped her hand and took a step backward. "Good night, Aggie. Sleep well." And then, with another warm smile, he turned away, leaving her to climb the stairs and to tell herself, not very convincingly, that she was quite pleased he hadn't kissed her. After all, she did not want to go through *that* again.

Chapter Fourteen

The next morning Aggie woke to the sound of Dillydums's cheerful chattering. The monkey was swinging gleefully from the bed curtains. His little black eyes gleamed at her impishly as he reached out a tiny paw toward another hold.

"Cecilie," Aggie called. It was time to get up anyway. She was rather interested in hearing what Cecilie would have to say about the previous evening. She did not intend to mention Lord Gale herself, of course; the less said about that Bond Street fribble the better. But if he had appealed to Cecilie, *she* might mention the fact and it would certainly be good to discover what she could.

Aggie pushed back the covers and reached for her robe. It was impossible to sleep with the little monkey chattering and swinging overhead. She smiled briefly. It was really no wonder that Denby had been startled by Dillydums, especially since he had not even known there was such a creature in the house.

As she moved toward the wardrobe to choose a morning gown, Aggie's smile turned to a frown. She was having far too much good feeling for the man who had deserted her. The whole thing still seemed impossible. Surely she could not have imagined the feeling that had existed between them. It was true she had been young and naive, but still... She sighed, choosing a gown temporarily forgotten. It seemed incredible that he could have departed as he had, without so much as a word. Yet he had done it. She sighed deeply. The more she saw him in relation to Cecilie the more she realized that he was a good man. If he showed perhaps more temper than was comfortable for those living in his establishment, that was to be expected. At times Cecilie's behavior was enough to make anyone enraged. And always he seemed to have Cecilie's best interests at heart. It was not uncommon for a guardian to marry his ward where and when it would benefit *him* and not every man would give consideration to the wants and wishes of the young woman involved. *Yes,* Aggie thought, *his lordship was behaving very well where Cecilie was concerned.*

As for herself – She brushed the thought aside and reached hurriedly for the gown. She would not think of him in relation to herself; he meant nothing to her.

But the gown that Aggie withdrew, a sprigged rose muslin several years old, had a rip in the side seam, which she discovered as she was about to draw it over her head. With an exasperated noise, not at the rip but at the thought of his lordship and the new gowns which it evoked, she tossed it on the bed and went to look for another. The next, of blue dotted muslin, was also faded, but at least its seams were intact. She pulled it on.

"Good morning, Aggie." She turned as the gown fell around her to see Cecilie standing barefoot, rubbing her eyes.

"Good morning. Did you sleep well?"

Cecilie nodded. "Yes, of course." She opened her arms to Dillydums, who jumped into them and began to play with a stray curl that had escaped her nightcap. "What are you doing in here bothering Aggie?" Cecilie asked the monkey in cooing tones.

"He wasn't bothering me," said Aggie. "It's time to get up."

Cecilie nodded. "Yes, it looks like a lovely day. I was wondering if we might go to Somerset House and see the paintings from the Royal Society's Exhibit. I should like to see some of Lawrence's latest portraits."

Aggie considered. "I think you had best ask his lordship for permission."

"There are many great and beautiful paintings on display there," said Cecilie soberly. "I am sure it would be good for me to see them."

Aggie smiled dryly. "I should not tell the Earl that they are educational," she said. "Your last attempt at education was very difficult for us all."

"I know," said Cecilie in a repentant voice. "And I'm truly sorry for it. But it was great fun," she added, her eyes sparkling at the memory. "It's such a shame that young Mr. Sadler didn't want an aeronautical wife. It would be a perfect life."

Aggie looked grim. "I'm afraid our ideas of perfection differ considerably. But if you want to go out today, you'd better get to his lordship right away. Before he leaves."

Cecilie nodded and went off to be dressed.

When she met Aggie at the breakfast table a little later, Cecilie was smiling happily. "His lordship has already eaten," she said gaily. "He thinks it's a grand idea to go to see the paintings. He even says I may take Dillydums along."

This piece of news was not particularly gratifying to Aggie. It was not that she disliked the monkey. Dillydums was a good little animal. It was only that it was hard enough to keep Cecilie in hand without having to trouble oneself with her pet. Well, she told herself with resignation, she would just have to do the best she could.

So it was that some time later she and Cecilie came down in walking dresses and bonnets, ready to appreciate the great works that the Royal Academy Exhibit offered to the public. Cecilie wore one of her new walking dresses of pale blue sarcenet embellished with white ribbons. Her bonnet was rather small, of white straw trimmed with blue flowers, and looked much better than the gigantic shovel-shaped one she had first settled on. Aggie was glad that she had been prevailed upon to change her mind.

Aggie's own gown of dove gray jaconet, though old, had not had much wear in Dover and was still presentable. She wore the bonnet designed to go with the dress, a small unobtrusive affair that was probably quite outdated. She did not really care.

Dillydums, in his blue trousers and red jacket, seemed to have sensed that he, too, was going out and he clung to Cecilie and chattered excitedly.

Aggie glanced around as they came down the stairs, but his lordship was not in evidence. Quite probably he was out, attending to his business. At least, she thought with an inward smile, he was probably not with Lady Alicia, not this early in the day. It was unlikely that the lady had even one eye open by now.

As the carriage moved through the crowded streets, Cecilie and the monkey peered excitedly out the window. "Be sure you have a good hold on the leash," urged Aggie. "If Dillydums gets loose out here, we shall never find him."

"Yes, Aggie, I'm being careful," Cecilie replied without turning her head. "But the city is so exciting. How I wish I might be free to roam about. There is so much to see."

"Cecilie!" Aggie tried to keep her voice even, but was not successful. "It is very dangerous for a young woman to be about in the street alone."

"I don't see why," said Cecilie stubbornly.

242

"Look, over there there's a girl just my age. *She's* alone."

Aggie looked. The girl in question was wearing a stained and torn muslin gown. Her hair was tangled and her feet bare. She moved about offering her flowers to passers-by. To Cecilie she probably looked happy and carefree, but Aggie saw the signs of hunger in the brown eyes cast so prettily upon the customers and under the city grime she glimpsed several large bruises. This poor child did not lead a pleasant life. "That girl is very poor," she said to Cecilie. "It may look like fun to sell flowers for a little while, but to be forced to do it every day for long hours and to go hungry if you fail – that would not be so good."

Cecilie turned sobered eyes upon her companion. "Oh, Aggie, I know you're right, but it just looks so exciting out there and I seem always to be kept in." She reached into her reticule. "We must buy some of her flowers." She leaned forward to direct the coachman and minutes later several large bunches of marigolds lay on the floor of the carriage. They would undoubtedly wilt long before their return to Grosvenor Square, but Aggie made no comment.

As the carriage drove on, Cecilie said no more about becoming part of the crowd, but

243

her eyes watched everything avidly. Finally the carriage reached Somerset House and a groom helped them descend. Cecilie's eyes sparkled as she surveyed the people about her. "I do so like to be out in public," she said happily. "It makes me feel so much more alive."

Their admission paid, they entered one of the great halls where paintings hung one above the other reached four and five high to the elevated ceiling. Some seemed so high up that they were difficult to see properly. Cecilie gazed round in awe. "My word, Aggie. I never realized there were so many."

"Take your time looking at them," Aggie advised. "One cannot rush an appreciation of art. We must give it time to sink into our senses."

Cecilie nodded. She seemed to be studying a painting that depicted the hazards of the steeplechase. Aggie let her eyes drift till they came to rest on a peaceful sylvan scene. Some people might like the great battle scenes or historical portrayals; others seemed to favor the portraits of well-known personages such as those the newly knighted Sir Thomas Lawrence was wont to do. But she herself favored the charm of a quiet landscape or sometimes the more rugged look of a seascape.

"Look there," said Cecilie. "Aren't those figures from the Bible?"

Aggie nodded. "Yes, if I'm not mistaken, that is one of the works of Benjamin West." Privately she thought the painting a trifle insipid, but she did not say so.

They moved on around the room. "Someone must like horses," cried Cecilie.

Aggie smiled. "George Stubbs excels at painting horses. I believe he has done a book on the anatomy of the horse."

Cecilie looked at her. "You mean all about bones and such?"

"Yes, I understand a really good painter must know what is under the surface."

Cecilie looked thoughtful. "I suppose that would help. Here are some portraits by Sir Thomas Lawrence," she continued. "I wish he would paint me as he did that lovely lady."

Leaning closer, Aggie read the name on the portrait and examined it again. She had known the woman whose likeness the painting was supposed to represent, and she felt somewhat surprised at the freedom Lawrence had taken with reality. The subject of the portrait seemed much younger than she had even five years ago. And there was a certain refinement to her features that was lacking in the original. Her hands seemed far too delicate and beautiful and her eyes excessively brilliant. In fact, but for the evidence of the name card, which clearly could not be denied, Aggie would not have recognized the lady at all. *Perhaps,* she thought to herself a bit ironically, *perhaps this was what accounted for Lawrence's great popularity.*

Cecilie paused to stare up at a fine country scene. One of David Wilkie's, Aggie had no doubt, though she could not see up far enough to distinguish the name. It was not difficult, however, to recognize his fine feeling for color and his enthusiasm for depicting a story of humble contemporary life.

Cecilie pointed to a painting showing rough shaggy horses at feeding time. "I like that," she said.

Aggie smiled. "So do I. I believe it is one of George Morland's. He also does country scenes. That one further up, of the gypsy encampment, looks like this work." She indicated it to Cecilie.

Cecilie sighed. "I suppose it takes a great deal of study to be a painter."

"It does indeed," agreed Aggie. "And then a man is often not given the regard due his talents."

"Are there no women painters?" asked Cecilie with the beginning of a pout.

"There was one in the last century," said Aggie. "Angelica Kauffmann. She often painted the intricate ceilings and friezes of houses designed by the great architect Robert Adam. If I am not mistaken, she also did some portraits and allegorical scenes. Of course, her father was an artist, too."

Cecilie shook her head. "I suppose I should not like to go clambering about on ladders and such. And I suppose the Earl would frown upon a painter for a husband."

Aggie hid her smile. "I'm afraid so, my dear. Unless he were someone of great renown. And in that case he would most likely already have a wife."

Cecilie grinned. "And, too, it might be calamitous if Dillydums were to get loose among all those paints!"

Aggie could no longer hide her smile. "Indeed it would," she replied. "I expect you are much wiser to look elsewhere for a husband."

Cecilie nodded. "Yes, I suppose so. But I should hope to get riveted soon. I am tired of hanging out for a husband."

"Really, Cecilie. Riveted is hardly an appropriate word for entering the state of matrimony."

Cecilie shrugged. "I don't see why not. That's what the Earl called it the other day when he was speaking to his friend."

Aggie's heart skipped a beat. Of course he would be cynical about marriage. He had managed to escape being leg-shackled for this long. Surely that was indicative of something.

"Drat," said Cecilie suddenly, recapturing Aggie's attention. "I should have been smart enough not to wear these new shoes. Could we go sit down on one of those benches in the middle of the hall?"

"Of course. We shall have to send the shoes to be stretched."

"Yes," said Cecilie. "I suppose so."

They found two empty places together and sat down. Cecilie looked hurriedly around and then began to pat Dillydums, who seemed rather anxious for the chance of further exploration. "There are certainly a large number of people here," Cecilie said.

"Yes," agreed Aggie. "I guess Londoners like to be out and about – to be seen."

"I suppose they do," replied Cecilie. "That seems rather normal to me. It's stuffy and terribly dull to be shut up in the house all the time." She leaned back to consider a painting very near the ceiling and Aggie relaxed. It was lovely just to sit there and

248

look around. She was lost in contemplation of a picture of a sunny tidewater. The water sparkled as if real and she wondered idly if it were the work of Calcott. He was not a great painter, but occasionally he did quite lovely things with water. How pleasant it had been in the days of her youth to wander here for whole afternoons, her maid trailing behind, her gaze resting on some picture while her mind was off in flights of fancy or serving up for her delectation memories of times with the handsome young Viscount. Just so had he looked at her, just these words had fallen from his lips. Her eyelids slowly closed as memories crept in upon her.

She almost jumped to her feet, so startled was she when Cecilie said, "Oh, Aggie, look who's here." Recovering herself, Aggie opened her eyes to find Lord Gale beaming down on her. Today his attire was a little more decorous. There was nothing explicitly wrong with any particular piece of it. But taken together there was the feeling of something not quite right: a cravat too intricately tied or too high, a coat not quite as it should be. She could not be sure, but the effect of the whole made her uneasy.

Lord Gale, however, seemed in high spirits. He beamed down on her with cheerful friendliness and kissed her hand.

Then he returned his admiring gaze to Cecilie. "Miss Winthrop, what a pleasant surprise to find you here. Do let me offer you my arm and we shall make a grand tour."

Cecilie got to her feet with great alacrity. "Oh, that would be capital. Why don't you wait here, Aggie, and rest? Lord Gale will take care of me."

Aggie got to her feet too, shaking her head. "It's very kind of Lord Gale to offer himself as escort. And we shall be pleased to have his services, but you know you cannot be going about alone."

Lord Gale's friendliness abated not a jot. "Of course," he told Cecilie. "Miss Trimble knows best."

Cecilie was obviously not of the same opinion, but she made no further demurrer, merely prettily taking the arm Lord Gale offered and smiling up at him engagingly. That smile gave Aggie some concern, for it was decidedly that of a female on the catch for a husband. Still, she told herself, she would do well not to worry yet. Lord Gale might be a graceful dancer, and even a prime rider, though he had nothing of the athlete about him to indicate it. He might be (or say that he was) excessively fond of animals *and* children, but it was obvious from his shock of brilliant red curls that his chest could not possibly be covered with a tangled mat of black. Just wait, she counseled herself, and Cecilie would see his weaknesses. She must.

As she followed them from place to place, only half listening to the bits of wisdom with which Lord Gale hoped to impress Cecilie, she caught herself wondering how the girl could possibly think this popinjay a man – when every day she had before her the example of the Earl – a gentleman of the first caliber. Of course, there was no accounting for taste and Cecilie was young and impressionable, easy prey for a man who knew how to offer extravagant compliments.

A sudden cry from Cecilie shattered her musings and with horror Aggie looked up to see Dillydums making his way across the crowded room by jumping from shoulder to elegant shoulder, with an occasional excursion across some frantic lady's bonnet. "Oh, Aggie, do catch him!" Cecilie cried. "He'll be so frightened."

In indecision Aggie looked from Cecilie to the monkey. "Oh quick, he'll be lost forever!" Cecilie cried, tears standing out in her eyes.

"Stay right here," Aggie commanded, "until I get back." Then she set out in pursuit of the monkey. It was not difficult to tell his direction since pandemonium seemed to follow in his wake. Several rather stout ladies had been so startled by his rapid advance across their ample shoulders that they had fallen victim to the spasms and were laid out prone upon the floor, being fanned and comforted by their hardier sisters.

Aggie tried to ignore the sharp looks that more than one patron of the exhibition gave her as she hurried on through the path of devastation. Finally, after skirting several fallen ladies, she reached the door and was most relieved to find that Dillydums had taken refuge in the arms of the man who guarded it. The monkey raised his little head and, spying Aggie, scrabbled into her arms.

"The little feller was just scared," said the guard, glancing with contempt at the ladies whose palpitating hearts had so unnerved them. "And no wonder," he continued, a twinkle in his eyes. "Them great creatures is enough to sceer anyone. And him such a little thing." And he gave Aggie a wink.

"Thank you so much for holding him," she said, giving the guard a warm smile. "I'm dreadfully sorry for the trouble he caused."

The guard grinned. "To tell you the truth, miss, I get terrible tired standing here. You understand. The same old thing everday, a man gets tired. But today now, that was something else. Just wait'll I get home and tell my little one about it." He chuckled. "Her eyes'll get bigger 'an saucers."

Aggie returned his smile. "Well, thank you for your help. I have to get back to my charge."

The guard nodded and, Aggie, clasping the monkey tightly, turned back to where she had left Cecilie. But to her dismay when she reached the spot, she found neither the girl nor Lord Gale. Quickly, ignoring the baleful glances that were coming her way from everyone now that she held the monkey, she made a survey of the large hall, but Cecilie was not in it.

Making her second circuit of the room, she again passed the friendly guard and on an impulse stopped to ask him, "Have you seen a young lady in a blue gown and a gentleman with red hair? I seem to have lost them."

"The gentleman's hair was real bright! And the lady, hers was golden?"

"Yes. Did you see them?" Aggie asked eagerly.

"Well, miss, it seems to me I saw such a pair going through that door over there."

"Thank you."

"Miss," said the guard, "there's a little parlor through there. Like as not the gentleman was taking the lady in there to

253

rest. It appeared like she was faintish. She leaned on him heavy like."

"Thank you." As quickly as possible Aggie made her way toward the door. There was something very wrong here. Cecilie had never been faintish in her life. The vapors and the spasms were equally unknown to her. Oh, why had she consented to bringing the monkey? Aggie asked herself.

She opened the door and hurried through. She was standing in a long hall and for a moment she hesitated, not knowing which way to go. Then she heard a soft girlish giggle from a room several doors down. The giggle sounded like Cecilie's. *It must be her,* thought Aggie, clutching the monkey and hurrying in that direction. She burst through the door to find Cecilie reclining on a divan and Lord Gale bending solicitously over her. He straightened as Aggie entered. "Ahh, Miss Trimble. I was just about to come looking for you. Miss Winthrop seems to have recovered from her feeling of faintness."

Seeing the look on Aggie's face, Cecilie quickly sat up. "Oh, you've got Dillydums! What a bad boy you are. Give him to me, Aggie."

Aggie shook her head. "No, Cecilie, I will keep the monkey. I have had quite enough of chasing him for one day. Since you are feeling better, I believe Lord Gale had best escort us to the carriage."

"Oh, but Aggie, I am quite recovered now. Really I am."

"That may well be," replied Aggie dryly. "However, the patrons of the Royal Society are not. Nor is Dillydums. Have you no concern for him?"

She did not miss the quick exchange of looks that took place between Cecilie and Lord Gale. Then the young man smiled and added his entreaties to Aggie's. "Of course. Miss Trimble is quite correct. You must both go home and recuperate from this dreadful accident." And Cecilie, though she was plainly unconvinced by his argument, nodded in acquiescence and got to her feet.

In silence Aggie followed the pair to the street and watched while Lord Gale helped Cecilie into the carriage and gallantly kissed her hand. "Until we meet again, fair lady."

And that, thought Aggie as she climbed into the carriage, was going to be quite a long time if *she* had anything to say about it. She was not at all convinced that Dillydums's escapade was an accident and even less sure that Cecilie's meeting with Lord Gale had not been arranged. There was too much coincidence here for comfort and the knowledge that she would have to inform Denby of the day's events did nothing to alleviate her feelings of unease.

But, as they reached home after a quiet ride and she inquired of Bates concerning when she might see the Earl, she discovered that he was to dine out and did not expect to be home until very late. So, leaving a message with Bates that she wished a moment to speak to his lordship, she went about her other business.

Chapter Fifteen

The next day did not get off to a judicious beginning. After tossing and turning far into the night, Aggie finally fell asleep near dawn, with the result that she did not waken until far later than her usual hour. Her first act after dressing was to seek out Bates, from whom she learned that his lordship had already gone out and would speak to her later in the day. The usually even-tempered Aggie also snapped at the butler when given this piece of dismaying news and she took herself off to the garden to settle her nerves. She could not go about on edge like this until the

Earl returned. And why, she asked herself angrily, hadn't he had courtesy enough to have her wakened? Surely he knew she would not bother him about mere trifles.

She reached the garden and sank down on the stone bench among the roses. Where had he been last night anyway? Probably in Lady Alicia's boudoir. Aggie clenched her fists angrily. That woman made her so irritated. But at least he could have seen Aggie this morning. Her head went up sharply at a sudden thought. Perhaps he had not come home at all! Perhaps he had spent the entire night with Lady Alicia – and Bates was protecting him! *That must be it,* she thought, her anger fleeing and leaving behind only despair. She had no right to anger. She had refused his offer of carte blanche, refused it before he had really had a chance to make it. She sighed deeply. Much as she loved him, she could not so demean herself – in her own eyes, and eventually in his. Lady Alicia, however, seemed to have avoided any such qualms. She obviously gave her favors when and where she pleased. And right now she pleased to give them to the Earl of Denby.

Aggie jumped suddenly to her feet. This kind of thinking was futile. She would go to the library and find something to expand her mind – and none of the poetry of that notorious Lord Byron either. That would only make matters worse. She would read in Boswell's *Life of Johnson* or perhaps Gibbon's *Decline and Fall of the Roman Empire.* What she needed was something heavy enough to occupy her thoughts.

But shortly after midday Aggie had to admit that her plan had not worked. Dr. Johnson's witticisms had failed to engage her attention and she had gotten no further than Gibbon's first discussion of Roman civilization, which she had read some three or four times without taking the real sense of it. The truth of the matter was that until Denby returned and she had her chance to talk to him, she was going to remain uncomfortable in spite of all her efforts.

It was about this time that Cecilie entered the library. They had not spoken about the incident at Somerset House: Aggie from fear she would lose her tightly-held temper and say something she regretted and Cecilie, quite probably, because she feared what such discussion might uncover.

"I wonder if anyone will call today," mused Cecilie as she nibbled on a hot scone and sipped the tea that Bates had brought them.

"We can only wait and see," said Aggie absently, her mind still on her coming interview with the Earl. She poured herself some tea and sat sipping it. If only they could get Cecilie safely married. Then she could free herself of the Earl, and open her school for young ladies. The prospect did not fill her with a great deal of enthusiasm, but she ignored that.

The two sat in silence. Aggie tried to keep the Earl out of her mind by concentrating on Gibbon, an attempt doomed to failure. And Cecilie toyed with her scone and then her teacup, and finally having finished eating, got up to wander among the shelves as though seeking something to read.

Because of her own abstracted state of mind it took Aggie some time to realize that Cecilie was not herself. There was an unusual brightness to her eyes and she seemed unable to settle anywhere.

Just at this time there came the sound of the door knocker. Immediately Cecilie threw herself in a chair and clasped her hands lightly in her lap. Her face bore a look of bright expectancy and Aggie knew then that she had been correct. Cecilie was expecting someone.

Aggie's heart fell as she recalled the surprised look between the girl and Lord Gale when finally she had found them. She bent her head to her book, determined not to say anything. If Lord Gale *had* called, it was entirely probable that the Earl had given orders that he was not to be admitted.

Some moments later Bates appeared at the door. "A Lord Gale, Miss Trimble." The old butler's face reflected the merest hint of distaste and Aggie knew that he, too, found the young man unsuitable.

"Please show him in," said Aggie calmly. If the Earl allowed the man to call, it was not up to her to refuse him.

Lord Gale appeared at the door and rushed across the room to grab Cecilie's hand and convey it to his lips. "Ah, the hours have seemed like days since last I saw you," he declared dramatically.

Aggie choked back a laugh. The boy was really amusing. That's all he was, really, a boy in his calf-time, hardly out of leading strings. How could Cecilie be so taken with him?

She thought back to her own youth and the remembered joy she had felt when Denby had signaled her out for his attentions. But even then Denby had been a man, already on the town for some years, what was now called a prime article. This young man was just a youngster, hardly older than Cecilie herself.

Gibbon went unheeded as Aggie covertly

watched the two young people. Of course, Lord Gale was not a suitable husband for Cecilie, but at least he was not malicious and he might well be stricken by Cecilie's fresh young charm.

Young Gale made a long visit, all of which was entirely proper if somewhat effusive, and as he rose to go he kissed Cecilie's hand and informed her that his life would be barren until he was once again privileged to gaze upon her loveliness. Whereupon he took his departure, beaming all the way out the door.

"Isn't he just the first style in elegance?" breathed Cecilie with a sigh.

Aggie was pondering this, wondering how she could answer truthfully without pushing Cecilie into an impassioned defense of her suitor, when Bates appeared in the doorway to announce, "His lordship has returned and wishes to see you in the drawing room, Miss Trimble."

"Yes, of course." Aggie rose to her feet, wondering as she did so if Denby had seen their caller. "I'll be right there." And she hurried past the butler, trying once more to calm her flurried nerves.

She paused outside the drawing room for a moment, taking a deep breath. Already she was feeling shaky, knowing that she would soon be near him. She forced herself to enter the room. He was looking out the window at the street and she felt a rush of relief at the fact that he was wearing day clothes. He had not stayed out all night. Then he turned to face her and her knees began to tremble.

"Bates said you wished to speak to me." He was not glaring, but there was something about his calmness that seemed forced.

"Yes, milord."

"Did it have to do with that Bond Street fribble that just left?"

"Yes, milord."

Denby sighed heavily. "You may as well sit down and tell me about it."

Aggie sank somewhat gratefully into a chair. "You know that yesterday Cecilie and I visited the Royal Academy Exhibit at Somerset House."

Denby nodded. "I gave her permission. I didn't see how she could get into mischief there."

It was Aggie's turn to sigh. "She did. The monkey got loose and went rushing through the crowd. He caused considerable furor, especially among the older ladies."

The Earl grimaced. "Continue, there must be more to it than that."

Aggie nodded. "There is. I went after the monkey. When I returned with him, Cecilie had gone. I found her in a private room with

Lord Gale. He had joined us shortly before the monkey got loose." She took a deep breath. "I suspect that Cecilie let Dillydums loose on purpose. So as to be alone with the man. And I'm quite certain she knew he would call today."

"So much for your theory," the Earl replied dryly. He seemed determined not to lose his temper again, but Aggie almost wished he would. She did not like the lines of weariness around his mouth or the cold way his eyes regarded her.

"There is nothing wrong with my theory," she said. "If we could find a suitable man, I am confident we could guide her into his arms. But perhaps we are worried too soon over Lord Gale."

One of Denby's dark brows shot up. "I think not. The young fool simpered at me on his way out and said something about seeing me soon on a matter of some importance."

"Oh, dear!" Aggie could not keep back the exclamation of dismay. To turn Lord Gale away at this time might well cause serious problems with Cecilie. And yet he was obviously unsuitable. She tried to think. "Perhaps you could be out to him if he comes to call. At least for a little while." She was conscious of Denby's frown, but she knew she must continue. "You see, the problem is that Cecilie is really taken with him."

Denby's other brow shot up momentarily. "I had begun to think the girl had some sense. Now I am doubtful."

Aggie sighed. "You must remember, milord, Cecilie is very young. This boy is, too."

The Earl made a gesture of protest. "It is precisely for that reason that he won't do. Everything they had would be gone in a fortnight. Besides, I have reason to believe that his partiality for Cecilie is contrived."

"What do you mean?"

"I mean that young Gale needs an heiress just as much as Parrington did. And the object of his affections is not Cecilie, but a sweet little ladybird who sings at Vauxhall Gardens."

"You're lying!" Cecilie's voice came from the doorway, startling them both.

The Earl turned. "May I suggest that you come in and shut the door? People of quality do not shout at one another."

"I don't care what people of quality do," said Cecilie stubbornly, but she stepped into the room and shut the door.

"Since you've heard this much," said the Earl, "you may as well come sit down and hear the rest."

Cecilie sat down beside Aggie, but her chin jutted out stubbornly. "I know you're lying about this. Henry *adores* me."

The Earl made a moue of disgust. "Henry," he said with sarcastic emphasis, "adores your money. He has lost a great deal at White's and his own funds are limited."

"There is nothing wrong with frequenting White's," Cecilie averred stubbornly. "Many men do."

Denby looked grim. "Many men lose a great deal at the tables and seek to recoup their losses with their wives' funds. This is not a situation I should wish on my worst enemy, let alone on someone whose welfare is in my hands."

"He will stop gaming if I ask him," Cecilie pouted prettily, but the effect was lost on the Earl.

"A man does not give up gaming that easily," his lordship returned. "Least of all for a woman he has married merely for her purse."

Cecilie clenched her fists and shook her head. "Henry loves me," she repeated.

Frowning, the Earl ran a hand through his dark hair, leaving it tumbled. "Cecilie, you must be sensible. What I said before is true. It's common knowledge among the swells that Gale's ladybird has been set up in a nice place in the suburbs – on the expectation that he will soon marry an heiress and be able to pay for her little establishment."

Cecilie's face turned crimson. "You should not discuss such matters with me," she cried. "A gentleman would not do so."

The Earl sighed wearily. "A lady would not eavesdrop on what was obviously a private conversation."

Cecilie's chin went up. "I knew you were talking about me. And I thought maybe Henry had offered for me." She glared at him. "It's not fair. You treat me like a child."

"You *are* a child," said the Earl, ignoring her protest. "You know very little of the ways of the world. If you did, you would see that I am trying to do my best for you." He sighed again. "And you are making it very difficult for me." There was a moment's silence in which he seemed to be waiting for a reply, but Cecilie vouchsafed none. Denby looked at Aggie in resignation.

"Did he?" asked Cecilie suddenly.

The Earl looked at her in surprise. "Did he what?"

"Did Henry offer for me?"

Denby's brows began to draw together in that line Aggie knew so well. "No, he did not," he said sternly. "And if he had, I should have refused him."

There, thought Aggie, who was watching Cecilie's face, *was his second mistake.* The first had been in trying to destroy Cecilie's belief in her suitor's affection. In doing so he had attacked her image of herself, an image which she would fight bitterly to defend. And now he had erred again. A simple no would have been sufficient, but he had to go on and make matters worse.

Cecilie got unsteadily to her feet. "I don't care what you say," she sobbed. "Henry loves me. I know he does. I shall never marry if you keep continually thwarting me like this!" And with a heartbroken sob she ran weeping from the room, slamming the door behind her.

Aggie stared down at her hands. Part of her heart was crying for Cecilie. If she had genuinely formed an affection for young Gale (which was, after all, possible), this was very painful for her.

Denby shifted his gaze to her. "I suppose you'll tell me I did it all wrong," he said, fixing her with an angry eye.

Aggie found herself bristling. If he had not been out so late with that scheming Lady Alicia, she could have warned him about Gale and they might have prevented all this. But no, he had to go to that woman who cared for no one but herself and now he was going to yell at Aggie. She glared back at him. "Well," she said, getting to her feet and moving toward the fireplace, "you could have done better."

He, too, got to his feet and strode toward her. "How so?" he demanded truculently.

Aggie forced herself to meet his eyes. "First, you insulted her by telling her that her Henry doesn't love her."

"The fool doesn't," he interjected scornfully.

Aggie's temper was getting out of hand. The thought of him being tête-à-tête with Lady Alicia when she needed to talk to him about Cecilie grew more and more infuriating. "That is not the point," she snapped. "She had a picture of herself as a woman who is loved and you tried to destroy it. Now she must insist more than ever that it is true. She has her pride."

"This is utter nonsense," he said crossly.

"May I suggest, milord," replied Aggie icily, "that being a man you are hardly in a position to know *how* a woman thinks. A woman in love will forgive a man a great deal, even make excuses for his bad behavior." She paled as the thought of his desertion filled her mind. For a moment there was silence, then she managed to go on. "The more you attack, the more she will defend

268

– and overlook his faults – no matter how obvious."

Denby stepped still closer. "Is that all I did wrong?" If she had not had the fireplace at her back, she would have moved away.

"No. You should never have told her you intend to refuse his offer."

"But I do!"

"Milord," said Aggie coldly. "May I suggest that you use a little common sense?" He glared at her, but she continued. "In the mood Cecilie was in, telling her that only added fuel to the fire."

"I suppose you would have me accept the calfling's offer." His eyes smoldered at her.

"Of course not! But you could have just kept quiet. Then I might have persuaded her that the man is unsuitable. Now that will be next to impossible."

"All this deviousness is ridiculous," said the Earl. "The matter is a simple one. I fail to see why she makes it so complicated."

"You fail to see a great many things," snapped Aggie. She was aware that her anger was getting out of hand, but she could not seem to stop herself.

"Indeed!" Denby's eyes grew smoky and he took still another step closer. He was only inches away now and in spite of her anger she felt herself yearning toward him. To combat that terrible need for him she put even more acid into her voice. "You ignore a very basic fact. Cecilie is a woman, a young and innocent woman. She knows nothing of estates or suitability. She only knows how she *feels*. And Lord Gale, no matter what his deficiencies in your eyes, makes her feel loved and wanted. That is a very precious feeling only few women can ignore." Memories of the past swept over her suddenly and, feeling the tears spring to her eyes, she dropped her gaze.

Silence filled the room for long moments as Aggie fought to keep the tears from spilling over and betraying her. Finally he spoke. "You seem to know a lot about the feelings of a woman in love. Yet you are still unmarried."

Aggie did not raise her eyes. She did not dare. "I am a woman." She managed to get the words out over the lump in her throat. "And I need not have experienced love to know about it. After all, I have eyes." She kept her gaze resolutely on his waistcoat.

"You have loved someone," he said flatly. "You cannot fool me about that. I am well past my grasstime and not so easily deceived as you may believe."

She felt his hands grasp her arms and a tremor of excitement swept over her as he drew her closer. "I should very much like to know who the man was," he said in a voice hoarse with suppressed emotion. "Tell me, Aggie. Who was the man who stole you away from me? Who was that thief?"

Astonishment kept her silent and immobile. How had he twisted the past to arrive at such a conclusion? She struggled against the grip of his hands, but he pulled her against his chest and held her there. Under her ear she heard the rapid beating of his heart and hers thudded violently in unison. Still she did not raise her head.

With one hand he kept her tightly against him and with the other he tilted back her chin, forcing her to look at him. His eyes were dark with desire and Aggie shuddered a little at the sight of them. Then, without another word, he slowly lowered his head and kissed her. Actually, she had time to avoid his lips, or at least to try, but she did not even make a token resistance, her lips opening eagerly under his and her body melting against him. Her brain, of course, clamored that this behavior was wrong, but her body was completely out of control. When finally his lips left her mouth to slide across her throat and stop beneath her ear, she was limp in his arms.

And then he put her slowly from him and

smiled down at her tenderly. "Never mind, Aggie," he said, gently pushing back a curl on her forehead. "I see that he hurt you terribly, but never mind. I'll make it up to you, you'll see."

A strange coldness began to creep through Aggie's body. He was going to offer her carte blanche, she knew it. And the thought appalled her. Some women might consent to a "marriage by the left hand," as the *ton* so delicately put it, but she had too much respect for herself to descend to such a level. She must not let him make her such an offer. Carefully she extricated herself from his arms and, summoning all her strength, she said coldly, "I am afraid that you go too far, milord. I have told you before. I do not wish to alter our relationship. If you would only desist from taking these liberties with my person, we should deal together much more pleasantly."

For long moments he looked at her in surprise and then slowly the warmth faded from his eyes and his mouth, which moments before had possessed hers so passionately, drew into a grim line. "Very well, Miss Trimble. But one thing before you return to your charge."

"Yes?" She kept her tone cold and his reply was equally chill.

"I have decided to send for my mother, the dowager countess. Perhaps she may succeed with the girl where we cannot."

She was about to argue the point with him. Being ordered around by an overblown dowager would only infuriate Cecilie more. But she saw from his face that further discussion was useless and, besides that, she was afraid to stay alone with him any longer. Even now she yearned to move back into the arms that were so invitingly close. Resisting the impulse, she swung on her heel. "I'm sure you'll do just as you please – as usual," she added sharply and, not trusting herself to say more or to look at him again, she left the room.

Her first order of business was to find Cecilie and try to undo some of the damage the Earl had done. Later she would have leisure to consider the change to be wrought in their life by the advent of a dragonish dowager who, if she were anything like her overbearing son, was apt to be haughty, proud, excessively high in the instep – and a great deal of trouble.

Chapter Sixteen

Aggie did what she could to calm Cecilie, but the girl was obviously distraught. It was no light thing for her to have been deprived of her first genuine admirer and, when she was not crying, she sulked. The news that Denby's mother was arriving did nothing to elevate her spirits. And it was apparent that like Aggie she envisioned a heavyset dragon dowager given to loud yellow gowns and huge purple turbans.

Late in the second day after Lord Gale's disturbing visit, Cecilie and Aggie were walking the monkey in the garden when Bates came to announce, "The dowager countess has arrived, Miss Trimble, and is waiting for you both in the library."

Cecilie made a face, which fortunately Bates could not see as his back was toward her, and Aggie said, "Please tell her ladyship we will be there as soon as we send the monkey upstairs."

"Her ladyship is very interested in the monkey," said Bates soberly. Aggie could have sworn that his eyes twinkled, but she decided that her senses must be deceiving her. "And she asked that Miss Winthrop bring him along."

Aggie sighed. "Very well. Come along, Cecilie."

Cecilie looked about to make another face, but then, perhaps intrigued by the dowager's interest in the monkey, did not. "Come, Dillydums," she told the little animal. "You are going to meet a dowager countess."

As they left the courtyard Cecilie picked a red rose and stuck it in her hair. An expression of defiance, Aggie thought, but said nothing. The dowager countess would soon learn about Cecilie's character, if her son had not already told her what a hoyden he had on his hands.

Together she and Cecilie entered the library and together they stopped, amazed. Turning from the window to greet them was not the dragon they had imagined, but a little birdlike woman, dressed in a fashionable gown of pearl gray. She bore herself with dignity, but her gray eyes sparkled as she surveyed them. "You must be Miss Trimble," she said, giving Aggie a smile. "And this is the young woman my son calls the impossible Cecilie." The twinkle in her eye was more pronounced now and to Aggie's great relief Cecilie responded to it.

"His lordship can be impossible, too," she said with a gamine grin.

"Indeed he can," replied Lady Denby. "How well I remember what a trial that boy was to me. But one has to admit that he has a high sense of duty."

Cecilie hesitated only a moment. "I suppose one has to admit it," she said with a small grimace. "But one need not admire it."

"No, I suppose not," agreed Denby's mother. "Also, I'm afraid my son knows very little about dealing with young ladies. And he does behave in a rather lofty fashion." She smiled ruefully. "I'm much afraid that I'm responsible for that. You see, he was my only child and I'm afraid I doted on him. Spoiled him rotten, I think they call it."

"Oh, I shouldn't worry too much about it, milady," replied Cecilie with an innocent smile. "My papa spoiled me, too. But actually I have turned out rather well. No doubt his lordship will mellow with time."

A sort of sputtering sound, half laughter, half choking, issued from Lady Denby's small but firm mouth. "No doubt he will, my dear," she said finally. "But it will take time. And certainly you will not want to wait that long to marry."

"No, indeed not. You see," said Cecilie

confidently, "his lordship insists on sending away the men I favor. Of course," she paused as though just realizing it, "he was right about Lord Parrington's horses. But," she hurried on, "he cannot be right about Lord Gale. I *know* he adores me."

"I'm sure he does, my dear," said Lady Denby. "You are quite a lovely girl. But come, there is no need for us to stand. Let us be comfortable and Bates will bring us a little tea."

As Cecilie settled onto a divan and she and the countess found chairs, Aggie wondered that the Earl had not sent for his mother sooner. Never had she seen anyone who could handle Cecilie so well.

"You must tell me about Lord Gale and what it is you are looking for in a husband," said Lady Denby after Bates had brought the tea and macaroons.

"Of course," said Cecilie eagerly. "Lord Gale is young, not much older than me. He dresses very fashionably. You would notice him in any crowd."

Aggie caught the flicker in the dowager's eyes and knew that this piece of information did not work in Lord Gale's favor.

"And he's very attentive."

"I see." Lady Denby was suitably impressed. "And how does he fit your requirements for a husband?"

Cecilie looked thoughtful. "Well, I haven't yet seen him on the ballroom floor or on a horse, but I'm sure he must be good in both those places. I am quite certain that he loves animals. He and Dillydums get along famously." She looked down at the monkey who was sitting in her arms, silently regarding the stranger.

Though Aggie was not at all as certain of Lord Gale's accomplishments on horseback or the ballroom floor as Cecilie was, she would have to concede that he and Dillydums were quite compatible.

Lady Denby nodded. "So a love of animals is necessary for your husband?"

"Yes, indeed," said Cecilie. "It was that which finished Lord Parrington. He was really light on his feet, but I simply could not tolerate a man who is cruel to his animals."

"I see."

"And of course," continued Cecilie, "he must also love little ones. For, though I don't know much about them, I'm sure I shall want several."

Lady Denby kept her attentive expression through this recital and Aggie gave her great credit for it. "Yes, of course," the dowager agreed. Then, as Cecilie was silent for a

278

moment, she asked, "And have you any more requirements?"

Cecilie looked at Aggie and hesitated. "Come, come, my dear," said Lady Denby kindly. "We are all friends here. You can tell me."

"Aggie has told me it's wrong to speak of such matters," said Cecilie and Aggie closed her eyes in mute despair. What would Denby's mother think of them now? "And I do not want to get her in trouble."

"That is very commendable of you," said Lady Denby. "But, I assure you, there is nothing that can shock me at my age." She sent Aggie a reassuring smile. "And if I am to help you find the right man, I must know what we are looking for."

Cecilie nodded. "Yes, that's very true." Still she looked at Aggie as though for permission.

Aggie sighed. "Go ahead, you might as well tell her."

"Well, it needs some explaining. So you will understand and not blame Aggie."

"Of course, my dear. Tell me however you wish." Lady Denby's smile was warm.

"Well, the morning after we arrived Dillydums got loose and startled his lordship. Since then they do not deal well together," she confided. "Though I know his lordship

279

takes excellent care of his cattle. At any rate, he was yelling and shouting, his lordship, you see, because he hadn't known there was a monkey in the house and Dillydums had his razor. It must have been a terrible shock to him. And anyway, he came running out into the hallway in his breeches and boots, yelling. And I woke up and came to see what all the commotion was about. And I saw his chest."

Lady Denby's expression did not change as she repeated, "You saw his chest?"

"Yes, it was bare, you see. Because he had not finished dressing yet."

"Yes, of course." Lady Denby was clearly bewildered.

"And that's what I want," concluded Cecilie happily.

The dowager shook her head. "Cecilie, my dear, I'm afraid the journey has left me somewhat fatigued. My wits are not all they were. Exactly *what* is it that you want?"

"His lordship's chest. It looks so cute with all that tangled black hair on it."

If Aggie had not been so embarrassed, she might have found Lady Denby's expression of amazement amusing.

"Of course," continued Cecilie. "I should never think of marrying the Earl himself.

He's far too old and he still needs a great deal of mellowing."

"Yes, of course," agreed Lady Denby, obviously struggling to regain her composure. "Aggie – Miss Trimble – was quite right to caution you against speaking about such things. It is not considered proper. But I am very glad you told *me*. Because I do want to help you."

"Yes, I am quite sure of that." Cecilie's golden head nodded in absolute agreement.

"Tell me," said Lady Denby with a swift look of commiseration at Aggie, "how did you expect to discover this last – fact – about your intended?"

"I thought I would just ask him."

Again that curious choking sound came from Lady Denby.

"Of course, I should not ask him right away," Cecilie explained. "Not until I knew the other things about him. I did not ask Lord Parrington, nor even Lord Gale."

"That was very wise of you," said Lady Denby. "That question can be construed rather dangerously."

"Yes," agreed Cecilie. "That is what Aggie thought, I'm sure."

Lady Denby nodded. "This Lord Gale now. What is he like? Physically, that is. How does he look?"

"He is taller than I," said Cecilie. "Fair skinned, with red hair."

"I see." There was something in Lady Denby's voice that indicated to Aggie that she already possessed this information, but Cecilie did not notice. "Red hair."

Cecilie nodded.

"If this young man has red hair," said the dowager, "is it not likely, since the hair of his head is red, that that of his chest – providing of course that he has hair there – should also be red?"

Cecilie considered this. "Yes, milady. I suppose so. I had not thought of that."

"It is fairly certain to be so," said Lady Denby. "And I think I should tell you that fair men with hair of red are almost always without much hair on their chests."

Aggie waited for Cecilie to ask the grand little woman how she came by this piece of knowledge, but evidently Cecilie thought Lady Denby's age gave her all necessary information.

Cecilie sighed. "It's a dreadful business, this hunting for a husband."

"Yes, I know," replied Lady Denby. "I remember my own salad days. I was absolutely miserable until I found Denby's father." She smiled and her face revealed traces of the beauty that had once been hers.

"He was a real man, he was. What they call a prime article, these days." She smiled mischievously at Aggie, and then at Cecilie. "Do not tell anyone else this," she whispered with the look of a child about to say something wicked. "But Denby's chest is very like his father's."

Cecilie giggled and Aggie found herself smiling, too; but to her surprise Cecilie did not ask the question that was uppermost in Aggie's own mind – had Lady Denby known that before her marriage night?

"What you need," said Lady Denby, "is a dark man. Denby is too old, of course, and you do have some difficulty dealing together, but there are other dark men in London. Younger ones."

"Oh, Lady Denby," said Cecilie with great sincerity. "I am so pleased you have come to London."

"So am I," declared the dowager. "It appears that my presence here was very much needed."

What Cecilie might have replied to this, Aggie was never to know, for at that moment Lord Denby appeared in the doorway and drawled, "I hope your journey was a pleasant one, Mother."

She smiled at him. "The new carriage you sent me bounces less than most, son. I thank you for it. Actually, the journey was rather pleasant and I am in the mood to go out this evening. I have not been to Vauxhall Gardens for some time. Perhaps if you are free, you will escort me there – with Cecilie and Miss Trimble, too."

The Earl smiled, a smile that would melt any woman's heart, thought Aggie. "Of course, Mother. I should be glad to. Around seven?"

Lady Denby nodded and with another smile his lordship left the room.

"Oh, milady!" Cecilie clapped her hands with glee. "How wonderful. I have been wanting to go to Vauxhall Gardens."

"Perhaps," said Lady Denby, "I should lie upon my bed for a while. I am not as young as I once was and I do not want to tire in the middle of our outing."

"Of course, milady. Of course."

."But first, just let me see Dillydums," said the dowager. He jumped into her open arms quite cheerfully and peered up at her. "He reminds me of my own little Charleykins." She spoke to the monkey for a moment and then handed him back to Cecilie. "I shall see you both later."

"Oh!" said Cecilie as she stepped down from the carriage into Vauxhall Gardens later that evening. "It's just lovely." The little monkey sitting on her shoulder gazed somberly around. Aggie had wondered at the wisdom of bringing along the monkey. Not that it was an unusual thing to do, only that Dillydums *had* been known to cause trouble. But the Earl had said it was fine.

Aggie, descending in her turn, put thoughts of trouble from her mind and concentrated on the beauty around her. The multitude of colored lanterns, lining the walks and the pavilions, gave the whole an effect of fairyland grace. Well-dressed people, often in couples, sauntered up and down the numerous paths.

"Oh! Do let us walk about," said Cecilie eagerly.

The Earl looked to his mother. "Of course, my dear," she said to Cecilie. "We shall see all of the gardens. But before we explore the walks, I should like to hear the orchestra perform. I believe it is about that time."

"Yes, of course," replied Cecilie.

Aggie, glancing surreptitiously at the Earl, saw the look of satisfaction that he and his mother exchanged. This puzzled her somewhat, but then, remembering the Earl's words about Lord Gale's lightskirt, she thought perhaps they planned to point her out to Cecilie. If so, she doubted the wisdom of such a plan. Cecilie was not apt to take lightly being so shamed, as she would inevitably feel she had been.

Then the Earl offered his arm to Cecilie and led them off toward the orchestra. Aggie and the Countess followed.

The orchestra was housed in a shell-shaped pavilion. Glittering with colored lanterns, it stood out against the darkening sky. "Oh," breathed Cecilie, "oh, just look."

"It's quite as nice as I remembered it," said Lady Denby complacently, and Aggie nodded in agreement. The strains of a beautiful ballad drifted out over the warm night air. Around the stand, entranced spectators stood in listening silence.

Aggie suppressed a sigh. The numerous couples around her, the women looking up with smiles into the men's faces, filled her with a terrible yearning. She wanted so badly to be on Denby's arm, looking up at him with eyes full of adoration, but of course that was foolishness. Staring at his broad shoulders ahead of her, she blinked rapidly to keep back the sudden tears. She would have to stop thinking of Denby like this. She would just have to.

By the time they had listened to several songs, Aggie had conquered her feelings enough to dismiss the tears. Then the Earl turned to his mother. Just as he did so a young man approached them. His hair was dark, his eyes, too; and he smiled at them all with cheerful friendliness. "Denby. Lady Denby. How good to see you."

The Earl looked him over silently. "Good evening, Heatherton." His tone seemed excessively stiff to Aggie and she glanced at him swiftly. But no one else seemed to notice. The Earl performed the amenities, introducing first Cecilie, then Aggie. Heatherton spoke to each of them in the same cheerful tones; but as soon as he had done the civil thing, he turned again to Cecilie. "Perhaps you might like to take my arm," he said. "Then the Earl may escort his mother."

"Of course," replied Cecilie with alacrity. "How very thoughtful of you."

The Earl made a moue and looked at Cecilie sternly, but she ignored him and put her gloved hand on Heatherton's extended arm.

The Earl turned then to his mother and offered her his arm. "Not unless you give Aggie your other," she said gently. "I cannot permit her to be left to walk alone."

"The pleasure is mine," said the Earl, turning to her. Avoiding his eyes, Aggie took his arm. She did not see how she could avoid it without drawing too much awareness to herself. Lady Denby was far too astute not to deduce something from such a refusal.

The small group moved on. Heatherton and Cecilie ahead, and Denby following with the other two women. The young people seemed to want to move ahead, perhaps to be alone; but Denby diligently kept them in sight. The monkey seemed to have taken to the Viscount Heatherton, for he perched cheerfully on his shoulder, one tiny paw braced on the rim of the young man's curly-brimmed beaver.

The Earl and his mother exchanged glances again and Aggie wondered if Cecilie was to be again denied a suitor. Though she had seen him only temporarily, Aggie thought the Viscount by far the nicest of all Cecilie's suitors so far. His eyes had been clear and friendly, his clothes as neatly elegant as the Earl's. There was something about him that inspired confidence in her. And yet the Earl had seemed disgruntled, barely civil to him. There was something here that Aggie did not understand, some undercurrent that was unclear to her. But perhaps it was only her own uneasy nerves that made things seem unusual, she thought.

Being close to Denby made it difficult to think clearly. She was far too aware of his strong lean body so close to her own. Her arm, which he had tucked so casually through his, seemed to tingle with the heat of his side. Color came to her face as she realized that she was thinking of his kisses, the kisses that devastated her senses so. With a little sigh she reminded herself that it was useless to think such thoughts. She was a nameless, penniless governess-companion, not a young girl in her first London season. And the only kind of offer that the Earl was likely to make for her was illegitimate. And he would scarcely even do that now, not with his lady mother in the house.

She cast a glance up at him from under lowered lashes. He was gazing ahead at Cecilie and Lord Heatherton and his face held a most curious look... If she hadn't seen the almost rude way he had treated the Viscount, she might even have said that the look was one of satisfaction, but that was patently impossible. He had made his dislike of the young man rather clear.

They strolled for some moments in silence, and then Aggie finally asked the question that was uppermost in her mind. "Is there something wrong with Lord Heatherton?" She was sorry as soon as the words left her mouth, but it was too late to recall them.

Denby turned to look at her and she was

thankful that in the fitful illumination of the lanterns he could not see her face clearly. "Why do you ask?"

"You – you seemed a trifle –" She hesitated, afraid to irritate him.

"Rude?" offered Lady Denby.

Aggie was covered with confusion. "Oh no! Just a little formal." She felt the word was inadequate, but she could think of no other at the moment.

He smiled at her sardonically. "You need not be so sparing of my feelings. My mother was right. I *was* rude to him."

Under the scrutiny of those smoky eyes Aggie had to say something. "But why? Has he done something? That is," she floundered on, feeling more and more foolish, "is he unsuitable for Cecilie?"

The Earl frowned, his dark brows meeting in the inevitable line that indicated his displeasure. "I do not care to discuss the matter," he said harshly, and Aggie dared not mention the subject again.

After some more time spent in silent strolling, Aggie noticed they were approaching the Dark Walks, the proverbial place for young lovers, especially unchaperoned ones, to walk. She felt herself growing anxious. Surely Cecilie would not go into the Dark Walks with a man newly met. But Cecilie, as her companion well knew, might do anything. So Aggie watched in agonized suspense. Then, just as the young couple came parallel to the Walks the monkey leaped suddenly from his perch on Heatherton's shoulder and darted off into the darkness.

"Dillydums! Come back!" called a distraught Cecilie. "Oh, he will be lost forever!"

Aggie, casting a hurried look at his lordship, was surprised to find him again exchanging that curious glance with his mother. But by then they had reached Cecilie and she had little time to think about anything else as she bent all her efforts to allaying Cecilie's fears.

"Don't despair, Miss Winthrop," said Heatherton. "I'll get the little fellow back. Truly I will."

The Viscount's features were drawn into an expression of deep concern and as soon as he saw Cecilie safely into Aggie's hands he sped off into the darkness, whistling softly for the monkey. Denby began to follow him. Then, obviously remembering that the monkey did not regard him in a particularly favorable light, he stopped and waited, almost as though he wished not to be seen with the women and yet feeling it his duty to protect them.

Cecilie burst into great sobs and Aggie put an arm around her heaving shoulders. "Now, now, Cecilie. You must not take on so. I'm sure Lord Heatherton will find Dillydums."

"But it's so dreadfully dark in there," wailed Cecilie. "And you know how Dillydums hates the dark. It terrifies him."

"I know, my dear," replied Aggie in soothing tones. "But just consider this. Since Dillydums dislikes the dark he will come all the quicker when he sees his friend Lord Heatherton has come after him."

Cecilie's sobs lessened momentarily and Lady Denby took that moment to say softly, "Come, Cecilie. Tears only redden a woman's nose, you know. And there's no call for that. The Viscount will find that rascally monkey. Such a nice young man he is." Her eyes sought Aggie's for the merest fraction of a second before she continued in a lower tone, "A very nice *dark* young man."

Cecilie's sobs stopped almost immediately and she raised her head from her handkerchief to ask, "Is my nose red already?"

Lady Denby surveyed it seriously before she replied. "No, it still looks fine."

"Good," said Cecilie. "I shall not cry anymore. Surely Lord Heatherton will find Dillydums."

"Of course he will," said Lady Denby

with a strange smile. "And then you may thank him very sweetly."

"Oh, I shall. I really shall." Cecilie looked suddenly at her new friend. "You know Lord Heatherton well."

Lady Denby nodded. "His mother is a friend of mine."

"Does he dance well?" asked Cecilie. "And how does he ride?"

"He dances with the grace of the best dancing master and I have never seen a better man on horseback with the exception of Denby and his father," replied the Countess soberly.

"He loves animals," Cecilie said, almost to herself. "And children. He was telling me about the antics of his little brothers." She turned wide eyes on Lady Denby. "Do you suppose..."

Aggie suppressed an urge to stop her. Let Lady Denby handle this.

The Countess nodded and the light of mischief danced in the gray eyes so like her son's. "I think it very likely, my dear." She looked around her with the suspicious gaze of a conspirator and her voice dropped still a tone lower even though Denby was much too far away to hear. "You see, Heatherton's mama and I were bosom-bows at school and we married much around the same time."

A little sigh escaped her. "Dear Fannie always did love the babies. The two oldest are girls, then Heatherton. There must be six or seven altogether." She shook her head as though dismissing some unsettling thought. "Anyway, Fannie and I were bosom-bows and we used to live close when we were young brides. And one day, quite by chance, mind you, we happened to be discussing – hair. And she told me that Heatherton's father was also very..." She raised her brows eloquently. "So one might well suppose that his son –"

Cecilie clapped her hands in glee. "Dear Countess. What a wonderful, wonderful friend you are. He is perfect, absolutely perfect."

Aggie, who had been watching and listening in utter astonishment, found herself completely at a loss. She could hardly reprimand Cecilie for discussing such things when the Countess was so obviously encouraging her. But she felt the whole proceeding was highly irregular.

And then Cecilie spied Heatherton just as he emerged from the darkness with Dillydums again riding on his shoulder. She squealed with happiness and could barely be restrained from running to his side.

As Heatherton passed his lordship, the

Earl fell in step behind him, but there was a certain stiffness in his carriage that made Aggie uncomfortable. Surely now that Cecilie had found someone suitable to care about he would be pleased. But that did not seem to be the case.

Cecilie's effusiveness, however, made up for any cordiality lacking in the Earl. "Oh, what a wonderful man you are," she breathed. "It's just marvelous the way you found him."

"It seems rather marvelous to me how he got away in the first place," commented Denby in rather acid tones.

Aggie was shocked that he should behave so rudely. And so stupidly, she told herself. Any fool could see that Cecilie was taken with this man. Now why must his lordship complicate matters by disapproving of him? And apparently without sound reason.

Fortunately, Heatherton ignored the remark and so did everyone else. The rest of the evening passed in a very curious fashion. Cecilie and the Viscount ambled on, laughing and chatting, while behind them came a silent Denby, his mother on one arm and Aggie on the other, his face set in an expression of grim displeasure. Because of having his lordship between them, Aggie could not ask Lady Denby any questions and she found this excessively galling.

All in all, it was quite an odd outing, thought Aggie, as she stood beside the others at the close of their stroll, watching the skyrockets explode in the summer heavens. She could not get over the feeling that there was something very peculiar about his lordship's behavior, but exactly what it was, she could not say.

The fireworks over, they returned to the entrance and sought out their carriage. As Heatherton handed Cecilie up, he spoke softly, "I shall call upon you tomorrow."

Aggie waited, holding her breath, for the Earl to deny him that privilege; but at this moment his lordship was deep in conversation with his mother and the Viscount's words went unheeded.

The ride home was uneventful. Everyone seemed lost in their own thoughts, Cecilie smiling in silent happiness. And then, just as they reached the great stairs, the Earl spoke, "I cannot very well forbid Heatherton the house because of my mother's affection for his mother," he said harshly to Cecilie. "But do not allow yourself to form a partiality for him. I cannot abide the man."

He wheeled on his heel and was gone before Cecilie could answer and, as she opened her mouth to call after him, Aggie shook her head in warning. A hard look of determination settled on Cecilie's delicate features and then, without a word to Aggie or Lady Denby, she swept on up to her rooms.

Aggie looked at the Countess. There was something very odd about this whole business; but when she opened her mouth to ask about it, Lady Denby forestalled her. "I must speak to my son," she said. "Good night, Aggie."

Chapter Seventeen

The next several days were odd ones for Aggie. Lord Heatherton called daily and was met with joy by a radiant Cecilie. Bates ushered him in and out with quiet dignity and Aggie saw that her charge was properly chaperoned, but no one mentioned any of this. Lady Denby avoided all Aggie's attempts to discuss the matter with her and Denby absented himself so completely from the house that Aggie did not once see him.

Cecilie could do nothing but sing young Heatherton's praises. Aggie, torn between sympathy for the young woman in love and her awareness that Denby could never be expected to approve the match, hardly knew what to say. She was especially provoked by the fact that the more she saw of Heatherton the more she liked the man. His feeling for animals and youngsters was quite genuine, she felt sure; one only had to see him play with Dillydums to know that. And his affections for Cecilie seemed sincere and strong. Denby was being very unfair, Aggie thought angrily, unfair and stupid. For it was quite clear to her that Cecilie would make Lord Heatherton an affable and loving wife and his children a good mother. But some little thing, some stupid little thing, had made Denby dislike him.

One day about a week after their trip to Vauxhall, Aggie and Cecilie were sitting in the drawing room. Cecilie, with much enthusiasm, but not a great deal of success, was working on a fire screen. Aggie had long ago given up attempting to teach her the fine points of needlepointing; indeed, Cecilie had had so much difficulty in that area that Aggie had despaired of ever teaching her anything of the art. But on his last visit the Viscount had remarked on the design that Aggie was engaged on and Cecilie had hardly seen him out before she insisted on having some needlework of her own. Aggie had been glad to oblige and Cecilie now sat, happily stabbing the needle in and out, secure in the knowledge that whatever she did would be much admired by her suitor.

Aggie continued her own work, the top for a footstool, only giving Cecilie assistance from time to time as she tangled her wool or otherwise erred. "You know, Aggie," said Cecilie, her eyes still intent on her work, but her mouth curving in a little grin, "I still think I had a good idea about that marriage marketplace."

Aggie smiled. "Perhaps, dear. But consider. There are many things you know about the Viscount that you could not have learned in such a place."

Looking up, Cecilie stabbed her finger, but she ignored it to ask, "Like what, Aggie? I know that you know a great deal about love and I respect your judgment."

For some reason Aggie found a lump in her throat. She spoke over it. "Well, Cecilie, I suppose I know no more than most women. But I have experienced love."

Cecilie nodded. "Yes. That's what I mean." She sighed dreamily. "How pleasant it would be if we could both have the men we love."

Aggie swallowed, blinking back the tears.

She knew that Cecilie did not mean to hurt her. "Yes dear, but that cannot be. What I meant for you to consider were things like Dillydums running away into the Dark Walks. Now the sign above a man in your marketplace might *say* that he loved animals. But we all know how easy it is for a man to puff himself falsely. This way you saw the Viscount in action. Just as you observed Lord Parrington's horses, you had a chance to observe Lord Heatherton. You *saw* how the Viscount behaved with Dillydums and how much Dillydums liked him."

Cecilie nodded. "Yes, Aggie. That is very true."

"And of course, you also have a chance to see how he treats you. Though of necessity he is on his best behavior, it does give you some idea."

Cecilie smiled. "Oh yes. And the way he looks at me." Her smile broadened. "So eagerly and so warmly. I like that."

Aggie nodded. She was seeing the Earl's smile as he had once gazed tenderly upon her, once – before time and something else had separated them. She choked back a sob.

"And the way he takes my elbow," Cecilie continued, unaware of Aggie's pain, lost as she was in her own pleasure. "And when he shawls me, the way his fingers feel on my neck." She sat lost in thought for some moments and Aggie successfully banished her longing to weep. Cecilie looked up slyly. "I don't suppose you could leave us alone for just a moment."

"Cecilie!"

"But Aggie, when he kisses my hand, when I feel his warm breath on my fingers, I get all shivery inside."

Aggie forced herself to smile though she felt a pain deep inside, a pain like a twisted knife. Just so did the Earl make *her* shiver.

"Please, Aggie? I want to feel what it's like to have him kiss my lips."

"Cecilie! I cannot do such a thing. Whatever would the Earl say? I could not possibly do such a thing."

"Just for a little minute," pleaded Cecilie, her wide eyes begging. "I know he wouldn't hurt me."

"I know that, too, dear," replied Aggie. "But it would not be proper for me to allow such a thing."

"I don't know why not," said Cecilie. "Just for a little minute."

Aggie did not reply to this and finally Cecilie went back to her needlework. But after a few minutes she raised her head to ask, "Aggie, did your young man kiss you?"

"Cecilie!" Aggie began, but the youngster interrupted her.

"Aggie! I need to know these things. And I've no mama to ask."

Aggie recognized the truth of this and, much as the subject caused her pain, she decided to allow Cecilie to pursue it. "Yes, he did."

"And was it wonderful?" asked Cecilie eagerly. "Did it seem like stars shining and fireworks going off?"

Aggie could not forbear smiling. "It was rather like that, dear. But I think it is different for different people. Not everyone sees fireworks, at least not all the time. Sometimes it's very peaceful, like coming home."

"Oh." Cecilie digested this news in silence for some moments.

"Like belonging?"

"Yes, dear," Aggie replied. "Like belonging." Resolutely she pushed from her mind the memories that wanted to come flooding back.

"I truly think I am in love," said Cecilie with a contented little sigh. "And it does not seem nearly as painful as it is in Shakespeare's stories."

"Cecilie." Aggie knew she was not going to be heard, but she could not let the girl go on like this. "You know how the Earl feels about Lord Heatherton."

Cecilie shrugged slim shoulders. "I don't care. I let him drive away Lord Gale, who was really a very nice man who said the most beautiful things." She sighed speculatively, a faraway look in her eyes. "But I shall not let him send Heatherton away. I shall run away first," she added defiantly. "To that place you told me of, where the fortune hunters take young women."

"Cecilie –" Aggie began, but Bates appeared at the door at that moment to announce Lord Heatherton and Aggie could not say any more on the matter. She determined, however, that she must discuss the subject with the Countess. She must do something before matters got out of hand – if they had not already.

And so after the Viscount left, and without the opportunity for Cecilie to sample his kisses, Aggie sought out Denby's mother.

The Countess greeted her with a sweet smile. "And how is Cecilie today?"

"She is well," said Aggie, not quite able to keep a note of worry out of her voice. "And as usual she is raving about the incomparable Lord Heatherton. Who, incidentally, just finished his daily visit."

"He is a nice boy," said her ladyship complacently.

Aggie thought perhaps she was dreaming. The whole thing seemed so strange. "But the Earl – he would never approve. And Cecilie is really taken."

Lady Denby smiled. "Sit down, Aggie. Let me tell you something."

A small voice inside Aggie told her she should run, but she could not disobey the Countess.

"You must think my son is a strange fish," Lady Denby said. "But he says he has his reasons for objecting to Heatherton. And really, considering that in holding out for the proper husband for Cecilie he is delaying his own plans, I feel he is to be respected."

"Delaying?" Aggie's heart threatened to stop beating altogether.

"Yes. He is particularly anxious to get Cecilie settled because, you see, he wants to marry himself."

Now Aggie was sure her heart had stopped momentarily. Denby – to marry?

"He has fallen deeply in love with a beautiful and talented lady and he plans to marry her after Cecilie's future is assured."

Aggie nodded. She must keep her emotions from overcoming her. She had rejected him and he had gone to Lady Alicia.

"That's one of the reasons I came to the city," said the Countess. "To meet her and give him my approval."

Aggie nodded dumbly, wondering how Denby could hope his mother would approve of Lady Alicia. But then, the Countess was a real lady and she wanted her son to be happy.

Aggie sat stiffly erect as the Countess continued. "So you see, all this delay is most disturbing to him. Especially since he feels that he can't marry until Cecilie is settled."

A shiver trembled over Aggie. Thank God! To live in the same house with a triumphant Lady Alicia would be more than she could stand. Much more.

"He does want to do his best for Cecilie," Lady Denby was saying.

"Then why does he behave so foolishly about Heatherton?" Aggie forced herself to push Denby to the back of her mind. She must concentrate on Cecilie.

Lady Denby shrugged. "You will have to ask him yourself, Aggie. I cannot say. Heatherton seems a most suitable young man to me."

Aggie nodded. The more she thought about it the more she believed that Denby was making a mistake about his ward, but with this news causing her heart to thud

305

madly in her throat she did not think she dared face him.

"Aggie. Aggie!"

She realized that Lady Denby had already spoken her name several times. "Yes, milady?"

"You are looking rather pale. Perhaps you have taken a chill. Why don't you go lie down for a while?"

Aggie slipped off her shoes and stretched out on the bed. To think of Denby actually marrying Lady Alicia seemed so strange. She simply could not sort all of it out, she thought, the tears rising to her eyes. The one clear thing seemed that whatever Denby's feelings had once been, he was now in love with another woman.

The tears overflowed then and she allowed them to course down her cheeks unheeded. She must see that Cecilie was soon married, even though it meant Denby's marriage to Lady Alicia. She must get out of this house and away from him. Once she opened her school there should be little chance of running into him again. She was not likely to be visiting in any of the *ton's* usual haunts. And it seemed the only way to cure this terrible ache in her heart, or at least to make it somewhat bearable, was to get away from him. If she did not have to see him, she might in time manage to forget the feel of his arms and the wild warm ecstasy of his kisses. Perhaps eventually she could achieve some degree of contentment. That was all she could hope for now. A reasonably contented life as a spinster schoolmarm.

Finally sleep overcame her, but it was not a restful sleep, haunted as it was by dreams of Denby. It was several hours later when a brisk tapping on her door aroused her. It took a moment for her to regain her senses. Then she called, "Yes? Who is it?"

The door opened. "It's me, miss," said Millie. "Bates sent me up to get you. His lordship is just in and it seems he wants to have a word with you. In the library."

Aggie sat up rather groggily. "Please tell his lordship I have been lying down. I will be there shortly."

"Yes, miss."

As the door closed behind the maid, Aggie forced herself from the bed. She did not want to see Denby. She would have given a great deal at that moment to be able to run away, but no such opportunity was available to her.

She splashed cold water on her face and patted down a few stray wisps of hair. Then, before her fear could immobilize her, she made herself go downstairs. Nothing would be gained by avoiding this moment. She knew that and yet . . .

Her knees were trembling long before she reached the library door and she did not pause before she entered. She got halfway across the room before her legs threatened to fail her. "Milord, you asked for me?" His back was to her and she noted absently that he was wearing a new coat, perfectly tailored. And then he turned to her and she had to fight the waves of longing that threatened to overwhelm her.

"Yes." His tone was formal, his eyes guarded. "My mother seemed to feel that you wished to discuss Cecilie." His eyes watched her closely.

"I – I do."

He gestured toward a chair and she sank into it gratefully. He pulled up another and straddled it. "Well?"

"I – I do not understand your attitude toward Viscount Heatherton," she began. "He seems to me to be very suitable. And Cecilie is quite taken with him. Why do you dislike him so much?"

"I have my reasons," he said quietly, his eyes never leaving her face.

She waited for him to go on, but he remained silent. "You must understand, milord," she said then. "This is much more serious than Lord Gale. The Viscount has a very real hold on Cecilie's affections."

"So my mother informs me," he replied calmly.

"But if you find him unsuitable, you should not allow Cecilie to see him," Aggie cried.

The Earl frowned. "I have told you. Heatherton's mama and mine are bosom-bows. I cannot forbid him the house."

"But your duty to Cecilie?"

"I have informed Cecilie as to my feelings on the matter," said his lordship dryly.

Aggie began to feel that everyone was going mad. "I told you that your stubbornness would drive her into a man's arms."

"So you did," he agreed.

Suddenly Aggie wanted to scream. For the moment she forget her feelings about herself. "Why must you be so – so –"

"Stupid?" he volunteered dryly.

"Yes!" Her temper was flaring now and she did not care. "You are ruining her life. Gretna Green is not unknown to her." She glared at him. "If you deny Heatherton's suit, she may well elect to run off with him."

"And you will assist in her packing?" he inquired, still in that strangely formal tone.

"Of course not!" she blazed. "I could not, in good conscience, do such a thing. But you must understand. Cecilie is wild about this man. And you have advanced no legitimate reasons against him."

"I need not do so," he said calmly. "I simply cannot abide him."

"But –" Aggie felt that they were talking in circles. There was something here she did not comprehend.

The Earl consulted his timepiece. "I'm sorry, Miss Trimble, but my time is limited. I must dress for dinner now. A pressing engagement. I'm sure you understand."

Aggie forced herself to nod. She was suddenly unable to speak, for the knowledge came to her quite clearly that the Earl's pressing engagement was with Lady Alicia and the thought filled her with despair.

Dumbly she rose and made her way toward the door. "Do not worry about Cecilie, Aggie. I am confident we will get her well settled." There was something strange about the tone of his voice, but her eyes were full of tears and she dared not turn to look at him for fear they would betray her.

Blindly she turned down the corridor toward the courtyard. She must have a chance to think. There was something quite extraordinary in Denby's behavior. It was certainly clear that he remembered her words concerning how opposition affected Cecilie.

Quite clear that he knew that his opposition would drive her *toward* a man rather than *away* from him. And still he behaved as he did, by his actions causing her to be even more enamored of young Heatherton.

Aggie stopped dead in her tracks. Was that his intent? Was he taking the advice she had given him? But if he were – Then he *expected* Cecilie to elope. Aggie shook her throbbing head. If he had such a plan, why hadn't he told her about it?

She sank down on the stone bench among the roses, absently inhaling their rich fragrance. Had Denby and his mother concocted this plot? With Heatherton's connivance? All the facts seemed to indicate so: the Earl's strange, almost unreal, stiffness with Heatherton; Lady Denby's encouragement of Cecilie's affections; the Earl's opposition which yet left the way clear for the Viscount; and even, Aggie realized suddenly, that first meeting at Vauxhall Gardens, which she could now see had almost certainly been arranged. They wanted Cecilie to elope! That must be it; it explained so much.

But why hadn't they enlisted her help? She could not tell. At any rate, she told herself, it seemed clear to her now. She must think about what to do. Absently she picked

311

a pink rose and held it to her nostrils. As she inhaled its sweet fragrance, a terrible sadness stole over her. Cecilie's love for Heatherton was sweet and innocent, as her love for Denby had been.

Sitting there in the sunshine, Aggie knew that Cecilie was right in her devotion to Heatherton. In the same situation, if Denby had asked her, she would have run off with him. And then the tears escaped the control Aggie had imposed on them and rolled down her cheeks, falling unheeded upon the rose. She had lost her chance at happiness, but Cecilie should not. If it was Denby's plan that the two elope, she would make the way clear for them.

Chapter Eighteen

And so the next day when Heatherton came to call, Aggie had made her decision. The Viscount gave her his usual cheerful greeting and sat down to admire Cecilie's needlepoint. "I am only just learning to do it," said Cecilie truthfully. "Aggie's is much better."

"You will learn," said the Viscount with

a smile. "It's the wanting to learn that counts."

"Yes, milord," said Cecilie with a smile of pleasure. "I want to learn everything I need to know to make you a perfect wife."

Heatherton reached out to take her hand in his. "None of us is perfect, my dear. I love you as you are."

Aggie attended diligently to her needlework, pretending that she heard nothing of what they were saying.

"I must speak to Denby about you," Heatherton said.

Cecilie sighed. "Aggie says it will do no good. He says he cannot abide you. How *can* that be?" she asked in genuine bewilderment. "You are the most wonderful man I have ever seen."

The Viscount chuckled. "Cecilie, my dear. you are love-bitten."

"Yes, I know," she replied with a little laugh. Then her tone sobered. "But I am afraid of Denby. He is so – so hard."

Heatherton's voice dropped. "I told you. Don't worry about him. I know what to do."

It was at this point that Aggie yelled "ouch!" causing both the young people to glance up in surprise. "I'm afraid I have stabbed my finger rather badly."

"Oh, Aggie, how dreadful! Do let me see."

Aggie shook her head. "No, no, dear. You stay here with your guest. I will just go out and ask Millie for a little piece of cloth to wrap it in. I should not like to stain my needlepoint."

"Oh!" Cecilie seemed suddenly to have realized something. "Yes, Aggie. That does seem the best thing to do."

So Aggie, her heart pounding, left Cecilie with her visitor. She was sure she was no more than a few paces down the hall before Cecilie was receiving her first kiss. Aggie found that her own hands were trembling. Was she doing the right thing leaving the two of them alone? She really felt she could trust Cecilie with Heatherton. But what if she could not? The thought seemed to add wings to her feet as she sped toward the kitchen. Without something on her finger she could not go back, especially as there was no sign of a needle hole anywhere in it.

It was only a few minutes later that she returned to the drawing room. Cecilie and Lord Heatherton still sat as she had left them, but a faint flush on Cecilie's cheeks and an extra brightness to her eyes told Aggie that her little stratagem had been successful. Cecilie no longer had to speculate as to the nature of her suitor's kisses; she had experienced at least one.

"Is your finger all right?" asked Cecilie as Aggie reentered the room.

Aggie nodded. "Yes." She lifted it to show them. "Millie helped me find a strip of cloth. And it will soon heal."

With these amenities observed, Aggie returned to her needlework and Cecilie and Heatherton to their conversation. The Viscount never overstayed himself and so in due course he rose to go, bowing low over Aggie's hand and saying gravely, "I hope your finger will soon heal."

And Aggie replied with equal gravity, "I'm sure it will not take long."

When Cecilie returned from walking the Viscount to the door, she was wearing a radiant smile. "I'm very sorry about your finger, Aggie."

Aggie nodded. "It was nothing dear, Such things happen."

"Yes, I suppose they do," agreed Cecilie, reaching for her needlework. She stitched in silence for some moments. Then she looked up with the merest of smiles. "Aggie?"

"Yes, dear."

"Do you suppose that a kiss could be both?"

"Both what?" asked Aggie, carefully keeping her eyes on her work.

"Both fireworks *and* coming home," said Cecilie softly.

Again Aggie could feel the treacherous tears rising. If only she had not lost Denby. If only she could feel his arms around her once more. Some seconds passed before she could master her emotions enough to speak. "Yes, Cecilie," she said finally. "Sometimes it's like that. Both at once."

Cecilie nodded. "That's what I thought."

No more was said of kisses that day, or later. But whenever Lord Heatherton called, Aggie contrived in one way or another to leave them to themselves for a few minutes.

And then one day it happened. Aggie had known it would, but still it was a shock. She woke early to find Cecilie's bed empty. A note pinned to the pillow said simply,

We've run off. Dillydums, too.

For long moments Aggie stood staring down at the note. Her heart was pounding in her throat and her mouth was suddenly dry. They had done it. As she had known they would. Done it without Heatherton even approaching Denby. Aggie had to admire the plan. For if the Viscount had approached Denby and been refused, he could certainly not have called again and there would have been no opportunity to arrange the elopement.

She was turning from the room, wondering how long she should wait before informing his lordship what she had discovered, when her foot kicked a piece of crumpled paper on the floor. Absently Aggie picked it up and smoothed it out. Then her heart rose up in her throat and she almost cried out in her alarm. Dear God! This was a letter from Lord Gale! An effusive letter full of flowery compliments and begging Cecilie to run off with him.

Aggie's fingers trembled so that the paper almost fell from them. No! Cecilie could not have gone with Gale. And yet – she could not risk it. Cecilie was so young and so easily swayed by compliments.

On trembling legs Aggie hurried to seek out his lordship. She found him still in the breakfast room. "Milord!" she cried. "Cecilie has run off." She was too distraught to notice the expression on his face, though later she was to wish she had. "At first I thought it was with the Viscount, but it may be with Lord Gale!"

"What!" His face darkened and his brows began to draw together in that line she dreaded, while the gray of his eyes turned stormy.

Silently she passed him the letter. He scanned it quickly, then bellowed, "Bates! Order my horse. And get my pistols."

"Yes, milord."

"Pistols!" Aggie grasped the back of a chair for support.

"If it's Gale," he said, "I may need them." He looked down at her, his eyes clouded. "Go to my mother and wait. She'll be up. And don't worry."

Then he was gone and all the words filling her heart were left unsaid. A shudder raced over her. If Cecilie *had* gone with Gale, and if Denby didn't catch them in time, Cecilie's life would be miserable. And it would be Aggie's fault.

Finally, realizing that she was still standing where he had left her, she made her way up the stairs to Lady Denby's room. Her soft tap on the door brought the call, "Come in." Lady Denby turned from the window where she stood fully clothed in a becoming gown of palest lavender. "Aggie!" she said, coming immediately across the room and taking Aggie's cold hands in her own. "Whatever is wrong? You look absolutely haggard. Do sit down, my dear, and tell me what is wrong." She pulled Aggie onto a divan beside her.

"Cecilie has run off," said Aggie in despair.

Lady Denby did not seem surprised.

"She's run off," Aggie repeated.

"I rather think the Viscount will take good care of her," soothed the dowager.

"But that's just it," cried Aggie, the tears trembling on her lashes. "We don't know if it's Heatherton she went with."

Lady Denby eyed her sharply. "Whatever makes you say that?"

"I found a letter on her floor. From Lord Gale. She might have gone with him." Aggie pressed her trembling hands together in her lap.

"But she seemed so fond of Heatherton." Now the Countess looked worried.

"She is," agreed Aggie dully. "But she is also easily impressed by flowery compliments. And Lord Gale is very good at those."

Lady Denby looked thoughtful. "I suppose you have been to my son."

Aggie nodded. "I took the letter to him. I thought at first it was Heatherton she had run off with. Till I found the letter. Oh, Lady Denby. If she has really gone off with Gale, it is my fault."

"How can that be?" Lady Denby's tone was even.

"I suspected she would run away," Aggie said. "Only I thought it would be with Heatherton."

"So did we."

"You *did* plan it then," cried Aggie.

The Countess nodded. "Yes, we deliberately introduced Cecilie and Heatherton and Denby deliberately snubbed him."

"Then there is nothing wrong with him? He *is* suitable for Cecilie?" Aggie asked anxiously.

Lady Denby smiled. "He is quite suitable and he has formed a real affection for the girl. We were both very pleased."

Aggie put a hand to her throbbing head. "Why didn't you tell me?"

"I wanted to," said the Countess, "but Denby said not to. He felt that you were not good at dissembling and that Cecilie might suspect something. You will agree that it was imperative that she not suspect?"

Aggie sighed. Her head felt as though it might explode into a million throbbing pieces. "Yes. But I have been so confused. I did not know how to behave."

"It must have been difficult for you," agreed Lady Denby with a sigh. "But you know how I am with Denby. I find myself always doing as he wants."

Aggie nodded. She knew only too well how charming Denby could be. "Yes, I understand. But I am so worried. He – he took his pistols."

Lady Denby did not seem surprised. "I should not be concerned over that. Denby is a careful person and an excellent shot. What he will probably do is check out the usual route. How fortunate for us that Lord Gale has red hair and that Cecilie took Dillydums."

Aggie sniffed and pressed a handkerchief to her eyes. "Why?"

"Because Denby need not catch up to them to be sure whom she is with. After all, there cannot be too many young ladies with fair hair, traveling with a monkey toward Gretna Green. He can simply ask at inns and turnpike gates. I also imagine he knows which horses the Viscount planned to drive. I believe they are the ones he recently bought from Denby. They are on the best of terms with each other, you know. All that other business was for Cecilie's sake."

Aggie was beginning to feel somewhat better. She only hoped that it was the Viscount with whom Cecilie had gone. "I think perhaps I presumed too much," she said. "It was wrong of me. We took a terrible chance with Cecilie's life."

"Perhaps," said the Countess. "But we had to do something. We could not know that she was in communication with that dreadful Gale. It must have been one of the maids who brought the letter in." She frowned. "I shall have to speak to them."

Aggie nodded. She sat silent, not knowing what to do or say. Finally she asked, "How long do you think we shall have to wait?"

Lady Denby shrugged. "It is hard to say. They may have left in the night or early this morning." She patted Aggie's hand comfortingly. "Come, child. Do not be so downcast. Denby will more than likely find she has gone with Heatherton. Then the two of you will be free to lead your own lives."

Aggie nodded, but the prospect held little pleasure for her. She knew that she could not stay on in Denby's house once Cecilie was wed. She knew it was ridiculous, even dangerous, to see Denby or be near him. And clearly she would never be able to bear the sight of him as Lady Alicia's husband. But the prospect of a life without him in it seemed unbearably empty. She suppressed a sigh. She would start her school for young ladies; she would be forced to do so because of her financial situation. And perhaps that would actually be the best thing. At least she would be unable to sit dumbly and mourn. There would be a great deal to do to get things organized. That would occupy her mind for a while.

She tried to set herself to making plans, but it was a useless effort. Her thoughts could not be diverted from the Earl. His face seemed permanently etched in her mind. The busy brows, the smoky gray eyes, the proud aristocratic nose, the firm lips. A shiver ran over her as she recalled his kisses. Dear God! Could she really live without him? It seemed impossible, yet she knew it must be done. Other women had lived through unrequited love, she told herself sternly. And so would she. She had done it once already.

"Let us go have some breakfast," said Lady Denby. "The day may well be a long one."

"I cannot eat now," protested Aggie.

"Nonsense," said the Countess sternly. "You must keep up your strength."

So Aggie followed her to the breakfast room where she managed to down a cup of tea and half a piece of toast.

The day passed slowly. Aggie, her ears always alert, jumped at every little sound. Finally, at the Countess's suggestion, she picked up her needlework. More than once she pricked a finger, but she persisted in the sewing. There was something to be said for physical activity. The fact of doing something – anything – seemed to be helpful.

Sometimes she felt hopeful. His lordship must have learned the truth by now. Quite soon he would return to reassure them that it was indeed Heatherton Cecilie had gone off with.

But other times her imagination ran rampant and she imagined Cecilie as the neglected wife of Lord Gale, clad in a shabby gown and surrounded by crying little ones.

She had stitched, read aloud, and been persuaded into nibbling on the luncheon Bates had provided, and returned again to stitching and reading, and still there was no word from his lordship. And then, finally, as the sun was beginning to sink in the sky, she heard the sound of the front door and Denby's voice in the hall. She leaped to her feet, scattering needlework and thread, but entirely unheeding of it as she sped out into the hall. Lady Denby was right behind her.

"Denby!" Aggie cried. "Oh, please. Is Cecilie all right?"

The Earl handed Bates his hat and gloves and turned to them. "Cecilie is fine. And so is the Viscount."

For a moment Aggie thought she would sink from pure relief, but she rallied herself. "Thank God."

"That is all I wish to hear," said the Countess. "The day has been a trying one. I believe I shall take a nap before dinner." She glanced at her son. "Why don't you take Aggie into the library and tell her all about it? I will get the details at dinner."

The Earl inclined his head and, taking Aggie by the elbow, guided her back into the library and seated her on a divan. She was uncomfortably aware of his nearness when he settled himself beside her, but her first concern was for Cecilie. "Please," she begged, "tell me."

He glanced down at her. "I told you not to worry," he said gently.

Aggie found a great lump in her throat. "I – I could not help it."

He nodded as though understanding her feelings. "I followed them. It was easy enough – a young woman with golden hair and a monkey. But I went to several of their stops to be sure. At the fourth place they had delayed to eat and the kitchen maid definitely remembered Heatherton's dark hair. Set your mind at rest, my dear, Cecilie now has a husband. Or will shortly."

And I must leave you, Aggie's heart cried, but her lips said only, "I am very glad."

"Except for the small hitch caused by Gale's letter I thought my plan worked famously."

His grin was infectious and even in her pain she managed a smile. *"Your* plan, milord?"

"Well, at least I put it into effect. And it worked."

Aggie nodded. "Yes, it did. Most fortunately for us all."

Denby reached out and took her hands in his. "We did it, Aggie. We actually got Cecilie well married."

She nodded, finding it difficult to speak. She tried to pull her hands away, but he held them fast. "Now," she said, her voice low, "now I can open my school. I should be ready to leave in a few days."

"I think not." His tone had become harsh and in confusion Aggie raised her eyes to his.

"I must," she said over the lump in her throat. "I cannot remain here."

The Earl's brows drew together. "You are not going anywhere," he said crisply. "At least, not until you have explained something to me."

Again Aggie struggled to release her hands, but he only sqeezed them tighter. "I

326

can conceive of nothing more that need be discussed between us," she said.

"That," he replied as his dark brows grew even closer, "is immaterial since *I* can. Stay here," he said and there was no disobeying what was plainly a command.

With a sigh Aggie sank back against the cushions. She would simply have to bear it as best she could. He must let her go sometime. As he took a key from his pocket and opened a drawer in the desk, he kept glancing at her as though she might disobey him. Then, taking a letter from the drawer, he returned to her side.

Aggie felt her body respond to his nearness as he stood towering over her. "Read this," he ordered brusquely.

She took the letter in fingers that trembled. She was so very tired; but there was no use in trying to explain that to him. His face was set in harsh implacable lines. Best to do as he said, to get it over with.

"Note the direction," he commanded.

Obediently she let her eyes rest there. It was an old letter, she saw now, wrinkled and stained, and it was directed to the Viscount Acton.

"Open it."

Her fingers moved to do his will. The letter lay unfolded before her.

"Read it aloud."

Aggie swallowed several times, moistening her dry lips with her tongue. In spite of all her efforts she couldn't stop the trembling of her hands. That, and the blur of tears in her eyes, made the words well nigh unreadable. "I – I cannot," she managed to stammer.

Strong white fingers plucked the paper ruthlessly from hers. "Then listen. 'Acton – This is to deny you permission to wait upon my daughter. She wants no more to do with you and laughs at the suggestion of an alliance between you. Young women, as you well know, like to play with the affections of men. Unfortunately, my daughter has set her cap for a certain man who shall remain unnamed. She has merely been using you to raise jealousy in another.'"

He paused and glared at her. Aggie could feel the heat of his stare even though she did not look at him.

"What do you say to that?" he demanded.

She shook her head in bewilderment. "What should I say? Why are you reading such things to me?"

Cursing volubly, the Earl yanked her to her feet. Thrown against the expanse of his waistcoat, Aggie could only remain there until, his hands gripping her upper arms, he pushed her back from him. "I warn you, Aggie. No more of this missish innocence." He shook her roughly, causing her hair to tumble loose from its knot, and fall to her shoulders in a rich brown cloud.

"I – I don't know what you mean," she gasped when she could regain her breath. "Please, Denby, just let me go."

"No!" The word reverberated through the room. "I want to know why, Aggie." He glared down at her.

"Why what?" She was growing more and more bewildered. His actions seemed those of a madman, but she hadn't the strength left to fight him.

"Aggie! Stop this." Even though her eyes were swimming with tears, she could see the agony in his face. "Why did you use me and reject me like that?"

For some moments shock kept her silent. Finally she found her tongue. "Me! Use you!" Her laugh was tinged with hysteria. "It was you who used me. You who left me without a word. How could you?" Her legs gave way then and without his grasp on her arms she would have slipped to the floor at his feet. But she forgot that in her amazement at the look of incredulity on his face.

"Aggie! What are you saying? You heard

the letter. Who was he? I must know." His brows met in that darkening scowl which signified his anger.

She shook her head, her loosened hair floating in a caress across his fingers. "What has that letter to do with me?"

His jaw jutted grimly. "As you well know, it was written by your father. At your request, no doubt."

"No!" The cry was a wild wail. "I didn't! I never –" Then she collapsed into wild sobbing.

Denby half led and half carried her to the divan and held her patiently while she sobbed against his waistcoat. Finally she raised her head. The green eyes were dimmed by tears and her nose reddened, but the Earl did not notice. "What do you mean – you didn't?" he asked softly.

Aggie sniffed and he pressed a clean white handkerchief into her hands. She dabbed at her face. "How can you accuse me of such a thing? I waited and waited, but you were gone."

"Aggie." His arm was warm around her sholders. "You mean you knew nothing of this letter?"

"Nothing."

"But why, why would your father do such a thing?"

Aggie shook her head. "Please, let me see it."

He took the letter from the table beside him and put it in her hands.

Aggie studied it for some moments. "It is my father's hand," she said finally. "But I knew nothing of it. He – he behaved very strangely sometimes in those last years. But I never thought he would do such a thing." She raised pleading eyes. "You must believe me, Denby. He said no word to me of it. I–" She took a deep breath. "I concluded that you – had tired of me."

The hand that clasped her shoulder tightened. "Never! The receipt of this so unnerved me that I left immediately to join the forces fighting Napoleon."

"If only you had come to me first." The words were out before she belatedly recalled that his lordship was now pledged to another.

He did not notice her expression of dismay. "I thought of it," he replied. "But my rage was so excessive that I could trust myself with you. And I did not wish to cause a public scandal."

He drew her toward him and she felt her resistance melting. But she must resist him, she told herself grimly. They had straightened out the past, but that had little effect on the future. Denby was going to marry Lady Alicia Temple.

He pulled her into his arms. Aggie, trying to stem her feelings of longing, stammered, "Your lady mother tells me you plan to marry."

"I do. As soon as possible." His eyes were bright and Aggie's heart sank. Why must she love this man?

"I – I see. I wish you every happiness," she murmured, bending every effort to keep back the tears.

"I'm sure I am quite blessed in my choice of a bride," he said, his eyes staring down into hers.

Privately, Aggie thought Lady Alicia quite the reverse of a blessing, but she did not say so. For one thing, to do so was not proper. And for another, the warmth in the Earl's eyes seemed to be pulling at her, drawing her into their enticing depths.

"I –" Aggie began, but the rest of her sentence was silenced by the Earl's lips on hers. Tender and persuasive at first, they grew more and more passionate. His lips were giving, and yet taking, and as her own mouth opened to admit his seeking tongue a sweet pang of longing coursed through her.

It seemed that by the touch of his lips he reached the very depths of her soul, reached them and stirred some part of herself she had never known existed. Her awareness of the outside world vanished. All she knew was this warmth, this joy, this terrible pressing need to blend herself with him body and soul, to melt into him so that they were no longer two separate entities, but one merged being.

She tried, but she could not withstand him. And, her heart cried, surely she could be allowed this one last kiss before he left her life forever. But when he released her, she forced herself to say, "Your lady wife, milord, would surely object to this."

He shook his head. "I think not. Aggie, my dear, now that we know the truth, surely you will not hold the past against me."

"No, of course not," she said. "But it is unseemly to be kissing me now when –"

"Aggie, Aggie." His arm clasped her close against his side. "How I have wanted you. Wanted you to distraction. And you so cold and icy." He wound a long strand of hair around his finger.

Aggie tried to free herself from his grasp. Surely he would not offer her carte blanche. Not now. Not when they had just spoken of his marriage. "Milord." She strove to make her voice cold. "Release me. This is unseemly."

"I shall never do that," he said, his lips seeking her throat.

Aggie sagged against him. She seemed to be fighting a losing battle, but she would not – could not – give in. "I – cannot – do – such – a – thing."

There was silence in the room as the Earl ceased moving. Aggie, captive in the circle of his arms, wished herself dead and buried, but the thunderous response she had expected did not come. "You cannot marry me?" he said, his tone dangerously soft.

"Marry you?" Her voice rose sharply.

"Of course – Aggie! You thought I meant you dishonor?"

She could only nod. "I – what else could I believe?"

He touched her cheek with a gentle finger, sending echoes of delight over her whole trembling body. "I understand, Aggie. But believe me, I have had matrimony in mind." A shadow of pain crossed his strong features. "At first I was angry. I meant to get revenge. But then I realized that I still loved you."

"And I you," she whispered. "But I could not believe you meant to do honorably by me. I have nothing." She bowed her head. "I thought you meant me to take Lady Alicia's former place. So, I fear, did she."

"Look me in the eyes, Aggie," he

334

commanded. She raised her eyes to his, those smoky eyes that seemed to pierce her very heart. "Lady Alicia *was* once what you thought she was to me. I am a man with a man's needs. But I swear to you – on our love." His voice was hoarse with emotion. "That since you entered this house Alicia has been nothing to me."

She looked long into his eyes, her heart thudding madly in her breast. "Your wife," she repeated. "Really your wife."

He drew her closer still. "Yes, my darling, my wife. We have lost five years, but we will have the rest of our lives together."

She sighed in contentment. "Oh, yes, Denby."

He was again gathering her into his arms when a slight tap on the open door caused them both to look up. "I could not wait till dinner," said Lady Denby from the doorway with a mischievous smile. "But I see that everything has gone well."

"Yes, indeed, Mother," replied the Earl, "exactly as we wished." And, while the Countess looked on in approbation, his lordship once more gathered his bride-to-be into his arms and kissed her soundly.